"There are tales of Middle-earth from times long before *The Lord of the Rings*, and the story told in this book is set in the great country that lay beyond the Grey Havens in the West: lands where Treebeard once walked, but which were drowned in the great cataclysm that ended the First Age of the World.

"In that remote time Morgoth, the first Dark Lord, dwelt in the vast fortress of Angband, the Hells of Iron, in the North; and the tragedy of Túrin and his sister Niënor unfolded within the shadow of the fear of Angband and the war waged by Morgoth against the lands and secret cities of the Elves.

"Their brief and passionate lives were dominated by the elemental hatred that Morgoth bore them as the children of Húrin, the man who had dared to defy and to scorn him to his face. Against them he sent his most formidable servant, Glaurung, a powerful spirit in the form of a huge wingless dragon of fire. Into this story of brutal conquest and flight, of forest hiding-places and pursuit, of resistance with lessening hope, the Dark Lord and the Dragon enter in direly articulate form. Sardonic and mocking, Glaurung manipulated the fates of Túrin and Niënor by lies of diabolic cunning and guile, and the curse of Morgoth was fulfilled.

"The earliest versions of this story by J.R.R. Tolkien go back to the end of the First World War and the years that followed; but long afterwards, when *The Lord of the Rings* was finished, he wrote it anew and greatly enlarged it in complexities of motive and character: it became the dominant story in his later work on Middle-earth. But he could not bring it to a final and finished form. In this book I have endeavoured to construct, after long study of the manuscripts, a coherent narrative without any editorial invention."

CHRISTOPHER TOLKIEN

D0939421

NARN I CHÎN HÚRIN
The Tale of the Children of Húrin

BY
J.R.R. Tolkien

Edited by Christopher Tolkien

Illustrated by Alan Lee

HarperCollins*Publishers*

To
BAILLIE TOLKIEN

HarperCollins*Publishers*
77–85 Fulham Palace Road,
Hammersmith, London W6 8JB

www.tolkien.co.uk

www.tolkienestate.com

Special overseas edition 2008

2

First published in Great Britain by HarperCollins*Publishers* 2007

Map, Preface, Introduction, Note on Pronunciation, Appendix and List of Names
© Christopher Reuel Tolkien 2007
The Tale of the Children of Húrin © The J.R.R. Tolkien Copyright Trust
and Christopher Reuel Tolkien 2007
Illustrations © Alan Lee 2007

 ® and 'Tolkien'® are registered trade marks of
The J.R.R. Tolkien Estate Limited

A CIP catalogue record for this book is available from the British Library

ISBN-13 978 0 00 730936 8

Printed and bound in Great Britain by Clays Ltd, St Ives plc

Mixed Sources
Product group from well-managed
forests and other controlled sources
www.fsc.org Cert no. SW-COC-1806
© 1996 Forest Stewardship Council

FSC is a non-profit international organisation established to promote the
responsible management of the world's forests. Products carrying the FSC
label are independently certified to assure consumers that they come
from forests that are managed to meet the social, economic and
ecological needs of present and future generations.

Find out more about HarperCollins and the environment at
www.harpercollins.co.uk/green

CONTENTS

ILLUSTRATIONS

PREFACE

It is undeniable that there are a very great many readers of *The Lord of the Rings* for whom the legends of the Elder Days (as previously published in varying forms in *The Silmarillion*, *Unfinished Tales*, and *The History of Middle-earth*) are altogether unknown, unless by their repute as strange and inaccessible in mode and manner. For this reason it has seemed to me for a long time that there was a good case for presenting my father's long version of the legend of the Children of Húrin as an independent work, between its own covers, with a minimum of editorial presence, and above all in continuous narrative without gaps or interruptions, if this could be done without distortion or invention, despite the unfinished state in which he left some parts of it.

I have thought that if the story of the fate of Túrin and Niënor, the children of Húrin and Morwen, could be presented in this way, a window might be opened onto a scene and a story set in an unknown Middle-earth that are vivid and immediate, yet conceived as handed down from remote ages: the drowned lands in the west beyond the Blue Mountains where Treebeard walked in his youth, and the life of Túrin Turambar, in Dor-lómin, Doriath, Nargothrond, and the Forest of Brethil.

This book is thus primarily addressed to such readers as may perhaps recall that the hide of Shelob was so horren-dously hard that it 'could not be pierced by any strength of men, not though Elf or Dwarf should forge the steel or the

hand of Beren or of Túrin wield it', or that Elrond named
Túrin to Frodo at Rivendell as one of 'the mighty Elf-friends
of old'; but know no more of him.

When my father was a young man, during the years of the
First World War and long before there was any inkling of the
tales that were to form the narrative of *The Hobbit* or *The
Lord of the Rings*, he began the writing of a collection of
stories that he called *The Book of Lost Tales*. That was his
first work of imaginative literature, and a substantial one, for
though it was left unfinished there are fourteen completed
tales. It was in *The Book of Lost Tales* that there first
appeared in narrative the Gods, or Valar; Elves and Men as
the Children of Ilúvatar (the Creator); Melkor-Morgoth the
great Enemy; Balrogs and Orcs; and the lands in which the
Tales are set, Valinor 'land of the Gods' beyond the western
ocean, and the 'Great Lands' (afterwards called 'Middle-
earth', between the seas of east and west).

Among the *Lost Tales* three were of much greater length
and fullness, and all three are concerned with Men as well as
Elves: they are *The Tale of Tinúviel* (which appears in brief
form in *The Lord of the Rings* as the story of Beren and
Lúthien that Aragorn told to the hobbits on Weathertop; this
my father wrote in 1917), *Turambar and the Foalókë* (Túrin
Turambar and the Dragon, certainly in existence by 1919, if
not before), and *The Fall of Gondolin* (1916–17). In an often-
quoted passage of a long letter describing his work that my
father wrote in 1951, three years before the publication of *The*

Fellowship of the Ring, he told of his early ambition: 'once upon a time (my crest has long since fallen) I had a mind to make a body of more or less connected legend, ranging from the large and cosmogonic, to the level of romantic fairy-story – the larger founded on the lesser in contact with the earth, the lesser drawing splendour from the vast backcloths ... I would draw some of the great tales in fullness, and leave many only placed in the scheme, and sketched.'

It is seen from this reminiscence that from far back it was a part of his conception of what came to be called *The Silmarillion* that some of the 'Tales' should be told in much fuller form; and indeed in that same letter of 1951 he referred expressly to the three stories which I have mentioned above as being much the longest in *The Book of Lost Tales*. Here he called the tale of Beren and Lúthien 'the chief of the stories of *The Silmarillion*', and of it he said: 'the story is (I think a beautiful and powerful) heroic-fairy-romance, receivable in itself with only a very general vague knowledge of the background. But it is also a fundamental link in the cycle, deprived of its full significance out of its place therein.' 'There are other stories almost equally full in treatment,' he went on, 'and equally independent, and yet linked to the general history': these are *The Children of Húrin* and *The Fall of Gondolin*.

It thus seems unquestionable, from my father's own words, that if he could achieve final and finished narratives on the scale he desired, he saw the three 'Great Tales' of the Elder Days (Beren and Lúthien, the Children of Húrin, and the Fall of Gondolin) as works sufficiently complete in themselves as not to demand knowledge of the great body of legend known as *The Silmarillion*. On the other hand, as my father observed in the same place, the tale of the Children of Húrin is integral to the history of Elves and Men in the Elder Days, and there are necessarily a good many references to events and circumstances in that larger story.

It would be altogether contrary to the conception of this book to burden its reading with an abundance of notes giving information about persons and events that are in any case seldom of real importance to the immediate narrative. However, it may be found helpful here and there if some such assistance is provided, and I have accordingly given in the Introduction a very brief sketch of Beleriand and its peoples near the end of the Elder Days, when Túrin and Niënor were born; and, as well as a map of Beleriand and the lands to the North, I have included a list of all names occurring in the text with very concise indications concerning each, and simplified genealogies.

At the end of the book is an Appendix in two parts: the first concerned with my father's attempts to achieve a final form for the three tales, and the second with the composition of the text in this book, which differs in many respects from that in *Unfinished Tales*.

I am very grateful to my son Adam Tolkien for his indispensable help in the arrangement and presentation of the material in the Introduction and Appendix, and for easing the book into the (to me) daunting world of electronic transmission.

INTRODUCTION

Middle-earth in the Elder Days

The character of Túrin was of deep significance to my father, and in dialogue of directness and immediacy he achieved a poignant portrait of his boyhood, essential to the whole: his severity and lack of gaiety, his sense of justice and his compassion; of Húrin also, quick, gay, and sanguine, and of Morwen his mother, reserved, courageous, and proud; and of the life of the household in the cold country of Dor-lómin during the years, already full of fear, after Morgoth broke the Siege of Angband, before Túrin was born.

But all this was in the Elder Days, the First Age of the world, in a time unimaginably remote. The depth in time to which this story reaches back was memorably conveyed in a passage in *The Lord of the Rings*. At the great council in Rivendell Elrond spoke of the Last Alliance of Elves and Men and the defeat of Sauron at the end of the Second Age, more than three thousand years before:

Thereupon Elrond paused a while and sighed. 'I remember well the splendour of their banners,' he said. 'It recalled to me the glory of the Elder Days and the hosts of Beleriand, so many great princes and captains were assembled. And yet not so many, nor so fair, as when Thangorodrim was broken, and the Elves deemed that evil was ended for ever, and it was not so.'

'You remember?' said Frodo, speaking his thought aloud in his astonishment. 'But I thought,' he stammered as Elrond turned towards him, 'I thought that the fall of Gil-galad was a long age ago.'

'So it was indeed,' answered Elrond gravely. 'But my memory reaches back even to the Elder Days. Eärendil was my sire, who was born in Gondolin before its fall; and my mother was Elwing, daughter of Dior, son of Lúthien of Doriath. I have seen three ages in the West of the world, and many defeats, and many fruitless victories.'

Some six and a half thousand years before the Council of Elrond was held in Rivendell, Túrin was born in Dor-lómin, 'in the winter of the year,' as is recorded in the *Annals of Beleriand*, 'with omens of sorrow'.

But the tragedy of his life is by no means comprehended solely in the portrayal of character, for he was condemned to live trapped in a malediction of huge and mysterious power, the curse of hatred set by Morgoth upon Húrin and Morwen and their children, because Húrin defied him, and refused his will. And Morgoth, the Black Enemy, as he came to be called, was in his origin, as he declared to Húrin brought captive before him, 'Melkor, first and mightiest of the Valar, who was before the world.' Now become permanently incarnate, in form a gigantic and majestic, but terrible, King in the northwest of Middle-earth, he was physically present in his huge fortress of Angband, the Hells of Iron: the black reek that issued from the summits of Thangorodrim, the mountains that he piled above Angband, could be seen far off staining the northern sky. It is said in the *Annals of Beleriand* that 'the gates of Morgoth were but one hundred and fifty leagues distant from the bridge of Menegroth; far and yet all too near.' These words refer to the bridge leading to the dwellings of the Elvish king Thingol, who took Túrin to be his fosterson: they were called Menegroth, the Thousand Caves, far south and east of Dor-lómin.

But being incarnate Morgoth was afraid. My father wrote of him: 'As he grew in malice, and sent forth from himself the evil that he conceived in lies and creatures of wickedness, his power passed into them and was dispersed, and he himself became ever more earth-bound, unwilling to issue from his dark strongholds.' Thus when Fingolfin, High King of the Noldorin Elves, rode alone to Angband to challenge Morgoth to combat, he cried at the gate: 'Come forth, thou coward king, to fight with thine own hand! Den-dweller, wielder of thralls, liar and lurker, foe of Gods and Elves, come! For I would see thy craven face.' Then (it is told) 'Morgoth came. For he could not refuse such a challenge before the face of his captains.' He fought with the great hammer Grond, which at each blow made a great pit, and he beat Fingolfin to the ground; but as he died he pinned the great foot of Morgoth to the earth, 'and the black blood gushed forth and filled the pits of Grond. Morgoth went ever halt thereafter.' So also, when Beren and Lúthien, in the shapes of a wolf and a bat, made their way into the deepest hall in Angband, where Morgoth sat, Lúthien cast a spell on him: and 'suddenly he fell, as a hill sliding in avalanche, and hurled like thunder from his throne lay prone upon the floors of hell. The iron crown rolled echoing from his head.'

The curse of such a being, who can claim that 'the shadow of my purpose lies upon Arda [the Earth], and all that is in it bends slowly and surely to my will', is unlike the curses or imprecations of beings of far less power. Morgoth is not 'invoking' evil or calamity on Húrin and his children, he is not 'calling on' a higher power to be the agent: for he, 'Master of the fates of Arda' as he named himself to Húrin, intends to bring about the ruin of his enemy by the force of his own gigantic will. Thus he 'designs' the future of those whom he hates, and so he says to Húrin: 'Upon all whom you love *my thought* shall weigh as *a cloud of Doom*, and it shall bring them down into darkness and despair.'

The torment that he devised for Húrin was 'to see with Morgoth's eyes'. My father gave a definition of what this meant: if one were forced to look into Morgoth's eye he would 'see' (or receive in his mind from Morgoth's mind) a compellingly credible picture of events, distorted by Morgoth's bottomless malice; and if indeed any could refuse Morgoth's command, Húrin did not. This was in part, my father said, because his love of his kin and his anguished anxiety for them made him desire to learn all that he could of them, no matter what the source; and in part from pride, believing that he had defeated Morgoth in debate, and that he could 'outstare' Morgoth, or at least retain his critical reason and distinguish between fact and malice.

Throughout Túrin's life from the time of his departure from Dor-lómin, and the life of his sister Niënor who never saw her father, this was the fate of Húrin, seated immovably in a high place of Thangorodrim in increasing bitterness inspired by his tormentor.

In the tale of Túrin, who named himself Turambar 'Master of Fate', the curse of Morgoth seems to be seen as power unleashed to work evil, seeking out its victims; so the fallen Vala himself is said to fear that Túrin 'would grow to such a power that the curse that he had laid upon him would become void, and he would escape the doom that had been designed for him' (p. 147). And afterwards in Nargothrond Túrin concealed his true name, so that when Gwindor revealed it he was angered: 'You have done ill to me, friend, to betray my right name, and call down my doom upon me, from which I would lie hid.' It was Gwindor who had told Túrin of the rumour that ran through Angband, where Gwindor had been held prisoner, that Morgoth had laid a curse on Húrin and all his kin. But now he replied to Túrin's wrath: 'the doom lies in yourself, not in your name.'

So essential is this complex conception in the story that my father even proposed an alternative title to it: *Narn e·'Rach Morgoth*, The Tale of the Curse of Morgoth. And his view of it is seen in these words: 'So ended the tale of Túrin the hapless; the worst of the works of Morgoth among Men in the ancient world.'

When Treebeard strode through the forest of Fangorn carrying Merry and Pippin each in the crook of his arm he sang to them of places that he had known in remote times, and of the trees that grew there:

In the willow-meads of Tasarinan I walked in the Spring.
Ah! the sight and the smell of the Spring in Nan-tasarion!
And I said that was good.
I wandered in Summer in the elm-woods of Ossiriand.
Ah! the light and the music in the Summer by the Seven
*   Rivers of Ossir!*
And I thought that was best.
To the beeches of Neldoreth I came in the Autumn.
Ah! the gold and the red and the sighing of leaves in the
*   Autumn in Taur-na-Neldor!*
It was more than my desire.
To the pine-trees upon the highland of Dorthonion I
*   climbed in the Winter.*
Ah! the wind and the whiteness and the black branches
*   of Winter upon Orod-na-Thôn!*
My voice went up and sang in the sky.
And now all those lands lie under the wave,
And I walk in Ambarona, in Tauremorna, in Aldalómë,
In my own land, in the country of Fangorn,

Where the roots are long,
And the years lie thicker than the leaves
In Tauremornalómë.

The memory of Treebeard, 'Ent the earthborn, old as mountains', was indeed long. He was remembering ancient forests in the great country of Beleriand, which was destroyed in the tumults of the Great Battle at the end of the Elder Days. The Great Sea poured in and drowned all the lands west of the Blue Mountains, called Ered Luin and Ered Lindon: so that the map accompanying *The Silmarillion* ends in the east with that mountain-chain, whereas the map accompanying *The Lord of the Rings* ends in the west with the same range; and the coastal lands beyond the mountains named on that map Forlindon and Harlindon (North Lindon and South Lindon) were all that remained in the Third Age of the country called both Ossiriand, Land of Seven Rivers, and also Lindon, in whose elm-woods Treebeard once walked.

He walked also among the great pine-trees on the highland of Dorthonion ('Land of Pines'), which afterwards came to be called Taur-nu-Fuin, 'the Forest under Night', when Morgoth turned it into 'a region of dread and dark enchantment, of wandering and despair' (p. 152); and he came to Neldoreth, the northern forest of Doriath, realm of Thingol.

It was in Beleriand and the lands to the north that Túrin's terrible destiny was played out; and indeed both Dorthonion and Doriath where Treebeard walked were crucial in his life. He was born into a world of warfare, though he was still a child when the last and greatest battle in the wars of Beleriand was fought. A very brief sketch of how this came about will answer questions that arise and references that are made in the course of the narrative.

In the north the boundaries of Beleriand seem to have been formed by the Ered Wethrin, the Mountains of Shadow, beyond which lay Húrin's country, Dor-lómin, a part of Hithlum; while in the east Beleriand extended to the feet of the Blue Mountains. Further east lay lands that scarcely appear in the history of the Elder Days; but the peoples that shaped that history came out of the east by the passes of the Blue Mountains.

The Elves appeared on earth far off in the distant east, beside a lake that was named Cuiviénen, Water of Awakening; and thence they were summoned by the Valar to leave Middle-earth, and passing over the Great Sea to come to the 'Blessed Realm' of Aman in the west of the world, the land of the Gods. Those who accepted the summons were led on a great march across Middle-earth from Cuiviénen by the Vala Oromë, the Hunter, and they are called the Eldar, the Elves of the Great Journey, the High Elves: distinct from those who, refusing the summons, chose Middle-earth for their land and their destiny. They are the 'lesser Elves', called Avari, the Unwilling.

But not all the Eldar, though they had crossed the Blue Mountains, departed over the Sea; and those who remained in Beleriand are named the Sindar, the Grey Elves. Their high king was Thingol (which means 'Grey-cloak'), who ruled from Menegroth, the Thousand Caves in Doriath. And not all the Eldar who crossed the Great Sea remained in the land of the Valar; for one of their great kindreds, the Noldor (the 'Loremasters'), returned to Middle-earth, and they are called the Exiles. The prime mover in their rebellion against the Valar was Fëanor, 'Spirit of Fire': he was the eldest son of Finwë, who had led the host of the Noldor from Cuiviénen, but was now dead. This cardinal event in the history of the Elves was thus briefly conveyed by my father in Appendix A to *The Lord of the Rings*:

Fëanor was the greatest of the Eldar in arts and lore, but also the proudest and most selfwilled. He wrought the Three Jewels, the *Silmarilli*, and filled them with the radiance of the Two Trees, Telperion and Laurelin, that gave light to the land of the Valar. The Jewels were coveted by Morgoth the Enemy, who stole them and, after destroying the Trees, took them to Middle-earth, and guarded them in his great fortress of Thangoro-drim [the mountains above Angband]. Against the will of the Valar Fëanor forsook the Blessed Realm and went in exile to Middle-earth, leading with him a great part of his people; for in his pride he purposed to recover the Jewels from Morgoth by force. Thereafter followed the hopeless war of the Eldar and the Edain against Thangorodrim, in which they were at last utterly defeated.

Fëanor was slain in battle soon after the return of the Noldor to Middle-earth, and his seven sons held wide lands in the east of Beleriand, between Dorthonion (Taur-nu-Fuin) and the Blue Mountains; but their power was destroyed in the terrible Battle of Unnumbered Tears which is described in *The Children of Húrin*, and thereafter 'the Sons of Fëanor wandered as leaves before the wind' (p. 61).

The second son of Finwë was Fingolfin (the half-brother of Fëanor), who was held the overlord of all the Noldor; and he with his son Fingon ruled Hithlum, which lay to the north and west of the great chain of Ered Wethrin, the Mountains of Shadow. Fingolfin dwelt in Mithrim, by the great lake of that name, while Fingon held Dor-lómin in the south of Hithlum. Their chief fortress was Barad Eithel (the Tower of the Well) at Eithel Sirion (Sirion's Well), where the river Sirion rose in the east face of the Mountains of Shadow: Sador, the old crippled servant of Húrin and Morwen, served as a soldier there for many years, as he told Túrin (pp. 41–42). After Fingolfin's death in single combat with Morgoth Fingon became the High King of the Noldor in his stead. Túrin saw him once, when he 'and many of his lords had ridden through Dor-lómin and passed over the bridge of Nen Lalaith, glittering in silver and white' (p. 40).

The second son of Fingolfin was Turgon. He dwelt at first, after the return of the Noldor, in the house named Vinyamar, beside the sea in the region of Nevrast, west of Dor-lómin; but he built in secret the hidden city of Gondolin, which stood on a hill in the midst of the plain called Tumladen, wholly surrounded by the Encircling Mountains, east of the river Sirion. When Gondolin was built, after many years of labour, Turgon removed from Vinyamar and dwelt with his people, both Noldor and Sindar, in Gondolin; and for centuries this Elvish redoubt of great beauty was preserved in the most profound secrecy, its only entry undiscoverable and heavily guarded, so that no stranger could ever pass in; and Morgoth was unable to learn where it lay. Not until the Battle of Unnumbered Tears, when more than three hundred and fifty years had passed since he left Vinyamar, did Turgon emerge with his great army from Gondolin.

The third son of Finwë, the brother of Fingolfin and half-brother of Fëanor, was Finarfin. He did not return to Middle-earth, but his sons and daughter came with the host of Fingolfin and his sons. The eldest son of Finarfin was Finrod, who, inspired by the magnificence and beauty of Menegroth in Doriath, founded the underground fortress-city of Nargothrond, for which he was named Felagund, interpreted to mean 'Lord of Caves' or 'Cave-hewer' in the tongue of the Dwarves. The doors of Nargothrond opened onto the gorge of the river Narog in West Beleriand, where that river passed through the high hills called Taur-en-Faroth, or the High Faroth; but Finrod's realm extended far and wide, east to the river Sirion, and west to the river Nenning that reached the sea at the haven of Eglarest. But Finrod was slain in the dungeons of Sauron, chief servant of Morgoth, and Orodreth, the second son of Finarfin, took the

crown of Nargothrond: this took place in the year following
the birth of Túrin in Dor-lómin.

The other sons of Finarfin, Angrod and Aegnor, vassals of
their brother Finrod, dwelt on Dorthonion, looking northwards over the vast plain of Ard-galen. Galadriel, Finrod's
sister, dwelt long in Doriath with Melian the Queen. Melian
was a Maia, a spirit of great power who took human form and
dwelt in the forests of Beleriand with King Thingol: she was
the mother of Lúthien, and the foremother of Elrond. Not
long before the return of the Noldor from Aman, when great
armies out of Angband came south into Beleriand, Melian (in
the words of *The Silmarillion*) 'put forth her power and fenced
all that dominion [the forests of Neldoreth and Region] round
about with an unseen wall of shadow and bewilderment: the
Girdle of Melian, that none thereafter could pass against her
will or the will of King Thingol, unless one should come with
a power greater than that of Melian the Maia.' Thereafter the
land was named Doriath, 'the Land of the Fence'.

In the sixtieth year after the return of the Noldor, ending
many years of peace, a great host of Orcs came down from
Angband, but was utterly defeated and destroyed by the
Noldor. This was called *Dagor Aglareb*, the Glorious Battle;
but the Elvish lords took warning from it, and set the Siege
of Angband, which lasted for almost four hundred years.

It was said that Men (whom the Elves called *Atani* 'the
Second', and *Hildor* 'the Followers') arose far off in the east
of Middle-earth towards the end of the Elder Days; but of

their earliest history the Men who entered Beleriand in the days of the Long Peace, when Angband was besieged and its gates shut, would never speak. The leader of these first Men to cross the Blue Mountains was named Bëor the Old; and to Finrod Felagund, King of Nargothrond, who first encountered them Bëor declared: 'A darkness lies behind us; and we have turned our backs on it, and we do not desire to return thither even in thought. Westwards our hearts have been turned, and we believe that there we shall find Light.' Sador, the old servant of Húrin, spoke in the same way to Túrin in his boyhood (p. 43). But it was said afterwards that when Morgoth learned of the arising of Men he left Angband for the last time and went into the East; and that the first Men to enter Beleriand 'had repented and rebelled against the Dark Power, and were cruelly hunted and oppressed by those that worshipped it, and its servants'.

These Men belonged to three Houses, known as the House of Bëor, the House of Hador, and the House of Haleth. Húrin's father Galdor the Tall was of the House of Hador, being indeed his son; but his mother was of the House of Haleth, while Morwen his wife was of the House of Bëor, and related to Beren.

The people of the Three Houses were the *Edain* (the Sindarin form of *Atani*), and they were called Elf-friends. Hador dwelt in Hithlum and was given the lordship of Dorlómin by King Fingolfin; the people of Bëor settled in Dorthonion; and the people of Haleth at this time dwelt in the Forest of Brethil. After the ending of the Siege of

Angband Men of a very different sort came over the mountains; they were commonly referred to as Easterlings, and some of them played an important part in the story of Túrin.

The Siege of Angband ended with a terrible suddenness (though long prepared) on a night of midwinter, 395 years after it had begun. Morgoth released rivers of fire that ran down from Thangorodrim, and the great grassy plain of Ardgalen that lay to the north of the highland of Dorthonion was transformed into a parched and arid waste, known thereafter by a changed name, *Anfauglith*, the Gasping Dust.

This catastrophic assault was called *Dagor Bragollach*, the Battle of Sudden Flame. Glaurung Father of Dragons emerged from Angband now for the first time in his full might; vast armies of Orcs poured southwards; the Elvish lords of Dorthonion were slain, and a great part of the warriors of Bëor's people. King Fingolfin and his son Fingon were driven back with the warriors of Hithlum to the fortress of Eithel Sirion in the east face of the Mountains of Shadow, and in its defence Hador Goldenhead was killed. Then Galdor, Húrin's father, became the lord of Dor-lómin; for the torrents of fire were stopped by the barrier of the Mountains of Shadow, and Hithlum and Dor-lómin remained unconquered.

It was in the year after the Bragollach that Fingolfin, in a fury of despair, rode to Angband and challenged Morgoth. Two years later Húrin and Huor went to Gondolin. After four more years, in a renewed assault on Hithlum, Húrin's father Galdor was slain in the fortress of Eithel Sirion: Sador was there, as he told Túrin (p. 42), and saw Húrin (then a young man of twenty-one) 'take up his lordship and his command'.

All these things were fresh in memory in Dor-lómin when Túrin was born, nine years after the Battle of Sudden Flame.

NOTE ON PRONUNCIATION

The following note is intended to clarify a few main features in the pronunciation of names.

Consonants

C   always has the value of *k*, never of *s*; thus *Celebros* is '*Kelebros*', not '*Selebros*'.

CH   always has the value of *ch* in Scots *loch* or German *buch*, never that of *ch* in English *church*; examples are *Anach*, *Narn i Chîn Húrin*.

DH   is always used to represent the sound of a voiced ('soft') *th* in English, that is the *th* in *then*, not the *th* in *thin*. Examples are *Glóredhel*, *Eledhwen*, *Maedhros*.

G   always has the sound of English *g* in *get*; thus *Region* is not pronounced like English *region*, and the first syllable of *Ginglith* is as in English *begin*, not as in *gin*.

Vowels

AI   has the sound of English *eye*; thus the second syllable of *Edain* is like English *dine*, not *Dane*.

AU   has the value of English *ow* in *town*; thus the first vowel of *Sauron* is like English *sour*, not *sore*.

EI   as in *Teiglin* has the sound of English *grey*.

IE   should not be pronounced as in English *piece*, but with both the vowels *i* and *e* sounded, and run together; thus *Ni-enor*, not '*Neenor*'.

AE   as in *Aegnor, Nirnaeth*, is a combination of the individual vowels, *a-e*, but may be pronounced in the same way as AI.

EA and EO   are not run together, but constitute two syllables; these combinations are written *ëa* and *ëo*, as in *Bëor*, or at the beginning of names *Eä, Eö*, as in *Eärendil*.

Ú   in names like *Húrin, Túrin*, should be pronounced *oo*; thus '*Toorin*', not '*Tyoorin*'.

IR, UR before a consonant (as in *Círdan, Gurthang*) should not be pronounced as in English *fir, fur*, but as in English, *eer, oor*.

E   at the end of words is always pronounced as a distinct vowel, and in this position is written *ë*. It is always pronounced in the middle of words like *Celebros, Menegroth*.

NARN I CHÎN HÚRIN

The Tale of the Children of Húrin

CHAPTER I

THE CHILDHOOD OF TÚRIN

Hador Goldenhead was a lord of the Edain and well-beloved by the Eldar. He dwelt while his days lasted under the lordship of Fingolfin, who gave to him wide lands in that region of Hithlum which was called Dor-lómin. His daughter Glóredhel wedded Haldir son of Halmir, lord of the Men of Brethil; and at the same feast his son Galdor the Tall wedded Hareth, the daughter of Halmir.

Galdor and Hareth had two sons, Húrin and Huor. Húrin was by three years the elder, but he was shorter in stature than other men of his kin; in this he took after his mother's people, but in all else he was like Hador, his grandfather, strong in body and fiery of mood. But the fire in him burned steadily, and he had great endurance of will. Of all Men of the North he knew most of the counsels of the Noldor. Huor his brother was tall, the tallest of all the Edain save his own son Tuor only, and a swift runner; but if the race were long and hard Húrin would be the first home, for he ran as strongly at the end of the course as at the beginning. There was great love between the brothers, and they were seldom apart in their youth.

Húrin wedded Morwen, the daughter of Baragund son of Bregolas of the House of Bëor; and she was thus of close kin to Beren One-hand. Morwen was dark-haired and tall, and for the light of her glance and the beauty of her face men called her Eledhwen, the elven-fair; but she was some-what stern of mood and proud. The sorrows of the House of Bëor saddened her heart; for she came as an exile to Dor-lómin from Dorthonion after the ruin of the Bragollach.

Túrin was the name of the eldest child of Húrin and Morwen, and he was born in that year in which Beren came to Doriath and found Lúthien Tinúviel, Thingol's daughter. Morwen bore a daughter also to Húrin, and she was named Urwen; but she was called Lalaith, which is Laughter, by all that knew her in her short life.

Huor wedded Rían, the cousin of Morwen; she was the daughter of Belegund son of Bregolas. By hard fate was she born into such days, for she was gentle of heart and loved neither hunting nor war. Her love was given to trees and to the flowers of the wild, and she was a singer and a maker of songs. Two months only had she been wedded to Huor when he went with his brother to the Nirnaeth Arnoediad, and she never saw him again.

But now the tale returns to Húrin and Huor in the days of their youth. It is said that for a while the sons of Galdor dwelt in Brethil as foster-sons of Haldir their uncle, after the custom of Northern men in those days. They often went to battle with the Men of Brethil against the Orcs, who now harried the northern borders of their land; for Húrin, though only seventeen years of age, was strong, and Huor the younger was already as tall as most full-grown men of that people.

On a time Húrin and Huor went with a company of scouts, but they were ambushed by the Orcs and scattered, and the brothers were pursued to the ford of Brithiach. There they would have been taken or slain but for the power of Ulmo that was still strong in the waters of Sirion; and it is said that a mist arose from the river and hid them from their enemies, and they escaped over the Brithiach into Dimbar. There they wandered in great hardship among the hills beneath the sheer walls of the Crissaegrim, until they were bewildered in the deceits of that land and knew not the way to go on or to return. There Thorondor espied them, and he sent two of his Eagles to their aid; and the Eagles bore them up and brought them beyond the Encircling Mountains to the secret vale of Tumladen and the hidden city of Gondolin, which no Man had yet seen.

There Turgon the King received them well, when he learned of their kin; for Hador was an Elf-friend, and Ulmo, moreover, had counselled Turgon to deal kindly with the sons of that House, from whom help should come to him at need. Húrin and Huor dwelt as guests in the King's house for well nigh a year; and it is said that in this time Húrin, whose mind was swift and eager, gained much lore of the Elves, and learned also something of the counsels and purposes of the King. For Turgon took great liking for the sons of Galdor, and spoke much with them; and he wished indeed to keep them in Gondolin out of love, and not only for his law that no stranger, be he Elf or Man, who found the way to the secret kingdom or looked upon the city should ever depart again, until the King should open the leaguer, and the hidden people should come forth.

But Húrin and Huor desired to return to their own people and share in the wars and griefs that now beset them. And Húrin said to Turgon: 'Lord, we are but mortal Men, and unlike the Eldar. They may endure for long years awaiting battle with their enemies in some far distant day; but for us the time is short, and our hope and strength soon wither. Moreover we did not find the road to Gondolin, and indeed we do not know surely where this city stands; for we were brought in fear and wonder by the high ways of the air, and in mercy our eyes were veiled.' Then Turgon granted his prayer, and he said: 'By the way that you came you have leave to return, if Thorondor is willing. I grieve at this parting; yet in a little while, as the Eldar account it, we may meet again.'

But Maeglin, the King's sister-son, who was mighty in Gondolin, grieved not at all at their going, though he begrudged them the favour of the King, for he had no love for any of the kindred of Men; and he said to Húrin: 'The King's grace is greater than you know, and some might wonder wherefore the strict law is abated for two knave-children of Men. It would be safer if they had no choice but to abide here as our servants to their life's end.'

'The King's grace is great indeed,' answered Húrin, 'but if our word is not enough, then we will swear oaths to you.' And the brothers swore never to reveal the counsels of Turgon, and to keep secret all that they had seen in his realm. Then they took their leave, and the Eagles coming bore them away by night, and set them down in Dor-lómin before the dawn. Their kinsfolk rejoiced to see them, for messengers from Brethil had reported that they were lost; but they would not tell even to their father where they had been, save that they were rescued in the wilderness by the Eagles that brought them home. But Galdor said: 'Did you then dwell a year in the wild? Or did the Eagles house you in their eyries? But you found food and fine raiment, and return as young princes, not as waifs of the wood.' 'Be content, father,' said Húrin, 'that we have returned; for only under an oath of silence was this permitted. That oath is still on us.' Then Galdor questioned them no more, but he and many others guessed at the truth. For both the oath of silence and the Eagles pointed to Turgon, men thought.

So the days passed, and the shadow of the fear of Morgoth lengthened. But in the four hundred and sixty-ninth year after the return of the Noldor to Middle-earth there was a stirring of hope among Elves and Men; for the rumour ran among them of the deeds of Beren and Lúthien, and the putting to shame of Morgoth even upon his throne in Angband, and some said that Beren and Lúthien yet lived, or had returned from the Dead. In that year also the great counsels of Maedhros were almost complete, and with the reviving strength of the Eldar and the Edain the advance of Morgoth was stayed, and the Orcs were driven back from Beleriand. Then some began to speak of victories to come, and of redressing the Battle of the Bragollach, when Maedhros should lead forth the united hosts, and drive Morgoth underground, and seal the Doors of Angband.

But the wiser were uneasy still, fearing that Maedhros revealed his growing strength too soon, and that Morgoth would be given time enough to take counsel against him. 'Ever will some new evil be hatched in Angband beyond the guess of Elves and Men,' they said. And in the autumn of that year, to point their words, there came an ill wind from the North under leaden skies. The Evil Breath it was called, for it was pestilent; and many sickened and died in the fall of the year in the northern lands that bordered on the Anfauglith, and they were for the most part the children or the rising youth in the houses of Men.

In that year Túrin son of Húrin was yet only five years old, and Urwen his sister was three in the beginning of spring. Her hair was like the yellow lilies in the grass as she ran in the fields, and her laughter was like the sound of the merry stream that came singing out of the hills past the walls of her father's house. Nen Lalaith it was named, and after it all the people of the household called the child Lalaith, and their hearts were glad while she was among them.

But Túrin was loved less than she. He was dark-haired as his mother, and promised to be like her in mood also; for he was not merry, and spoke little, though he learned to speak early and ever seemed older than his years. Túrin was slow to forget injustice or mockery; but the fire of his father was also in him, and he could be sudden and fierce. Yet he was quick to pity, and the hurts or sadness of living things might move him to tears; and he was like his father in this also, for Morwen was stern with others as with herself. He loved his mother, for her speech to him was forthright and plain; but his father he saw little, for Húrin was often long away from home with the host of Fingon that guarded Hithlum's eastern borders, and when he returned his quick speech, full of strange words and jests and half-meanings, bewildered Túrin and made him uneasy. At that time all the warmth of his heart was for Lalaith his sister; but he played with her seldom, and liked better to guard her unseen and to watch her going upon grass or under tree, as she sang such songs as the children of the Edain made long ago when the tongue of the Elves was still fresh upon their lips.

'Fair as an Elf-child is Lalaith,' said Húrin to Morwen; 'but briefer, alas! And so fairer, maybe, or dearer.' And Túrin hearing these words pondered them, but could not

understand them. For he had seen no Elf-children. None of
the Eldar at that time dwelt in his father's lands, and once
only had he seen them, when King Fingon and many of his
lords had ridden through Dor-lómin and passed over the
bridge of Nen Lalaith, glittering in silver and white.

But before the year was out the truth of his father's
words was shown; for the Evil Breath came to Dor-lómin,
and Túrin took sick, and lay long in a fever and dark
dream. And when he was healed, for such was his fate and
the strength of life that was in him, he asked for Lalaith.
But his nurse answered: 'Speak no more of Lalaith, son of
Húrin; but of your sister Urwen you must ask tidings of
your mother.'

And when Morwen came to him, Túrin said to her: 'I
am no longer sick, and I wish to see Urwen; but why must
I not say Lalaith any more?'

'Because Urwen is dead, and laughter is stilled in this
house,' she answered. 'But you live, son of Morwen; and
so does the Enemy who has done this to us.'

She did not seek to comfort him any more than herself;
for she met her grief in silence and coldness of heart. But
Húrin mourned openly, and he took up his harp and would
make a song of lamentation; but he could not, and he broke
his harp, and going out he lifted up his hand towards the
North, crying: 'Marrer of Middle-earth, would that I might
see you face to face, and mar you as my lord Fingolfin did!'

But Túrin wept bitterly at night alone, though to
Morwen he never again spoke the name of his sister. To

one friend only he turned at that time, and to him he
spoke of his sorrow and the emptiness of the house. This
friend was named Sador, a house-man in the service of
Húrin; he was lame, and of small account. He had been a
woodman, and by ill-luck or the mishandling of his axe he
had hewn his right foot, and the footless leg had shrunken;
and Túrin called him Labadal, which is 'Hopafoot',
though the name did not displease Sador, for it was given
in pity and not in scorn. Sador worked in the outbuild-
ings, to make or mend things of little worth that were
needed in the house, for he had some skill in the working
of wood; and Túrin would fetch him what he lacked, to
spare his leg, and sometimes he would carry off secretly
some tool or piece of timber that he found unwatched, if
he thought his friend might use it. Then Sador smiled, but
bade him return the gifts to their places; 'Give with a free
hand, but give only your own,' he said. He rewarded as he
could the kindness of the child, and carved for him the
figures of men and beasts; but Túrin delighted most in
Sador's tales, for he had been a young man in the days of
the Bragollach, and loved now to dwell upon the short
days of his full manhood before his maiming.

'That was a great battle, they say, son of Húrin. I was
called from my tasks in the wood in the need of that year;
but I was not in the Bragollach, or I might have got my
hurt with more honour. For we came too late, save to bear
back the bier of the old lord, Hador, who fell in the guard
of King Fingolfin. I went for a soldier after that, and I was

in Eithel Sirion, the great fort of the Elf-kings, for many years; or so it seems now, and the dull years since have little to mark them. In Eithel Sirion I was when the Black King assailed it, and Galdor your father's father was the captain there in the King's stead. He was slain in that assault; and I saw your father take up his lordship and his command, though but new come to manhood. There was a fire in him that made the sword hot in his hand, they said. Behind him we drove the Orcs into the sand; and they have not dared to come within sight of the walls since that day. But alas! my love of battle was sated, for I had seen spilled blood and wounds enough; and I got leave to come back to the woods that I yearned for. And there I got my hurt; for a man that flies from his fear may find that he has only taken a short cut to meet it.'

In this way Sador would speak to Túrin as he grew older; and Túrin began to ask many questions that Sador found hard to answer, thinking that others nearer akin should have had the teaching. And one day Túrin said to him: 'Was Lalaith indeed like an Elf-child, as my father said? And what did he mean, when he said that she was briefer?'

'Very like,' said Sador; 'for in their first youth the children of Men and Elves seem close akin. But the children of Men grow more swiftly, and their youth passes soon; such is our fate.'

Then Túrin asked him: 'What is fate?'

'As to the fate of Men,' said Sador, 'you must ask those that are wiser than Labadal. But as all can see, we weary soon and die; and by mischance many meet death even sooner. But the Elves do not weary, and they do not die save by great hurt. From wounds and griefs that would slay Men they may be healed; and even when their bodies are marred they return again, some say. It is not so with us.'

'Then Lalaith will not come back?' said Túrin. 'Where has she gone?'

'She will not come back,' said Sador. 'But where she has gone no man knows; or I do not.'

'Has it always been so? Or do we suffer some curse of the wicked King, perhaps, like the Evil Breath?'

'I do not know. A darkness lies behind us, and out of it few tales have come. The fathers of our fathers may have had things to tell, but they did not tell them. Even their names are forgotten. The Mountains stand between us and the life that they came from, flying from no man now knows what.'

'Were they afraid?' said Túrin.

'It may be,' said Sador. 'It may be that we fled from the fear of the Dark, only to find it here before us, and nowhere else to fly to but the Sea.'

'We are not afraid any longer,' said Túrin, 'not all of us. My father is not afraid, and I will not be; or at least, as my mother, I will be afraid and not show it.'

It seemed then to Sador that Túrin's eyes were not the eyes of a child, and he thought: 'Grief is a hone to a hard mind.' But aloud he said: 'Son of Húrin and Morwen, how it will be with your heart Labadal cannot guess; but seldom and to few will you show what is in it.'

Then Túrin said: 'Perhaps it is better not to tell what you wish, if you cannot have it. But I wish, Labadal, that I were one of the Eldar. Then Lalaith might come back, and I should still be here, even if she were long away. I shall go as a soldier with an Elf-king as soon as I am able, as you did, Labadal.'

'You may learn much of them,' said Sador, and he sighed. 'They are a fair folk and wonderful, and they have a power over the hearts of Men. And yet I think sometimes that it might have been better if we had never met them, but had walked in lowlier ways. For already they are ancient in knowledge; and they are proud and enduring. In their light we are dimmed, or we burn with too quick a flame, and the weight of our doom lies the heavier on us.'

'But my father loves them,' said Túrin, 'and he is not happy without them. He says that we have learned nearly all that we know from them, and have been made a nobler people; and he says that the Men that have lately come over the Mountains are hardly better than Orcs.'

'That is true,' answered Sador; 'true at least of some of us. But the up-climbing is painful, and from high places it is easy to fall low.'

At this time Túrin was almost eight years old, in the month of Gwaeron in the reckoning of the Edain, in the year that cannot be forgotten. Already there were rumours among his elders of a great mustering and gathering of arms, of which Túrin heard nothing; though he marked that his father often looked steadfastly at him, as a man might look at something dear that he must part from.

Now Húrin, knowing her courage and her guarded tongue, often spoke with Morwen of the designs of the Elven-kings, and of what might befall, if they went well or ill. His heart was high with hope, and he had little fear for the outcome of the battle; for it did not seem to him that any strength in Middle-earth could overthrow the might and splendour of the Eldar. 'They have seen the Light in the West,' he said, 'and in the end Darkness must flee from their faces.' Morwen did not gainsay him; for in Húrin's company the hopeful ever seemed the more likely. But there was knowledge of Elven-lore in her kindred also, and to herself she said: 'And yet did they not leave the Light, and are they not now shut out from it? It may be that the Lords of the West have put them out of their thought; and how then can even the Elder Children overcome one of the Powers?'

No shadow of such doubt seemed to lie on Húrin Thalion; yet one morning in the spring of that year he awoke heavy as after unquiet sleep, and a cloud lay on his brightness that day; and in the evening he said suddenly: 'When I am summoned, Morwen Eledhwen, I shall leave in your keeping the heir of the House of Hador. The lives of Men are short, and in them there are many ill chances, even in time of peace.'

'That has ever been so,' she answered. 'But what lies under your words?'

'Prudence, not doubt,' said Húrin; yet he looked troubled. 'But one who looks forward must see this: that things will not remain as they were. This will be a great throw, and one side must fall lower than it now stands. If it be the Elven-kings that fall, then it must go evilly with the Edain; and we dwell nearest to the Enemy. This land might pass into his dominion. But if things do go ill, I will not say to you: *Do not be afraid!* For you fear what should be feared, and that only; and fear does not dismay you. But I say: *Do not wait!* I shall return to you as I may, but do not wait! Go south as swiftly as you can – if I live I shall follow, and I shall find you, though I have to search through all Beleriand.'

'Beleriand is wide, and houseless for exiles,' said Morwen. 'Whither should I flee, with few or with many?'

Then Húrin thought for a while in silence. 'There is my mother's kin in Brethil,' he said. 'That is some thirty leagues, as the eagle flies.'

'If such an evil time should indeed come, what help would there be in Men?' said Morwen. 'The House of Bëor has fallen. If the great House of Hador falls, in what holes shall the little Folk of Haleth creep?'

'In such as they can find,' said Húrin. 'But do not doubt their valour, though they are few and unlearned. Where else is hope?'

'You do not speak of Gondolin,' said Morwen.

'No, for that name has never passed my lips,' said Húrin. 'Yet the word is true that you have heard: I have been there. But I tell you now truly, as I have told no other, and will not: I do not know where it stands.'

'But you guess, and guess near, I think,' said Morwen.

'It may be so,' said Húrin. 'But unless Turgon himself released me from my oath, I could not tell that guess, even to you; and therefore your search would be vain. But were I to speak, to my shame, you would at best but come at a shut gate; for unless Turgon comes out to war (and of that no word has been heard, and it is not hoped) no one will come in.'

'Then if your kin are not hopeful, and your friends deny you,' said Morwen, 'I must take counsel for myself; and to me now comes the thought of Doriath.'

'Ever your aim is high,' said Húrin.

'Over-high, you would say?' said Morwen. 'But last of all defences will the Girdle of Melian be broken, I think; and the House of Bëor will not be despised in Doriath. Am I not now kin of the king? For Beren son of Barahir was grandson of Bregor, as was my father also.'

'My heart does not lean to Thingol,' said Húrin. 'No help will come from him to King Fingon; and I know not what shadow falls on my spirit when Doriath is named.'

'At the name of Brethil my heart also is darkened,' said Morwen.

Then suddenly Húrin laughed, and he said: 'Here we sit debating things beyond our reach, and shadows that come out of dream. Things will not go so ill; but if they do, then to your courage and counsel all is committed. Do then what your heart bids you; but do it swiftly. And if we gain our ends, then the Elven-kings are resolved to restore all the fiefs of Bëor's house to his heir; and that is you, Morwen daughter of Baragund. Wide lordships we should then wield, and a high inheritance come to our son. Without the malice in the North he should come to great wealth, and be a king among Men.'

'Húrin Thalion,' said Morwen, 'this I judge truer to say: that you look high, but I fear to fall low.'

'That at the worst you need not fear,' said Húrin.

That night Túrin half-woke, and it seemed to him that his father and mother stood beside his bed, and looked down on him in the light of the candles that they held; but he could not see their faces.

On the morning of Túrin's birthday Húrin gave his son a gift, an Elf-wrought knife, and the hilt and the sheath were silver and black; and he said: 'Heir of the House of Hador, here is a gift for the day. But have a care! It is a bitter blade, and steel serves only those that can wield it. It will cut your hand as willingly as aught else.' And setting Túrin on a table he kissed his son, and said: 'You overtop me already, son of Morwen; soon you will be as high on your own feet. In that day many may fear your blade.'

Then Túrin ran from the room and went away alone, and in his heart was a warmth like the warmth of the sun upon the cold earth that sets growth astir. He repeated to himself his father's words, Heir of the House of Hador; but other words came also to his mind: Give with a free hand, but give of your own. And he went to Sador and cried: 'Labadal, it is my birthday, the birthday of the heir of the House of Hador! And I have brought you a gift to mark the day. Here is a knife, just such as you need; it will cut anything that you wish, as fine as a hair.'

Then Sador was troubled, for he knew well that Túrin had himself received the knife that day; but men held it a grievous thing to refuse a free-given gift from any hand. He spoke then to him gravely: 'You come of a generous kin, Túrin son of Húrin. I have done nothing to equal your gift, and I cannot hope to do better in the days that are left to me; but what I can do, I will.' And when Sador drew the knife from the sheath he said: 'This is a gift indeed: a blade of elven steel. Long have I missed the feel of it.'

Húrin soon marked that Túrin did not wear the knife, and he asked him whether his warning had made him fear it. Then Túrin answered: 'No; but I gave the knife to Sador the woodwright.'

'Do you then scorn your father's gift?' said Morwen; and again Túrin answered: 'No; but I love Sador, and I am sorry for him.'

Then Húrin said: 'All three gifts were your own to give, Túrin: love, pity, and the knife the least.'

'Yet I doubt if Sador deserves them,' said Morwen. 'He is self-maimed by his own want of skill, and he is slow with his tasks, for he spends much time on trifles unbidden.'

'Give him pity nonetheless,' said Húrin. 'An honest hand and a true heart may hew amiss; and the harm may be harder to bear than the work of a foe.'

'But you must wait now for another blade,' said Morwen. 'Thus the gift shall be a true gift and at your own cost.'

Nonetheless Túrin marked that Sador was treated more kindly thereafter, and was set now to the making of a great chair for the lord to sit on in his hall.

There came a bright morning in the month of Lothron when Túrin was roused by sudden trumpets; and running to the doors he saw in the court a great press of men on foot and on horse, and all fully armed as for war. There also stood Húrin, and he spoke to the men and gave commands; and Túrin learned that they were setting out that day for Barad Eithel. These were Húrin's guards and household men; but all the men of his land that could be spared were summoned. Some had gone already with Huor his father's brother; and many others would join the Lord of Dor-lómin on the road, and go behind his banner to the great muster of the King.

Then Morwen bade farewell to Húrin without tears; and she said: 'I will guard what you leave in my keeping, both what is and what shall be.'

And Húrin answered her: 'Farewell, Lady of Dor-lómin; we ride now with greater hope than ever we have known before. Let us think that at this midwinter the feast shall be merrier than in all our years yet, with a fearless spring to follow after!' Then he lifted Túrin to his shoulder, and cried to his men: 'Let the heir of the House of Hador see the light of your swords!' And the sun glittered on fifty blades as they leaped forth, and the court rang with the battle-cry of the Edain of the North: *Lacho calad! Drego morn!* Flame Light! Flee Night!

Then at last Húrin sprang into his saddle, and his golden banner was unfurled, and the trumpets sang again in the morning; and thus Húrin Thalion rode away to the Nirnaeth Arnoediad.

But Morwen and Túrin stood still by the doors, until far away they heard the faint call of a single horn on the wind: Húrin had passed over the shoulder of the hill, beyond which he could see his house no more.

CHAPTER II

THE BATTLE OF UNNUMBERED TEARS

Many songs are yet sung and many tales are yet told by the Elves of the Nirnaeth Arnoediad, the Battle of Unnumbered Tears, in which Fingon fell and the flower of the Eldar withered. If all were now retold a man's life would not suffice for the hearing. Here then shall be recounted only those deeds which bear upon the fate of the House of Hador and the children of Húrin the Steadfast.

Having gathered at length all the strength that he could Maedhros appointed a day, the morning of Midsummer. On that day the trumpets of the Eldar greeted the rising of the Sun, and in the east was raised the standard of the sons of Fëanor; and in the west the standard of Fingon, King of the Noldor.

Then Fingon looked out from the walls of Eithel Sirion, and his host was arrayed in the valleys and woods upon the east of Ered Wethrin, well hid from the eyes of the Enemy; but he knew that it was very great. For there all the Noldor of Hithlum were assembled, and to them were gathered many Elves of the Falas and of Nargothrond; and he had great strength of Men. Upon the right were stationed the host of Dor-lómin and all the valour of Húrin and Huor his brother, and to them had come Haldir of Brethil, their kinsman, with many men of the woods.

Then Fingon looked east and his elven-sight saw far off a dust and the glint of steel like stars in a mist, and he knew that Maedhros had set forth; and he rejoiced. Then he looked towards Thangorodrim, and there was a dark cloud about it and a black smoke went up; and he knew that the wrath of Morgoth was kindled and that their challenge would be accepted, and a shadow of doubt fell upon his heart. But at that moment a cry went up, passing on the wind from the south from vale to vale, and Elves and Men lifted up their voices in wonder and joy. For unsummoned and unlooked-for Turgon had opened the leaguer of Gondolin, and was come with an army, ten thousand strong, with bright mail and long swords and spears like a forest. Then when Fingon heard afar the great trumpet of Turgon, the shadow passed and his heart was uplifted, and he shouted aloud: *'Utúlie'n aurë! Aiya Eldalië ar Atanatarni, utúlie'n aurë!* The day has come! Behold, people of the Eldar and Fathers of Men, the day has come!' And all those who heard his great voice echo in the hills answered crying: *'Auta i lómë!* The night is passing!'

It was not long before the great battle was joined. For Morgoth knew much of what was done and designed by his foes and had laid his plans against the hour of their assault. Already a great force out of Angband was drawing near to Hithlum, while another and greater went to meet Maedhros to prevent the union of the powers of the kings. And those that came against Fingon were clad all in dun raiment and showed no naked steel, and thus were already far over the sands of Anfauglith before their approach became known.

Then the hearts of the Noldor grew hot, and their captains wished to assail their foes on the plain; but Fingon spoke against this.

'Beware of the guile of Morgoth, lords!' he said. 'Ever his strength is more than it seems, and his purpose other than he reveals. Do not reveal your own strength, but let the enemy spend his first in assault on the hills.' For it was the design of the kings that Maedhros should march openly over the Anfauglith with all his strength, of Elves and of Men and of Dwarves; and when he had drawn forth, as he hoped, the main armies of Morgoth in answer, then Fingon should come on from the West, and so the might of Morgoth should be taken as between hammer and anvil and be broken to pieces; and the signal for this was to be the firing of a great beacon in Dorthonion.

But the Captain of Morgoth in the west had been commanded to draw out Fingon from his hills by whatever means he could. He marched on, therefore, until the front of his battle was drawn up before the stream of Sirion, from the walls of the Barad Eithel to the Fen of Serech; and the outposts of Fingon could see the eyes of their enemies. But there was no answer to his challenge, and the taunts of his Orcs faltered as they looked upon the silent walls and the hidden threat of the hills.

Then the Captain of Morgoth sent out riders with tokens of parley, and they rode up before the very walls of the outworks of the Barad Eithel. With them they brought Gelmir son of Guilin, a lord of Nargothrond, whom they had captured in the Bragollach, and had blinded; and their heralds showed him forth crying: 'We have many more such at home, but you must make haste if you would find them. For we shall deal with them all when we return, even so.' And they hewed off Gelmir's arms and legs, and left him.

By ill chance at that point in the outposts stood Gwindor son of Guilin with many folk of Nargothrond; and indeed he had marched to war with such strength as he could gather because of his grief for the taking of his brother. Now his wrath was like a flame, and he leapt forth upon horse-back, and many riders with him, and they pursued the heralds of Angband and slew them; and all the folk of Nargothrond followed after, and they drove on deep into the ranks of Angband. And seeing this the host of the Noldor was set on fire, and Fingon put on his white helm, and sounded his trumpets, and all his host leapt forth from the hills in sudden onslaught.

The light of the drawing of the swords of the Noldor was like a fire in a field of reeds; and so fell and swift was their onset that almost the designs of Morgoth went astray. Before the decoying army that he had sent west could be strengthened it was swept away and destroyed, and the banners of Fingon passed over the Anfauglith and were raised before the walls of Angband.

Ever in the forefront of that battle went Gwindor and the folk of Nargothrond, and even now they could not be restrained; and they burst through the outer gates and slew the guards within the very courts of Angband; and Morgoth trembled upon his deep throne, hearing them beat upon his doors. But Gwindor was trapped there and taken alive and his folk slain; for Fingon could not come to his aid. By many secret doors in Thangorodrim Morgoth let forth his main strength that he had held in waiting, and Fingon was beaten back with great loss from the walls of Angband.

Then in the plain of the Anfauglith, on the fourth day of the war, there began the Nirnaeth Arnoediad, all the sorrow of which no tale can contain. Of all that befell in the eastward battle: of the routing of Glaurung the Dragon by the Dwarves of Belegost; of the treachery of the Easterlings and the overthrow of the host of Maedhros and the flight of the sons of Fëanor, no more is here said. In the west the host of Fingon retreated over the sands, and there fell Haldir son of Halmir and most of the Men of Brethil. But on the fifth day as night fell, and they were still far from Ered Wethrin, the armies of Angband surrounded the army of Fingon, and they fought until day, pressed ever closer. In the morning came hope, for the horns of Turgon were heard, as he marched up with the main host of Gondolin; for Turgon had been stationed southward guarding the passes of Sirion, and he had restrained most of his folk from the rash onslaught. Now he hastened to the aid of his brother; and the Noldor of Gondolin were strong and their ranks shone like a river of steel in the sun, for the sword and harness of the least of the warriors of Turgon was worth more than the ransom of any king among Men.

Now the phalanx of the guard of the King broke through the ranks of the Orcs, and Turgon hewed his way to the side of his brother. And it is said that the meeting of Turgon with Húrin who stood beside Fingon was glad in the midst of the battle. For a while then the hosts of Angband were driven back, and Fingon again began his retreat. But having routed Maedhros in the east Morgoth had now great forces to spare, and before Fingon and Turgon could come to the shelter of the hills they were assailed by a tide of foes thrice greater than all the force that was left to them. Gothmog, high-captain of Angband, was come; and he drove a dark wedge between the Elvenhosts, surrounding King Fingon, and thrusting Turgon and Húrin aside towards the Fen of Serech. Then he turned upon Fingon. That was a grim meeting. At last Fingon stood alone with his guard dead about him, and he fought with Gothmog, until a Balrog came behind him and cast a thong of steel round him. Then Gothmog hewed him with his black axe, and a white flame sprang up from the helm of Fingon as it was cloven. Thus fell the King of the Noldor; and they beat him into the dust with their maces, and his banner, blue and silver, they trod into the mire of his blood.

The field was lost; but still Húrin and Huor and the remnant of the House of Hador stood firm with Turgon of Gondolin; and the hosts of Morgoth could not yet win the passes of Sirion. Then Húrin spoke to Turgon, saying: 'Go now, lord, while time is! For you are the last of the House of Fingolfin, and in you lives the last hope of the Eldar. While Gondolin stands Morgoth shall still know fear in his heart.'

'Not long now can Gondolin remain hidden, and being discovered it must fall,' said Turgon.

'Yet if it stands only a little while,' said Huor, 'then out of your house shall come the hope of Elves and Men. This I say to you, lord, with the eyes of death: though we part here for ever, and I shall not look on your white walls again, from you and from me a new star shall arise. Farewell!'

Maeglin, Turgon's sister-son, who stood by, heard these words and did not forget them.

Then Turgon took the counsel of Húrin and Huor, and he gave orders that his host should begin a retreat into the passes of Sirion; and his captains Ecthelion and Glorfindel guarded the flanks to right and left so that none of the enemy should pass them by, for the only road in that region was narrow and ran near the west bank of the growing stream of Sirion. But the Men of Dor-lómin held the rearguard, as Húrin and Huor desired; for they did not wish in their hearts to escape from the Northlands; and if they could not win back to their homes, there they would stand to the end. So it was that Turgon fought his way southward, until coming behind the guard of Húrin and Huor, he passed down Sirion and escaped; and he vanished into the mountains and was hidden from the eyes of Morgoth. But the brothers drew the remnant of the mighty men of the House of Hador about them, and foot by foot they withdrew, until they came behind the Fen of Serech, and had the stream of Rivil before them. There they stood and gave way no more.

Then all the hosts of Angband swarmed against them, and they bridged the stream with their dead, and encircled the remnant of Hithlum as a gathering tide about a rock. There, as the Sun westered and the shadows of the Ered Wethrin grew dark, Huor fell pierced with a venomed arrow in the eye, and all the valiant men of Hador were slain about him in a heap; and the Orcs hewed their heads and piled them as a mound of gold in the sunset.

Last of all Húrin stood alone. Then he cast aside his shield, and seized the axe of an orc-captain and wielded it two-handed; and it is sung that the axe smoked in the black blood of the troll-guard of Gothmog until it withered, and each time that he slew Húrin cried aloud: *'Aure entuluva!*

Day shall come again!' Seventy times he uttered that cry; but they took him at last alive, by the command of Morgoth, who thought thus to do him more evil than by death. Therefore the Orcs grappled Húrin with their hands, which clung to him still, though he hewed off their arms; and ever their numbers were renewed, till he fell buried beneath them. Then Gothmog bound him and dragged him to Angband with mockery.

Thus ended the Nirnaeth Arnoediad, as the Sun went down beyond the Sea. Night fell in Hithlum, and there came a great storm of wind out of the West.

Great was the triumph of Morgoth, though all the purposes of his malice were not yet accomplished. One thought troubled him deeply and marred his victory with unquiet: Turgon had escaped his net, of all his foes the one whom he had most desired to take or destroy. For Turgon of the great House of Fingolfin was now by right King of all the Noldor; and Morgoth feared and hated the House of Fingolfin, because they had scorned him in Valinor and had the friendship of Ulmo his foe; and because of the wounds that Fingolfin gave him in battle. And most of all Morgoth feared Turgon, for of old in Valinor his eye had lighted on him, and whenever he drew near a dark shadow had fallen on his spirit, foreboding that in some time that yet lay hidden in doom, from Turgon ruin should come to him.

CHAPTER III

THE WORDS OF HÚRIN AND MORGOTH

Now by the command of Morgoth the Orcs with great labour gathered all the bodies of their enemies, and all their harness and weapons, and piled them in a mound in the midst of the plain of Anfauglith, and it was like a great hill that could be seen from afar, and the Eldar named it Haudh-en-Nirnaeth. But grass came there and grew again long and green upon that hill alone in all the desert; and no servant of Morgoth thereafter trod upon the earth beneath which the swords of the Eldar and the Edain crumbled into rust. The realm of Fingon was no more, and the Sons of Fëanor wandered as leaves before the wind. To Hithlum none of the Men of Hador's House returned, nor any tidings of the battle and the fate of their lords. But Morgoth sent thither Men who were under his dominion, swarthy Easterlings; and he shut them in that

61

land and forbade them to leave it. This was all that he gave them of the rich rewards that he had promised them for their treachery to Maedhros: to plunder and harass the old and the children and womenfolk of Hador's people. The remnant of the Eldar of Hithlum, all those who did not escape into the wilds and the mountains, he took to the mines of Angband and they became his thralls. But the Orcs went freely through all the North and pressed ever southward into Beleriand. There Doriath yet remained, and Nargothrond; but Morgoth gave little heed to them, either because he knew little of them, or because their hour was not yet come in the designs of his malice. But his thought ever returned to Turgon.

Therefore Húrin was brought before Morgoth, for Morgoth knew by his arts and his spies that Húrin had the friendship of the King; and he sought to daunt him with his eyes. But Húrin could not yet be daunted, and he defied Morgoth. Therefore Morgoth had him chained and set in slow torment; but after a while he came to him, and offered him his choice to go free whither he would, or to receive power and rank as the greatest of Morgoth's captains, if he would but reveal where Turgon had his stronghold, and aught else that he knew of the King's counsels. But Húrin the Steadfast mocked him, saying: 'Blind you are, Morgoth Bauglir, and blind shall ever be, seeing only the dark. You know not what rules the hearts of Men, and if you knew you could not give it. But a fool is he who accepts what Morgoth offers. You will take first the price and then withhold the promise; and I should get only death, if I told you what you ask.'

Then Morgoth laughed, and he said: 'Death you may yet crave of me as a boon.' Then he took Húrin to the Haudh-en-Nirnaeth, and it was then new-built and the reek of death was upon it; and Morgoth set Húrin upon its top and bade him look west towards Hithlum, and think of his wife and his son and other kin. 'For they dwell now in my realm,' said Morgoth, 'and they are at my mercy.'

'You have none,' answered Húrin. 'But you will not come at Turgon through them; for they do not know his secrets.'

Then wrath mastered Morgoth, and he said: 'Yet I may come at you, and all your accursed house; and you shall be broken on my will, though you all were made of steel.' And he took up a long sword that lay there and broke it before the eyes of Húrin, and a splinter wounded his face; but Húrin did not blench. Then Morgoth stretching out his long arm towards Dor-lómin cursed Húrin and Morwen and their offspring, saying: 'Behold! The shadow of my thought shall lie upon them wherever they go, and my hate shall pursue them to the ends of the world.'

But Húrin said: 'You speak in vain. For you cannot see them, nor govern them from afar: not while you keep this shape, and desire still to be a King visible on earth.'

Then Morgoth turned upon Húrin, and he said: 'Fool, little among Men, and they are the least of all that speak! Have you seen the Valar, or measured the power of Manwë and Varda? Do you know the reach of their thought? Or do you think, perhaps, that their thought is upon you, and that they may shield you from afar?'

'I know not,' said Húrin. 'Yet so it might be, if they willed. For the Elder King shall not be dethroned while Arda endures.'

'You say it,' said Morgoth. 'I am the Elder King: Melkor, first and mightiest of all the Valar, who was before the world, and made it. The shadow of my purpose lies upon Arda, and all that is in it bends slowly and surely to my will. But upon all whom you love my thought shall weigh as a cloud of Doom, and it shall bring them down into darkness and despair. Wherever they go, evil shall arise. Whenever they speak, their words shall bring ill counsel. Whatsoever they do shall turn against them. They shall die without hope, cursing both life and death.'

But Húrin answered: 'Do you forget to whom you speak? Such things you spoke long ago to our fathers; but we escaped from your shadow. And now we have knowledge of you, for we have looked on the faces that have seen the Light, and heard the voices that have spoken with Manwë. Before Arda you were, but others also; and you did not make it. Neither are you the most mighty; for you have spent your strength upon yourself and wasted it in your own emptiness. No more are you now than an escaped thrall of the Valar, and their chain still awaits you.'

'You have learned the lessons of your masters by rote,' said Morgoth. 'But such childish lore will not help you, now they are all fled away.'

'This last then I will say to you, thrall Morgoth,' said Húrin, 'and it comes not from the lore of the Eldar, but is put into my heart in this hour. You are not the Lord of Men, and shall not be, though all Arda and Menel fall in your dominion. Beyond the Circles of the World you shall not pursue those who refuse you.'

'Beyond the Circles of the World I will not pursue them,' said Morgoth. 'For beyond the Circles of the World there is Nothing. But within them they shall not escape me, until they enter into Nothing.'

'You lie,' said Húrin.

'You shall see and you shall confess that I do not lie,' said Morgoth. And taking Húrin back to Angband he set him in a chair of stone upon a high place of Thangorodrim, from which he could see afar the land of Hithlum in the west and the lands of Beleriand in the south. There he was bound by the power of Morgoth; and Morgoth standing beside him cursed him again and set his power upon him, so that he could not move from that place, nor die, until Morgoth should release him.

'Sit now there,' said Morgoth, 'and look out upon the lands where evil and despair shall come upon those whom you have delivered to me. For you have dared to mock me, and have questioned the power of Melkor, Master of the fates of Arda. Therefore with my eyes you shall see, and with my ears you shall hear, and nothing shall be hidden from you.'

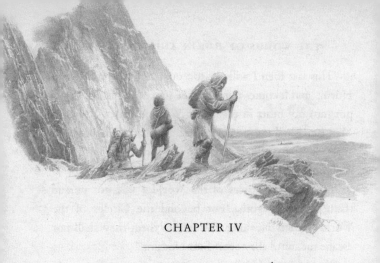

CHAPTER IV

THE DEPARTURE OF TÚRIN

To Brethil three men only found their way back at last through Taur-nu-Fuin, an evil road; and when Glóredhel Hador's daughter learned of the fall of Haldir she grieved and died.

To Dor-lómin no tidings came. Rían wife of Huor fled into the wild distraught; but she was aided by the Grey-elves of Mithrim, and when her child, Tuor, was born they fostered him. But Rían went to the Haudh-en-Nirnaeth, and laid herself down there, and died.

Morwen Eledhwen remained in Hithlum, silent in grief. Her son Túrin was only in his ninth year, and she was again with child. Her days were evil. The Easterlings came into the land in great numbers and they dealt cruelly with the people of Hador, and robbed them of all that they possessed and enslaved them. All the people of Húrin's homelands that could work or serve any purpose they took away, even young girls and boys, and the old they killed or drove out to starve. But they dared not yet lay hands on the Lady of Dor-lómin, or thrust her from her house; for the word ran among them that she was perilous, and a witch who had dealings with the white-fiends: for so they named the Elves, hating them, but fearing them more. For this reason they also feared and avoided the mountains, in which many of the Eldar had taken refuge, especially in the south of the land; and after plundering and harrying the Easterlings drew back northwards. For Húrin's house stood in the south-east of Dor-lómin, and the mountains were near; Nen Lalaith indeed came down from a spring under the shadow of Amon Darthir, over whose shoulder there was a steep pass. By this the hardy could cross Ered Wethrin and come down by the wells of Glithui into Beleriand. But this was not known to the Easterlings, nor to Morgoth yet; for all that country, while the House of Fingolfin stood, was secure from him, and none of his servants had ever come there. He trusted that Ered Wethrin was a wall insurmountable, both against escape from the north and against assault from the south; and there was indeed no other pass, for the unwinged, between Serech and far westward where Dor-lómin marched with Nevrast.

Thus it came to pass that after the first inroads Morwen was let be, though there were men that lurked in the woods about and it was perilous to stir far abroad. There still remained under Morwen's shelter Sador the woodwright

and a few old men and women, and Túrin, whom she kept
close within the garth. But the homestead of Húrin soon
fell into decay, and though Morwen laboured hard she was
poor, and would have gone hungry but for the help that
was sent to her secretly by Aerin, Húrin's kinswoman; for
a certain Brodda, one of the Easterlings, had taken her by
force to be his wife. Alms were bitter to Morwen; but she
took this aid for the sake of Túrin and her unborn child,
and because, as she said, it came of her own. For it was this
Brodda who had seized the people, the goods, and the cattle
of Húrin's homelands, and carried them off to his own
dwellings. He was a bold man, but of small account among
his own people before they came to Hithlum; and so,
seeking wealth, he was ready to hold lands that others of his
sort did not covet. Morwen he had seen once, when he rode
to her house on a foray; but a great dread of her had seized
him. He thought that he had looked in the fell eyes of a
white-fiend, and he was filled with a mortal fear lest some
evil should overtake him; and he did not ransack her house,
nor discover Túrin, else the life of the heir of the true lord
would have been short.

Brodda made thralls of the Strawheads, as he named
the people of Hador, and set them to build him a wooden
hall in the land to the northward of Húrin's house; and
within a stockade his slaves were herded like cattle in a
byre, but ill guarded. Among them some could still be
found uncowed and ready to help the Lady of Dor-lómin,
even at their peril; and from them came secretly tidings of

the land to Morwen, though there was little hope in the news they brought. But Brodda took Aerin as a wife and not a slave, for there were few women amongst his own following, and none to compare with the daughters of the Edain; and he hoped to make himself a lordship in that country, and have an heir to hold it after him.

Of what had happened and of what might happen in the days to come Morwen said little to Túrin; and he feared to break her silence with questions. When the Easterlings first came into Dor-lómin he said to his mother: 'When will my father come back, to cast out these ugly thieves? Why does he not come?'

Morwen answered: 'I do not know. It may be that he was slain, or that he is held captive; or again it may be that he was driven far away, and cannot yet return through the foes that surround us.'

'Then I think that he is dead,' said Túrin, and before his mother he restrained his tears; 'for no one could keep him from coming back to help us, if he were alive.'

'I do not think that either of those things are true, my son,' said Morwen.

As the time lengthened the heart of Morwen grew darker for her son Túrin, heir of Dor-lómin and Ladros; for she could see no hope for him better than to become a slave of the Easterling men, before he was much older. Therefore she remembered her words with Húrin, and her thought turned again to Doriath; and she resolved at last

to send Túrin away in secret, if she could, and to beg King
Thingol to harbour him. And as she sat and pondered
how this might be done, she heard clearly in her thought
the voice of Húrin saying to her: *Go swiftly! Do not wait
for me!* But the birth of her child was drawing near, and
the road would be hard and perilous; the more that went
the less hope of escape. And her heart still cheated her
with hope unadmitted; her inmost thought foreboded that
Húrin was not dead, and she listened for his footfall in the
sleepless watches of the night, or would wake thinking
that she had heard in the courtyard the neigh of Arroch
his horse. Moreover, though she was willing that her son
should be fostered in the halls of another, after the manner
of that time, she would not yet humble her pride to be an
alms-guest, not even of a king. Therefore the voice of
Húrin, or the memory of his voice, was denied, and the
first strand of the fate of Túrin was woven.

Autumn of the Year of Lamentation was drawing on
before Morwen came to this resolve, and then she was in
haste; for the time for journeying was short, but she
dreaded that Túrin would be taken, if she waited over
winter. Easterlings were prowling round the garth and
spying on the house. Therefore she said suddenly to
Túrin: 'Your father does not come. So you must go, and
soon. It is as he would wish.'

'Go?' cried Túrin. 'Whither shall we go? Over the
Mountains?'

'Yes,' said Morwen, 'over the Mountains, away south. South – that way some hope may lie. But I did not say *we*, my son. You must go, but I must stay.'

'I cannot go alone!' said Túrin. 'I will not leave you. Why should we not go together?'

'I cannot go,' said Morwen. 'But you will not go alone. I shall send Gethron with you, and Grithnir too, perhaps.'

'Will you not send Labadal?' said Túrin.

'No, for Sador is lame,' said Morwen, 'and it will be a hard road. And since you are my son and the days are grim, I will not speak softly: you may die on that road. The year is getting late. But if you stay, you will come to a worse end: to be a thrall. If you wish to be a man, when you come to a man's age, you will do as I bid, bravely.'

'But I shall leave you only with Sador, and blind Ragnir, and the old women,' said Túrin. 'Did not my father say that I am the heir of Hador? The heir should stay in Hador's house to defend it. Now I wish that I still had my knife!'

'The heir should stay, but he cannot,' said Morwen. 'But he may return one day. Now take heart! I will follow you, if things grow worse; if I can.'

'But how will you find me, lost in the wild? said Túrin; and suddenly his heart failed him, and he wept openly.

'If you wail, other things will find you first,' said Morwen. 'But I know whither you are going, and if you come there, and if you remain there, there I will find you, if I can. For I am sending you to King Thingol in Doriath. Would you not rather be a king's guest than a thrall?'

'I do not know,' said Túrin. 'I do not know what a thrall is.'

'I am sending you away so that you need not learn it,' Morwen answered. Then she set Túrin before her and looked into his eyes, as if she were trying to read some riddle there. 'It is hard, Túrin, my son,' she said at length. 'Not hard for you only. It is heavy on me in evil days to judge what is best to do. But I do as I think right; for why else should I part with the thing most dear that is left to me?'

They spoke no more of this together, and Túrin was grieved and bewildered. In the morning he went to find Sador, who had been hewing sticks for firing, of which they had little, for they dared not stray out in the woods; and now he leant on his crutch and looked at the great chair of Húrin, which had been thrust unfinished in a corner. 'It must go,' he said, 'for only bare needs can be served in these days.'

'Do not break it yet,' said Túrin. 'Maybe he will come home, and then it will please him to see what you have done for him while he was away.'

'False hopes are more dangerous than fears,' said Sador, 'and they will not keep us warm this winter.' He fingered the carving on the chair, and sighed. 'I wasted my time,' he said, 'though the hours seemed pleasant. But all such things are short-lived; and the joy in the making is their only true end, I guess. And now I might as well give you back your gift.'

Túrin put out his hand, and quickly withdrew it. 'A man does not take back his gifts,' he said.

'But if it is my own, may I not give it as I will?' said Sador.

'Yes,' said Túrin, 'to any man but me. But why should you wish to give it?'

'I have no hope of using it for worthy tasks,' Sador said. 'There will be no work for Labadal in days to come but thrall-work.'

'What is a thrall?' said Túrin.

'A man who was a man but is treated as a beast,' Sador answered. 'Fed only to keep alive, kept alive only to toil, toiling only for fear of pain or death. And from these robbers he may get pain or death just for their sport. I hear that they pick some of the fleet-footed and hunt them with hounds. They have learned quicker from the Orcs than we learnt from the Fair Folk.'

'Now I understand things better,' said Túrin.

'It is a shame that you should have to understand such things so soon,' said Sador; then seeing the strange look on Túrin's face: 'What do you understand now?'

'Why my mother is sending me away,' said Túrin, and tears filled his eyes.

'Ah!' said Sador, and he muttered to himself: 'But why so long delayed?' Then turning to Túrin he said: 'That does not seem news for tears to me. But you should not speak your mother's counsels aloud to Labadal, or to anyone. All walls and fences have ears these days, ears that do not grow on fair heads.'

'But I must speak with someone!' said Túrin. 'I have always told things to you. I do not want to leave you, Labadal. I do not want to leave this house or my mother.'

'But if you do not,' said Sador, 'soon there will be an end of the House of Hador for ever, as you must understand now. Labadal does not want you to go; but Sador servant of Húrin will be happier when Húrin's son is out of the reach of the Easterlings. Well, well, it cannot be helped: we must say farewell. Now will you not take my knife as a parting gift?'

'No!' said Túrin. 'I am going to the Elves, to the King of Doriath, my mother says. There I may get other things like it. But I shall not be able to send you any gifts, Labadal. I shall be far away and all alone.' Then Túrin wept; but Sador said to him: 'Hey now! Where is Húrin's son? For I heard him say, not long ago: *I shall go as a soldier with an Elf-king, as soon as I am able.*'

Then Túrin stayed his tears, and he said: 'Very well: if those were the words of the son of Húrin, he must keep them, and go. But whenever I say that I will do this or that, it looks very different when the time comes. Now I am unwilling. I must take care not to say such things again.'

'It would be best indeed,' said Sador. 'So most men teach, and few men learn. Let the unseen days be. Today is more than enough.'

Now Túrin was made ready for the journey, and he bade farewell to his mother, and departed in secret with his two companions. But when they bade Túrin turn and look back upon the house of his father, then the anguish of parting smote him like a sword, and he cried: 'Morwen, Morwen, when shall I see you again?' But Morwen standing on her threshold heard the echo of that cry in the wooded hills, and she clutched the post of the door so that her fingers were torn. This was the first of the sorrows of Túrin.

Early in the year after Túrin was gone Morwen gave birth to her child, and she named her Niënor, which is Mourning; but Túrin was already far away when she was born. Long and evil was his road, for the power of Morgoth was ranging far abroad; but he had as guides Gethron and Grithnir, who had been young in the days of Hador, and though they were now aged they were valiant, and they knew well the lands, for they had journeyed often through Beleriand in former times. Thus by fate and courage they passed over the Shadowy Mountains, and coming down into the Vale of Sirion they passed into the Forest of Brethil; and at last, weary and haggard, they reached the confines of Doriath. But there they became bewildered, and were enmeshed in the mazes of the Queen, and wandered lost amid the pathless trees, until all their food was spent. There they came near to death, for winter came cold from the North; but not so light was Túrin's doom. Even as they lay in despair they heard a horn sounded. Beleg the Strong-bow was hunting in that region, for he dwelt ever on the marches of Doriath, and he was the greatest woodsman of those days. He heard their cries and came to them, and when he had given them food and drink he learned their names and whence they came, and he was filled with wonder and pity. And he looked with liking upon Túrin, for he had the beauty of his mother and the eyes of his father, and he was sturdy and strong.

'What boon would you have of King Thingol?' said Beleg to the boy.

'I would be one of his knights, to ride against Morgoth, and avenge my father,' said Túrin.

'That may well be, when the years have increased you,' said Beleg. 'For though you are yet small you have the makings of a valiant man, worthy to be a son of Húrin the Steadfast, if that were possible.' For the name of Húrin was held in honour in all the lands of the Elves. Therefore Beleg gladly became the guide of the wanderers, and he led them to a lodge where he dwelt at that time with other hunters, and there they were housed while a messenger went to Menegroth. And when word came back that Thingol and Melian would receive the son of Húrin and his guardians, Beleg led them by secret ways into the Hidden Kingdom.

Thus Túrin came to the great bridge over the Esgalduin, and passed the gates of Thingol's halls; and as a child he gazed upon the marvels of Menegroth, which no mortal Man before had seen, save Beren only. Then Gethron spoke the message of Morwen before Thingol and Melian;

and Thingol received them kindly, and set Túrin upon his knee in honour of Húrin, mightiest of Men, and of Beren his kinsman. And those that saw this marvelled, for it was a sign that Thingol took Túrin as his foster-son; and that was not at that time done by kings, nor ever again by Elf-lord to a Man. Then Thingol said to him: 'Here, son of Húrin, shall your home be; and in all your life you shall be held as my son, Man though you be. Wisdom shall be given you beyond the measure of mortal Men, and the weapons of the Elves shall be set in your hands. Perhaps the time may come when you shall regain the lands of your father in Hithlum; but dwell now here in love.'

Thus began the sojourn of Túrin in Doriath. With him remained for a while Gethron and Grithnir his guardians, though they yearned to return again to their lady in Dor-lómin. Then age and sickness came upon Grithnir, and he stayed beside Túrin until he died; but Gethron departed, and Thingol sent with him an escort to guide him and guard him, and they brought words from Thingol to Morwen. They came at last to Húrin's house, and when Morwen learned that Túrin was received with honour in the halls of Thingol her grief was lightened; and the Elves brought also rich gifts from Melian, and a message bidding her return with Thingol's folk to Doriath. For Melian was wise and foresighted, and she hoped thus to avert the evil that was prepared in the thought of Morgoth. But Morwen would not depart from her house, for her heart was yet unchanged and her pride still high; moreover Niënor was a babe in arms. Therefore she dismissed the Elves of Doriath with her thanks, and gave them in gift the last small things of gold that remained to her, concealing her poverty; and she bade them take back to Thingol the Helm of Hador. But Túrin watched ever for the return of Thingol's messengers; and when they came back alone he fled into the woods and wept, for he knew of Melian's bidding and he had hoped that Morwen would come. This was the second sorrow of Túrin. When the messengers spoke Morwen's answer, Melian was moved with pity, perceiving her mind; and she saw that the fate which she foreboded could not lightly be set aside.

The Helm of Hador was given into Thingol's hands. That helm was made of grey steel adorned with gold, and on it were graven runes of victory. A power was in it that guarded any who wore it from wound or death, for the sword that hewed it was broken, and the dart that smote it sprang aside. It was wrought by Telchar, the smith of Nogrod, whose works were renowned. It had a visor (after the manner of those that the Dwarves used in their forges for the shielding of their eyes), and the face of one that wore it struck fear into the hearts of all beholders, but was itself guarded from dart and fire. Upon its crest was set in defiance a gilded image of Glaurung the dragon; for it had been made soon after he first issued from the gates of Morgoth. Often Hador, and Galdor after him, had borne it in war; and the hearts of the host of Hithlum were uplifted when they saw it towering high amid the battle, and they cried: 'Of more worth is the Dragon of Dor-lómin than the gold-worm of Angband!' But Húrin did not wear the Dragon-helm with ease, and in any case he would not use it, for he said: 'I would rather look on my foes with my true face.' Nonetheless he accounted the helm among the greatest heirlooms of his house.

Now Thingol had in Menegroth deep armouries filled with great wealth of weapons: metal wrought like fishes' mail and shining like water in the moon; swords and axes, shields and helms, wrought by Telchar himself or by his master Gamil Zirak the old, or by elven-wrights more skilful still. For some things he had received in gift that came out of Valinor and were wrought by Fëanor in his mastery, than whom no craftsman was greater in all the days of the world. Yet Thingol handled the Helm of Hador as though his hoard were scanty, and he spoke courteous words, saying: 'Proud were the head that bore this helm, which the sires of Húrin bore.'

Then a thought came to him, and he summoned Túrin, and told him that Morwen had sent to her son a mighty thing, the heirloom of his fathers. 'Take now the Dragon-head of the North,' he said, 'and when the time comes wear it well.' But Túrin was yet too young to lift the helm, and he heeded it not because of the sorrow of his heart.

CHAPTER V

TÚRIN IN DORIATH

In the years of his childhood in the kingdom of Doriath Túrin was watched over by Melian, though he saw her seldom. But there was a maiden named Nellas, who lived in the woods; and at Melian's bidding she would follow Túrin if he strayed in the forest, and often she met him there, as it were by chance. Then they played together, or walked hand in hand; for he grew swiftly, whereas she seemed no more than a maiden of his own age, and was so in heart for all her elven-years. From Nellas Túrin learned much concerning the ways and the wild things of Doriath, and she taught him to speak the Sindarin tongue after the manner of the ancient realm, older, and more courteous, and richer in beautiful words. Thus for a little while his mood was lightened, until he fell again under shadow, and that friendship passed like a morning of spring. For Nellas did not go to Menegroth, and was unwilling ever to walk under roofs of stone; so that as Túrin's boyhood passed and he turned his thoughts to deeds of men, he saw her less and less often, and at last called for her no more. But she watched over him still, though now she remained hidden.

Nine years Túrin dwelt in the halls of Menegroth. His heart and thought turned ever to his own kin, and at times he had tidings of them for his own comfort. For Thingol sent messengers to Morwen as often as he might, and she sent back words for her son; thus Túrin heard that Morwen's plight was eased, and that his sister Niënor grew in beauty, a flower in the grey North. And Túrin grew in stature until he became tall among Men and surpassed that of the Elves of Doriath, and his strength and hardihood were renowned in the realm of Thingol. In those years he learned much lore, hearing eagerly the histories of ancient days and great deeds of old, and he became thoughtful, and sparing in speech. Often Beleg Strongbow came to Menegroth to seek him, and led him far afield, teaching him woodcraft and archery and (which he liked more) the handling of swords; but in crafts of making he had less skill, for he was slow to learn his own strength, and often marred what he made with some sudden stroke. In other matters also it seemed that fortune was unfriendly to him, so that often what he designed went awry, and what he desired he did not gain; neither did he win friendship easily, for he was not merry, and laughed seldom, and a shadow lay on his youth. Nonetheless he was held in love and esteem by those who knew him well, and he had honour as the fosterling of the King.

Yet there was one in Doriath that begrudged him this, and ever the more as Túrin drew nearer to manhood: Saeros was his name. He was proud, dealing haughtily with those whom he deemed of lesser state and worth than himself. He became a friend of Daeron the minstrel, for he also was skilled in song; and he had no love for Men, and least of all for any kinsman of Beren One-hand. 'Is it not strange,' said he, 'that this land should be opened to yet another of this unhappy race? Did not the other do harm enough in Doriath?' Therefore he looked askance at Túrin and on all that he did, saying what ill he could of it; but his words were cunning and his malice veiled. If he met with Túrin alone, he spoke haughtily to him and showed plain his contempt; and Túrin grew weary of him, though for long he returned ill words with silence, for Saeros was great among the people of Doriath and a counsellor of the King. But the silence of Túrin displeased Saeros as much as his words.

In the year that Túrin was seventeen years old, his grief was renewed; for all tidings from his home ceased at that time. The power of Morgoth had grown yearly, and all Hithlum was now under his shadow. Doubtless he knew much of the doings of Húrin's people and kin, and had not molested them for a while, so that his design might be fulfilled; but now in pursuit of this purpose he set a close watch on all the passes of the Shadowy Mountains, so that none might come out of Hithlum nor enter it, save at great peril, and the Orcs swarmed about the sources of Narog and Teiglin and the upper waters of Sirion. Thus there came a time when the messengers of Thingol did not return, and he would send no more. He was ever loath to let any stray beyond the guarded borders, and in nothing had he shown greater good will to Húrin and his kin than in sending his people on the dangerous roads to Morwen in Dor-lómin.

Now Túrin grew heavy-hearted, not knowing what new evil was afoot, and fearing that an ill fate had befallen Morwen and Niënor; and for many days he sat silent, brooding on the downfall of the House of Hador and the Men of the North. Then he rose up and went to seek Thingol; and he found him sitting with Melian under Hírilorn, the great beech of Menegroth.

Thingol looked on Túrin in wonder, seeing suddenly before him in the place of his fosterling a Man and a stranger, tall, dark-haired, looking at him with deep eyes in a white face, stern and proud; but he did not speak.

'What do you desire, foster-son?' said Thingol, and guessed that he would ask for nothing small.

'Mail, sword, and shield of my stature, lord,' answered Túrin. 'Also by your leave I will now reclaim the Dragon-helm of my sires.'

'These you shall have,' said Thingol. 'But what need have you yet of such arms?'

'The need of a man,' said Túrin; 'and of a son who has kin to remember. And I need also companions valiant in arms.'

'I will appoint you a place among my knights of the sword, for the sword will ever be your weapon,' said Thingol. 'With them you may make trial of war upon the marches, if that is your desire.'

'Beyond the marches of Doriath my heart urges me,' said Túrin. 'For onset against our foe I long, rather than defence.'

'Then you must go alone,' said Thingol. 'The part of my people in the war with Angband I rule according to my wisdom, Túrin son of Húrin. No force of the arms of Doriath will I send out at this time; nor at any time that I can yet foresee.'

'Yet you are free to go as you will, son of Morwen,' said Melian. 'The Girdle of Melian does not hinder the going of those that passed in with our leave.'

'Unless wise counsel will restrain you,' said Thingol.

'What is your counsel, lord?' said Túrin.

'A Man you seem in stature, and indeed more than many already,' Thingol answered; 'but nonetheless you have not come to the fullness of your manhood that shall be. Until that is achieved, you should be patient, testing and training your strength. Then, maybe, you can remember your kin; but there is little hope that one Man alone can do more against the Dark Lord than to aid the Elf-lords in their defence, as long as that may last.'

Then Túrin said: 'Beren my kinsman did more.'

'Beren, and Lúthien,' said Melian. 'But you are over-bold to speak so to the father of Lúthien. Not so high is your destiny, I think, Túrin son of Morwen, though great-ness is in you, and your fate is twined with that of the Elven-folk, for good or for ill. Beware of yourself, lest it be ill.' Then after a silence she spoke to him again, saying: 'Go now, fosterson; and take the advice of the King. That will ever be wiser than your own counsel. Yet I do not think that you will long abide with us in Doriath beyond the coming of manhood. If in days to come you remem-ber the words of Melian, it will be for your good: fear both the heat and the cold of your heart, and strive for patience, if you can.'

Then Túrin bowed before them, and took his leave. And soon after he put on the Dragon-helm, and took arms, and went away to the north-marches, and was joined to the elven-warriors who there waged unceasing war upon the Orcs and all servants and creatures of Morgoth. Thus while yet scarcely out of his boyhood his strength and courage were proved; and remembering the wrongs of his kin he was ever forward in deeds of daring, and he received many wounds by spear or arrow or the crooked blades of the Orcs.

But his doom delivered him from death; and word ran through the woods, and was heard far beyond Doriath, that the Dragon-helm of Dor-lómin was seen again. Then many wondered, saying: 'Can the spirit of any man return from death; or has Húrin of Hithlum escaped indeed from the pits of Hell?'

One only was mightier in arms among the march-wardens of Thingol at that time than Túrin, and that was Beleg Strongbow; and Beleg and Túrin were companions in every peril, and walked far and wide in the wild woods together.

Thus three years passed, and in that time Túrin came seldom to Thingol's halls; and he cared no longer for his looks or his attire, but his hair was unkempt, and his mail covered with a grey cloak stained with the weather. But it chanced in the third summer after Túrin's departure, when he was twenty years old, that desiring rest and needing smithwork for the repair of his arms he came unlooked for to Menegroth, and went one evening into the hall. Thingol was not there, for he was abroad in the greenwood with Melian, as was his delight at times in the high summer. Túrin took a seat without heed, for he was wayworn, and filled with thought; and by ill-luck he set himself at a board among the elders of the realm, and in that place where Saeros was accustomed to sit. Saeros, entering late, was angered, believing that Túrin had done this in pride, and with intent to affront him; and his anger was not lessened to find that Túrin was not rebuked by those that sat there, but was welcomed as one worthy to sit among them.

For a while therefore Saeros feigned to be of like mind, and took another seat, facing Túrin across the board.

'Seldom does the march-warden favour us with his company,' he said; 'and I gladly yield my accustomed seat for the chance of speech with him.' But Túrin, who was in converse with Mablung the Hunter, did not rise, and said only a curt 'I thank you'.

Saeros then plied him with questions, concerning the news from the borders, and his deeds in the wild; but though his words seemed fair, the mockery in his voice could not be mistaken. Then Túrin became weary, and he looked about him, and knew the bitterness of exile; and for all the light and laughter of the Elven-halls his thought turned to Beleg and their life in the woods, and thence far away, to Morwen in Dor-lómin in the house of his father; and he frowned, because of the darkness of his thoughts, and made no answer to Saeros. At this, believing the frown aimed at himself, Saeros restrained his anger no longer; and he took out a golden comb, and cast it on the board before Túrin, crying: 'Doubtless, Man of Hithlum, you came in haste to this table, and may be excused your ragged cloak; but there is no need to leave your head untended as a thicket of brambles. And maybe if your ears were uncovered you would heed better what is said to you.'

Túrin said nothing, but turned his eyes upon Saeros, and there was a glint in their darkness. But Saeros did not heed the warning, and returned the gaze with scorn, saying for all to hear: 'If the Men of Hithlum are so wild and fell, of what sort are the women of that land? Do they run like the deer clad only in their hair?'

Then Túrin took up a drinking-vessel and cast it in Saeros' face, and he fell backward with great hurt; and Túrin drew his sword and would have run at him, but Mablung restrained him. Then Saeros rising spat blood upon the board, and spoke as best he could with a broken mouth: 'How long shall we harbour this woodwose? Who rules here tonight? The King's law is heavy upon those who hurt his lieges in the hall; and for those who draw blades there outlawry is the least doom. Outside the hall I could answer you, Woodwose!'

But when Túrin saw the blood upon the table his mood became cold; and with a shrug he released himself from Mablung and left the hall without a word.

Then Mablung said to Saeros: 'What ails you tonight? For this evil I hold you to blame; and maybe the King's law will judge a broken mouth a just return for your taunting.'

'If the cub has a grievance, let him bring it to the King's judgement,' answered Saeros. 'But the drawing of swords here is not to be excused for any such cause. Outside the hall, if the woodwose draws on me, I shall kill him.'

'It might well go otherwise,' said Mablung. 'But if either be slain it will be an evil deed, more fit for Angband than Doriath, and more evil will come of it. Indeed I feel that some shadow of the North has reached out to touch us tonight. Take heed, Saeros, lest you do the will of Morgoth in your pride, and remember that you are of the Eldar.'

'I do not forget it,' said Saeros; but he did not abate his wrath, and through the night his malice grew, nursing his injury.

In the morning he waylaid Túrin, as he set off early from Menegroth, intending to go back to the marches. Túrin had gone only a little way when Saeros ran out upon him from behind with drawn sword and shield on arm. But Túrin, trained in the wild to wariness, saw him from the corner of his eye, and leaping aside he drew swiftly and turned upon his foe. 'Morwen!' he cried, 'now your mocker shall pay for his scorn!' And he clove Saeros' shield, and then they fought together with swift blades. But Túrin had been long in a hard school, and had grown as agile as any Elf, but stronger. He soon had the mastery, and wounding Saeros' sword-arm he had him at his mercy. Then he set his foot on the sword that Saeros had let fall. 'Saeros,' he said, 'there is a long race before you, and clothes will be a hindrance; hair must suffice.' And suddenly throwing him to the ground he stripped him, and Saeros felt Túrin's great strength, and was afraid. But Túrin let him up, and then 'Run, run, mocker of women!' he cried. 'Run! And unless you go swift as the deer I shall prick you on from behind.' Then he set the point of the sword in Saeros' buttock; and he fled into the wood, crying wildly for help in his terror; but Túrin came after him like a hound, and however he ran, or swerved, still the sword was behind him to egg him on.

The cries of Saeros brought many others to the chase, and they followed after, but only the swiftest could keep up with the runners. Mablung was in the forefront of these, and he was troubled in mind, for though the taunting had seemed evil to him, 'malice that wakes in the morning is the mirth of Morgoth ere night'; and it was held moreover a grievous thing to put any of the Elven-folk to shame, self-willed, without the matter being brought to judgement. None knew at that time that Túrin had been assailed first by Saeros, who would have slain him.

'Hold, hold, Túrin!' he cried. 'This is Orc-work in the woods!' 'Orc-work there was; this is only Orc-play,' Túrin called back. Before Mablung spoke he had been on the point of releasing Saeros, but now with a shout he sprang after him again; and Saeros, despairing at last of aid and thinking his death close behind, ran wildly on, until he came suddenly to a brink where a stream that fed Esgalduin flowed in a deep cleft through high rocks, and it was wide for a deer-leap. In his terror Saeros attempted the leap; but he failed of his footing on the far side and fell back with a cry, and was broken on a great stone in the water. So he ended his life in Doriath; and long would Mandos hold him.

Túrin looked down on his body lying in the stream, and he thought: 'Unhappy fool! From here I would have let him walk back to Menegroth. Now he has laid a guilt upon me undeserved.' And he turned and looked darkly on Mablung and his companions, who now came up and stood near him on the brink. Then after a silence Mablung said gravely: 'Alas! But come back now with us, Túrin, for the King must judge these deeds.'

But Túrin said: 'If the King were just, he would judge me guiltless. But was not this one of his counsellors? Why should a just king choose a heart of malice for his friend? I abjure his law and his judgement.'

'Your words are too proud,' said Mablung, though he pitied the young man. 'Learn wisdom! You shall not turn runagate. I bid you return with me, as a friend. And there are other witnesses. When the King learns the truth you may hope for his pardon.'

But Túrin was weary of the Elven-halls, and he feared lest he be held captive; and he said to Mablung: 'I refuse your bidding. I will not seek King Thingol's pardon for nothing; and I will go now where his doom cannot find me. You have but two choices: to let me go free, or to slay me, if that would fit your law. For you are too few to take me alive.'

They saw by the fire in his eyes that this was true, and they let him pass. 'One death is enough,' said Mablung.

'I did not will it, but I do not mourn it,' said Túrin. 'May Mandos judge him justly; and if ever he return to the lands of the living, may he prove wiser. Farewell!'

'Fare free!' said Mablung; 'for that is your wish. To say *well* would be vain, if you go in this way. A shadow is over you. When we meet again, may it be no darker.'

To that Túrin made no answer, but left them, and went swiftly away, alone, none knew whither.

It is told that when Túrin did not return to the north-marches of Doriath and no tidings could be heard of him,

Beleg Strongbow came himself to Menegroth to seek him; and with heavy heart he gathered news of Túrin's deeds and flight. Soon afterwards Thingol and Melian came back to their halls, for the summer was waning; and when the King heard report of what had passed he said: 'This is a grievous matter, which I must hear in full. Though Saeros, my counsellor, is slain, and Túrin my foster-son has fled, tomorrow I will sit in the seat of judgement, and hear again all in due order, before I speak my doom.'

Next day the King sat upon his throne in his court, and about him were all the chiefs and elders of Doriath. Then many witnesses were heard, and of these Mablung spoke most and clearest. And as he told of the quarrel at table, it seemed to the King that Mablung's heart leaned to Túrin.

'You speak as a friend of Túrin son of Húrin?' said Thingol. 'I was, but I have loved truth more and longer,' Mablung answered. 'Hear me to the end, lord!'

When all was told, even to the parting words of Túrin, Thingol sighed; and he looked on those that sat before him, and he said: 'Alas! I see a shadow on your faces. How has it stolen into my realm? Malice is at work here. Saeros I accounted faithful and wise; but if he lived he would feel my anger, for his taunting was evil, and I hold him to blame for all that chanced in the hall. So far Túrin has my pardon. But I cannot pass over his later deeds, when wrath should have cooled. The shaming of Saeros and the hounding of him to his death were wrongs greater than the offence. They show a heart hard and proud.'

Then Thingol sat for a while in thought, and spoke sadly at last. 'This is an ungrateful foster-son, and in truth a man too proud for his state. How can I still harbour one who scorns me and my law, or pardon one who will not repent? This must be my doom. I will banish Túrin from Doriath. If he seeks entry he shall be brought to judgement before me; and until he sues for pardon at my feet he is my son no longer. If any here accounts this unjust, let him speak now!'

Then there was silence in the hall, and Thingol lifted up his hand to pronounce his doom. But at that moment Beleg entered in haste, and cried: 'Lord, may I yet speak?'

'You come late,' said Thingol. 'Were you not bidden with the others?'

'Truly, lord,' answered Beleg, 'but I was delayed; I sought for one whom I knew. Now I bring at last a witness who should be heard, ere your doom falls.'

'All were summoned who had aught to tell,' said the King. 'What can he tell now of more weight than those to whom I have listened?'

'You shall judge when you have heard,' said Beleg. 'Grant this to me, if I have ever deserved your grace.'

'To you I grant it,' said Thingol. Then Beleg went out, and led in by the hand the maiden Nellas, who dwelt in the woods, and came never into Menegroth; and she was afraid, as much of the great pillared hall and the roof of stone as of the company of many eyes that watched her. And when Thingol bade her speak, she said: 'Lord, I was sitting in a tree'; but then she faltered in awe of the King, and could say no more.

At that the King smiled, and said: 'Others have done this also, but have felt no need to tell me of it.'

'Others indeed,' said she, taking courage from his smile. 'Even Lúthien! And of her I was thinking that morning, and of Beren the Man.'

To that Thingol said nothing, and he smiled no longer, but waited until Nellas should speak again.

'For Túrin reminded me of Beren,' she said at last. 'They are akin, I am told, and their kinship can be seen by some: by some that look close.'

Then Thingol grew impatient. 'That may be,' he said. 'But Túrin son of Húrin is gone in scorn of me, and you will see him no more to read his kindred. For now I will speak my judgement.'

'Lord King!' she cried then. 'Bear with me, and let me speak first. I sat in a tree to look on Túrin as he went away; and I saw Saeros come out from the wood with sword and shield, and spring on Túrin at unawares.'

At that there was a murmur in the hall; and the King lifted his hand, saying: 'You bring graver news to my ear than seemed likely. Take heed now to all that you say; for this is a court of doom.'

'So Beleg has told me,' she answered, 'and only for that have I dared to come here, so that Túrin shall not be ill judged. He is valiant, but he is merciful. They fought, lord, these two, until Túrin had bereft Saeros of both shield and sword; but he did not slay him. Therefore I do not believe that he willed his death in the end. If Saeros were put to shame, it was shame that he had earned.'

'Judgement is mine,' said Thingol. 'But what you have told shall govern it.' Then he questioned Nellas closely; and at last he turned to Mablung, saying: 'It is strange to me that Túrin said nothing of this to you.'

'Yet he did not,' said Mablung, 'or I should have recounted it. And otherwise should I have spoken to him at our parting.'

'And otherwise shall my doom now be,' said Thingol. 'Hear me! Such fault as can be found in Túrin I now pardon, holding him wronged and provoked. And since it was indeed, as he said, one of my council who so misused him, he shall not seek for this pardon, but I will send it to him, wherever he may be found; and I will recall him in honour to my halls.'

But when the doom was pronounced, suddenly Nellas wept. 'Where can he be found?' she said. 'He has left our land, and the world is wide.'

'He shall be sought,' said Thingol. Then he rose, and Beleg led Nellas forth from Menegroth; and he said to her: 'Do not weep; for if Túrin lives or walks still abroad, I shall find him, though all others fail.'

On the next day Beleg came before Thingol and Melian, and the King said to him: 'Counsel me, Beleg; for

I am grieved. I took Húrin's son as my son, and so he shall remain, unless Húrin himself should return out of the shadows to claim his own. I would not have any say that Túrin was driven forth unjustly into the wild, and gladly would I welcome him back; for I loved him well.'

'Give me leave, lord,' said Beleg, 'and on your behalf I will redress this evil, if I can. For such manhood as he promised should not run to nothing in the wild. Doriath has need of him, and the need will grow more. And I love him also.'

Then Thingol said to Beleg: 'Now I have hope in the quest! Go with my good will, and if you find him, guard him and guide him as you may. Beleg Cúthalion, long have you been foremost in the defence of Doriath, and for many deeds of valour and wisdom have earned my thanks. Greatest of all I shall hold the finding of Túrin. At this parting ask for any gift, and I will not deny it to you.'

'I ask then for a sword of worth,' said Beleg; 'for the Orcs come now too thick and close for a bow only, and such blade as I have is no match for their armour.'

'Choose from all that I have,' said Thingol, 'save only Aranrúth, my own.'

Then Beleg chose Anglachel; and that was a sword of great fame, and it was so named because it was made of iron that fell from heaven as a blazing star; it would cleave all earth-dolven iron. One other sword only in Middle-earth was like to it. That sword does not enter into this tale, though it was made of the same ore by the same smith; and that smith was Eöl the Dark Elf, who took Aredhel Turgon's sister to wife. He gave Anglachel to Thingol as fee, which he begrudged, for leave to dwell in Nan Elmoth; but the other sword, Anguirel, its mate, he kept, until it was stolen from him by Maeglin, his son.

But as Thingol turned the hilt of Anglachel towards Beleg, Melian looked at the blade; and she said: 'There is malice in this sword. The heart of the smith still dwells in it, and that heart was dark. It will not love the hand that it serves; neither will it abide with you long.'

'Nonetheless I will wield it while I may,' said Beleg; and thanking the king he took the sword and departed. Far across Beleriand he sought in vain for tidings of Túrin, through many perils; and that winter passed away, and the spring after.

CHAPTER VI

TÚRIN AMONG THE OUTLAWS

Now the tale turns again to Túrin. He, believing himself an outlaw whom the King would pursue, did not return to Beleg on the north-marches of Doriath, but went away westward, and passing secretly out of the Guarded Realm came into the woodlands south of Teiglin. There before the Nirnaeth many men had dwelt in scattered homesteads; they were of Haleth's folk for the most part, but owned no lord, and they lived both by hunting and husbandry, keeping swine in the mast-lands, and tilling clearings in the forest which were fenced from the wild. But most were now destroyed, or had fled into Brethil, and all that region lay under the fear of Orcs, and of outlaws. For in that time of ruin houseless and desperate men went astray: remnants of battle and defeat, and lands laid waste; and some were men driven into the wild for evil deeds. They hunted and gathered such food as they could; but many took to robbery and became cruel, when hunger or other need drove them. In winter they were most to be feared, like wolves; and Gaurwaith, wolf-men, they were called by those who still defended their homes. Some sixty of these men had joined in one band, wandering in the woods beyond the western marches of Doriath; and they were hated scarcely less than Orcs, for there were among them outcasts hard of heart, bearing a grudge against their own kind.

The hardest of heart was one named Andróg, who had been hunted from Dor-lómin for the slaying of a woman; and others also came from that land: old Algund, the oldest of the fellowship, who had fled from the Nirnaeth, and Forweg, as he named himself, a man with fair hair and unsteady glittering eyes, big and bold, but far fallen from the ways of the Edain of the people of Hador. Yet he could still be wise and generous at times; and he was the captain of the fellowship. They had dwindled now to some fifty men, by deaths in hardship or affrays; and they were become wary, and set scouts or a watch about them, whether moving or at rest. Thus they were soon aware of Túrin when he strayed into their haunts. They trailed him, and they drew a ring about him, so that suddenly, as he came out into a glade beside a stream, he found himself within a circle of men with bent bows and drawn swords.

Then Túrin halted, but he showed no fear. 'Who are you?' he said. 'I thought that only Orcs waylaid men; but I see that I am mistaken.'

'You may rue the mistake,' said Forweg, 'for these are our haunts, and my men do not allow other men to walk in them. We take their lives as forfeit, unless they can ransom them.'

Then Túrin laughed grimly: 'You will get no ransom from me, an outcast and an outlaw. You may search me when I am dead, but it may cost you dearly to prove my words true. Many of you are likely to die first.'

Nonetheless his death seemed near, for many arrows were notched to the string, waiting for the word of the captain, and though Túrin wore elven-mail under his grey tunic and cloak, some would find a deadly mark. None of his enemies stood within reach of a leap with drawn sword. But suddenly Túrin stooped, for he had espied some stones at the stream's edge before his feet. At that moment an outlaw, angered by his proud words, let fly a shaft aimed at his face; but it passed over him, and he sprang up again like a bowstring released and cast a stone at the bowman with great force and true aim; and he fell to the ground with broken skull.

'I might be of more service to you alive, in the place of that luckless man,' said Túrin; and turning to Forweg he said: 'If you are the captain here, you should not allow your men to shoot without command.'

'I do not,' said Forweg; 'but he has been rebuked swiftly enough. I will take you in his stead, if you will heed my words better.'

'I will,' said Túrin, 'as long as you are captain, and in

all that belongs to a captain. But the choice of a new man to a fellowship is not his alone, I judge. All voices should be heard. Are there any here who do not welcome me?'

Then two of the outlaws cried out against him; and one was a friend of the fallen man. Ulrad was his name. 'A strange way to gain entry to a fellowship,' he said, 'the slaying of one of our best men!'

'Not unchallenged,' said Túrin. 'But come then! I will endure you both together, with weapons or with strength alone. Then you shall see if I am fit to replace one of your best men. But if there are bows in this test, I must have one too.' Then he strode towards them; but Ulrad gave back and would not fight. The other threw down his bow and walked up to meet Túrin. This man was Andróg of Dor-lómin. He stood before Túrin and looked him up and down.

'Nay,' he said at length, shaking his head. 'I am not a chicken-heart, as men know; but I am not your match. There is none here, I think. You may join us, for my part. But there is a strange light in your eyes; you are a danger-ous man. What is your name?'

'Neithan, the Wronged, I call myself,' said Túrin, and Neithan he was afterwards called by the outlaws; but though he claimed to have suffered injustice (and to any who claimed the like he ever lent too ready an ear), no more would he reveal concerning his life or his home. Yet they saw that he had fallen from high state, and that though he had nothing but his arms, those were made by elven-smiths. He soon won their praise, for he was strong and valiant, and had more skill in the woods than they, and they trusted him, for he was not greedy, and took little thought for himself; but they feared him, because of his sudden angers, which they seldom understood.

To Doriath Túrin could not, or in pride would not, return; to Nargothrond since the fall of Felagund none were admitted. To the lesser folk of Haleth in Brethil he did not deign to go; and to Dor-lómin he did not dare, for it was closely beset, and one man alone could not hope at that time, as he thought, to come through the passes of the Mountains of Shadow. Therefore Túrin abode with the outlaws, since the company of any men made the hardship of the wild more easy to endure; and because he wished to live and could not be ever at strife with them, he did little to restrain their evil deeds. Thus he soon became hardened to a mean and often cruel life, and yet at times pity and disgust would wake in him, and then he was perilous in his anger. In this evil and dangerous way Túrin lived to that year's end and through the need and hunger of winter, until stirring came and then a fair spring.

Now in the woods of Teiglin, as has been told, there were still some homesteads of Men, hardy and wary, though now few in number. Though they loved them not at all and pitied them little, they would in bitter winter put out such food as they could well spare where the Gaurwaith might find it; and so they hoped to avoid the banded attack of the famished. But they earned less gratitude so from the outlaws than from beasts and birds, and they were saved rather by their dogs and their fences. For each homestead had great hedges about its cleared land, and about the houses was a ditch and a stockade; and there were paths from stead to stead, and men could summon help at need by horn-calls.

But when spring was come it was perilous for the Gaurwaith to linger so near to the houses of the woodmen, who might gather and hunt them down; and Túrin wondered therefore that Forweg did not lead them away. There was more food and game, and less peril, away south where no Men remained. Then one day Túrin missed Forweg, and also Andróg his friend; and he asked where they were, but his companions laughed.

'Away on business of their own, I guess,' said Ulrad. 'They will be back before long, and then we shall move. In haste, maybe; for we shall be lucky if they do not bring the hive-bees after them.'

The sun shone and the young leaves were green, and Túrin was irked by the squalid camp of the outlaws, and he wandered away alone far into the forest. Against his will he remembered the Hidden Kingdom, and he seemed to hear the names of the flowers of Doriath as echoes of an old tongue almost forgotten. But on a sudden he heard cries, and from a hazel-thicket a young woman ran out; her clothes were rent by thorns, and she was in great fear, and stumbling she fell gasping to the ground. Then Túrin springing towards the thicket with drawn sword hewed down a man that burst from the hazels in pursuit; and he saw only in the very stroke that it was Forweg.

But as he stood looking down in amaze at the blood upon the grass, Andróg came out, and halted also astounded. 'Evil work, Neithan!' he cried, and drew his sword; but Túrin's mood ran cold, and he said to Andróg: 'Where are the Orcs, then? Have you outrun them to help her?'

'Orcs?' said Andróg. 'Fool! You call yourself an outlaw. Outlaws know no law but their needs. Look to your own, Neithan, and leave us to mind ours.'

'I will do so,' said Túrin. 'But today our paths have crossed. You will leave the woman to me, or you will join Forweg.'

Andróg laughed. 'If that is the way of it, have your will,' he said. 'I make no claim to match you, alone; but our fellows may take this slaying ill.'

Then the woman rose to her feet and laid her hand on Túrin's arm. She looked at the blood and she looked at Túrin, and there was delight in her eyes. 'Kill him, lord!' she said. 'Kill him too! And then come with me. If you bring their heads, Larnach my father will not be displeased. For two "wolf-heads" he has rewarded men well.'

But Túrin said to Andróg: 'Is it far to her home?'

'A mile or so,' he answered, 'in a fenced homestead yonder. She was straying outside.' 'Go then quickly,' said Túrin, turning back to the woman. 'Tell your father to keep you better. But I will not cut off the heads of my fellows to buy his favour, or aught else.'

Then he put up his sword. 'Come!' he said to Andróg. 'We will return. But if you wish to bury your captain, you must do so yourself. Make haste, for a hue and cry may be raised. Bring his weapons!'

The woman went off through the woods, and she looked back many times before the trees hid her. Then Túrin went on his way without more words, and Andróg watched him go, and he frowned as one pondering a riddle.

When Túrin came back to the camp of the outlaws he found them restless and ill at ease; for they had stayed too long already in one place, near to homesteads well-guarded, and they murmured against Forweg. 'He runs hazards to our cost', they said; 'and others may have to pay for his pleasures.'

'Then choose a new captain!' said Túrin, standing before them. 'Forweg can lead you no longer; for he is dead.'

'How do you know that?' said Ulrad. 'Did you seek honey from the same hive? Did the bees sting him?'

'No,' said Túrin. 'One sting was enough. I slew him. But I spared Andróg, and he will soon return.' Then he told all that was done, rebuking those that did such deeds; and while he yet spoke Andróg returned bearing Forweg's weapons. 'See, Neithan!' he cried. 'No alarm has been raised. Maybe she hopes to meet with you again.'

'If you jest with me,' said Túrin, 'I shall regret that I grudged her your head. Now tell your tale, and be brief.'

Then Andróg told truly enough all that had befallen. 'What business Neithan had there I now wonder,' he said. 'Not ours, it seems. For when I came up, he had already slain Forweg. The woman liked that well, and offered to go with him, begging our heads as a bride-price. But he did not want her, and sped her off; so what grudge he had against the captain I cannot guess. He left my head on my shoulders, for which I am grateful, though much puzzled.'

'Then I deny your claim to come of the People of Hador,' said Túrin. 'To Uldor the Accursed you belong rather, and should seek service with Angband. But hear me now!' he cried to them all. 'These choices I give you. You must take me as your captain in Forweg's place, or else let me go. I will govern this fellowship now, or leave it. But if you wish to kill me, set to! I will fight you all until I am dead – or you.'

Then many men seized their weapons, but Andróg cried out: 'Nay! The head that he spared is not witless. If we fight, more than one will die needlessly, before we kill the best man among us.' Then he laughed. 'As it was when he joined us, so it is again. He kills to make room. If it proved well before, so may it again; and he may lead us to better fortune than prowling about other men's middens.'

And old Algund said: 'The best man among us. Time was when we would have done the same, if we dared; but we have forgotten much. He may bring us home in the end.'

At that the thought came to Túrin that from this small band he might rise to build himself a free lordship of his own. But he looked at Algund and Andróg, and he said: 'Home, do you say? Tall and cold stand the Mountains of Shadow between. Behind them are the people of Uldor, and about them the legions of Angband. If such things do not daunt you, seven times seven men, then I may lead you homewards. But how far, before we die?'

All were silent. Then Túrin spoke again. 'Do you take me to be your captain? Then I will lead you first away into the wild, far from the homes of Men. There we may find better fortune, or not; but at the least we shall earn less hatred of our own kind.'

Then all those that were of the People of Hador gathered to him, and took him as their captain; and the others with less good will agreed. And at once he led them away out of that country.

Many messengers had been sent out by Thingol to seek Túrin within Doriath and in the lands near its borders; but in the year of his flight they searched for him in vain, for none knew or could guess that he was with the outlaws and enemies of Men. When winter came on they returned to the King, save Beleg only. After all others had departed still he went on alone.

But in Dimbar and along the north-marches of Doriath things had gone ill. The Dragon-helm was seen there in battle no longer, and the Strongbow also was missed; and the servants of Morgoth were heartened and increased ever in numbers and in daring. Winter came and passed, and with Spring their assault was renewed: Dimbar was overrun, and the Men of Brethil were afraid, for evil roamed now upon all their borders, save in the south.

It was now almost a year since Túrin had fled, and still Beleg sought for him, with ever lessening hope. He passed northwards in his wanderings to the Crossings of Teiglin, and there, hearing ill news of a new inroad of Orcs out of Taur-nu-Fuin, he turned back, and came as it chanced to the homes of the Woodmen soon after Túrin had left that region. There he heard a strange tale that went among them. A tall and lordly Man, or an Elf-warrior, some said, had appeared in the woods, and had slain one of the Gaurwaith, and rescued the daughter of Larnach whom they were pursuing. 'Very proud he was,' said Larnach's daughter to Beleg, 'with bright eyes that scarcely deigned to look at me. Yet he called the Wolf-men his fellows, and would not slay another that stood by, and knew his name. Neithan, he called him.'

'Can you read this riddle?' asked Larnach of the Elf.

'I can, alas,' said Beleg. 'The Man that you tell of is one whom I seek.' No more of Túrin did he tell the Woodmen; but he warned them of evil gathering northward. 'Soon the Orcs will come ravening in this country in strength too great for you to withstand,' he said. 'This year at last you must give up your freedom or your lives. Go to Brethil while there is time!'

Then Beleg went on his way in haste, and sought for the lairs of the outlaws, and such signs as might show him whither they had gone. These he soon found; but Túrin was now several days ahead, and moved swiftly, fearing the pursuit of the Woodmen, and he had used all the arts that he knew to defeat or mislead any that tried to follow him. He led his men westward, away from the Woodmen and from the borders of Doriath, until they came to the northern end of the great highlands that rose between the Vales of Sirion and Narog. There the land was drier, and the forest ceased suddenly on the brink of a ridge. Below it could be seen the ancient South Road, climbing up from the Crossings of Teiglin to pass along the western feet of the moorlands on its way to Nargothrond. There for a time the outlaws lived warily, remaining seldom two nights in one camp, and leaving little trace of their going or staying. So it was that even Beleg hunted them in vain. Led by signs that he could read, or by the rumour of the passing of Men among the wild things with whom he could speak, he came often near, but always their lair was deserted when he came to it; for they kept a watch about them by day and night, and at any rumour of approach they were swiftly up and away. 'Alas!' he cried. 'Too well did I teach this child of Men craft in wood and field! An Elvish band almost one might think this to be.' But they for their part became aware that they were trailed by some tireless pursuer, whom they could not see, and yet could not shake off; and they grew uneasy.

Not long afterwards, as Beleg had feared, the Orcs came across the Brithiach, and being resisted with all the force that he could muster by Handir of Brethil, they passed south over the Crossings of Teiglin in search of plunder. Many of the Woodmen had taken Beleg's counsel and sent their women and children to ask for refuge in Brethil. These and their escort escaped, passing over the Crossings in time; but the armed men that came behind were met by the Orcs, and the men were worsted. A few fought their way through and came to Brethil, but many were slain or captured; and the Orcs passed on to the homesteads, and sacked them and burned them. Then at once they turned back westwards, seeking the Road, for they wished now to return back north as swiftly as they could with their booty and their captives.

But the scouts of the outlaws were soon aware of them; and though they cared little enough for the captives, the plunder of the Woodmen aroused their greed. To Túrin it seemed perilous to reveal themselves to the Orcs, until their numbers were known; but the outlaws would not heed him, for they had need of many things in the wild, and already some began to regret his leading. Therefore taking one Orleg as his only companion Túrin went forth to spy upon the Orcs; and giving command of the band to Andróg he charged him to lie close and well hid while they were gone.

Now the Orc-host was far greater than the band of outlaws, but they were in lands to which Orcs had seldom dared to come, and they knew also that beyond the Road lay the Talath Dirnen, the Guarded Plain, upon which the scouts and spies of Nargothrond kept watch; and fearing danger they were wary, and their scouts went creeping through the trees on either side of the marching lines. Thus it was that Túrin and Orleg were discovered, for three scouts stumbled upon them as they lay hid; and though they slew two the third escaped, crying as he ran *Golug! Golug!* Now that was a name which they had for the Noldor. At once the forest was filled with Orcs, scattering silently and hunting far and wide. Then Túrin, seeing that there was small hope of escape, thought at least to deceive them and to lead them away from the hiding-place of his men; and perceiving from the cry of *Golug!* that they feared the spies of Nargothrond, he fled with Orleg westward. The pursuit came swiftly after them, until turn and dodge as they would they were driven at last out of the forest; and then they were espied, and as they sought to cross the Road Orleg was shot down by many arrows. But Túrin was saved by his elven-mail, and escaped alone into the wilds beyond; and by speed and craft he eluded his enemies, fleeing far into lands that were strange to him. Then the Orcs, fearing that the Elves of Nargothrond might be aroused, slew their captives and made haste away into the North.

Now when three days had passed, and yet Túrin and Orleg did not return, some of the outlaws wished to depart from the cave where they lay hid; but Andróg spoke against it. And while they were in the midst of this debate, suddenly a grey figure stood before them. Beleg had found them at last. He came forward with no weapon in his hands, and held the palms turned towards them; but they leapt up in fear and Andróg coming behind cast a noose over him, and drew it so that it pinioned his arms.

'If you do not wish for guests, you should keep better watch,' said Beleg. 'Why do you welcome me thus? I come as a friend, and seek only a friend. Neithan, I hear that you call him.'

'He is not here,' said Ulrad. 'But unless you have long spied on us, how know you that name?'

'He has long spied on us,' said Andróg. 'This is the shadow that has dogged us. Now perhaps we shall learn his true purpose.' Then he bade them tie Beleg to a tree beside the cave; and when he was hard bound hand and foot they questioned him. But to all their questions Beleg would give one answer only: 'A friend I have been to this Neithan since I first met him in the woods, and he was then but a child. I seek him only in love, and to bring him good tidings.'

'Let us slay him, and be rid of his spying,' said Andróg in wrath; and he looked on the great bow of Beleg and coveted it, for he was an archer. But some of better heart spoke against him, and Algund said to him: 'The captain may return yet; and then you will rue it, if he learns that he has been robbed at once of a friend and of good tidings.'

'I do not believe the tale of this Elf,' said Andróg. 'He is a spy of the King of Doriath. But if he has indeed any tidings, he shall tell them to us; and we shall judge if they give us reason to let him live.'

'I shall wait for your captain,' said Beleg.

'You shall stand there until you speak,' said Andróg.

Then at the egging of Andróg they left Beleg tied to the tree without food or water, and they sat near eating and drinking; but he said no more to them. When two days and nights had passed in this way they became angry and fearful, and were eager to be gone; and most were now ready to slay the Elf. As night drew down they were all gathered about him, and Ulrad brought a brand from the little fire that was lit in the cave-mouth. But at that moment Túrin returned. Coming silently, as was his custom, he stood in the shadows beyond the ring of men, and he saw the haggard face of Beleg in the light of the brand.

Then he was stricken as with a shaft, and as if at the sudden melting of a frost tears long unshed filled his eyes. He sprang out and ran to the tree. 'Beleg! Beleg!' he cried. 'How have you come hither? And why do you stand so?' At once he cut the bonds from his friend, and Beleg fell forward into his arms.

When Túrin heard all that the men would tell, he was angry and grieved; but at first he gave heed only to Beleg. While he tended him with what skill he had, he thought of his life in the woods, and his anger turned upon himself. For often strangers had been slain, when caught near the lairs of the outlaws, or waylaid by them, and he had not hindered it; and often he himself had spoken ill of King Thingol and of the Grey-elves, so that he must share the blame, if they were treated as foes. Then with bitterness he turned to the men. 'You were cruel,' he said, 'and cruel without need. Never until now have we tormented a prisoner; but to this Orc-work such a life as we lead has brought us. Lawless and fruitless all our deeds have been, serving only ourselves, and feeding hate in our hearts.'

But Andróg said: 'But whom shall we serve, if not ourselves? Whom shall we love, when all hate us?'

'At least my hands shall not again be raised against Elves or Men,' said Túrin. 'Angband has servants enough. If others will not take this vow with me, I will walk alone.'

Then Beleg opened his eyes and raised his head. 'Not alone!' he said. 'Now at last I can tell my tidings. You are no outlaw, and Neithan is a name unfit. Such fault as was found in you is pardoned. For a year you have been sought, to recall you to honour and to the service of the King. The Dragon-helm has been missed too long.'

But Túrin showed no joy in this news, and sat long in silence; for at Beleg's words a shadow fell upon him again. 'Let this night pass,' he said at length. 'Then I will choose. However it goes, we must leave this lair tomorrow; for not all who seek us wish us well.'

'Nay, none,' said Andróg, and he cast an evil look at Beleg.

In the morning Beleg, being swiftly healed of his pains, after the manner of the Elven-folk of old, spoke to Túrin apart.

'I looked for more joy at my tidings,' he said. 'Surely you will return now to Doriath?' And he begged Túrin to do this in all ways that he could; but the more he urged it, the more Túrin hung back. Nonetheless he questioned Beleg closely concerning the judgement of Thingol. Then Beleg told him all that he knew, and at the last Túrin said: 'Then Mablung proved my friend, as he once seemed?'

'The friend of truth, rather,' said Beleg, 'and that was best, in the end; though the doom would have been less just, were it not for the witness of Nellas. Why, why, Túrin, did you not speak of Saeros' assault to Mablung? All otherwise might things have gone. And,' he said, looking at the men sprawled near the mouth of the cave, 'you might have held your helm still high, and not fallen to this.'

'That may be, if fall you call it,' said Túrin. 'That may be. But so it went; and words stuck in my throat. There was reproof in his eyes, without question asked of me, for a deed I had not done. My Man's heart was proud, as the Elf-king said. And so it still is, Beleg Cúthalion. Not yet will it suffer me to go back to Menegroth and bear looks of pity and pardon, as for a wayward boy amended. I should give pardon, not receive it. And I am a boy no longer, but a man, according to my kind; and a hard man by my fate.'

Then Beleg was troubled. 'What will you do, then?' he asked.

'Fare free,' said Túrin. 'That wish Mablung gave me at our parting. The grace of Thingol will not stretch to receive these companions of my fall, I think; but I will not part with them now, if they do not wish to part with me. I love them in my way, even the worst a little. They are of my own kind, and there is some good in each that might grow. I think that they will stand by me.'

'You see with other eyes than mine,' said Beleg. 'If you try to wean them from evil, they will fail you. I doubt them, and one most of all.'

'How shall an Elf judge of Men?' said Túrin.

'As he judges of all deeds, by whomsoever done,' answered Beleg, but he said no more, and did not speak of Andróg's malice, to which his evil handling had been chiefly due; for perceiving Túrin's mood he feared to be disbelieved and to hurt their old friendship, driving Túrin back to his evil ways.

'Fare free, you say, Túrin, my friend,' he said. 'What is your meaning?'

'I would lead my own men, and make war in my own way,' Túrin answered. 'But in this at least my heart is changed: I repent every stroke save those dealt against the Enemy of Men and Elves. And above all else I would have you beside me. Stay with me!'

'If I stayed beside you, love would lead me, not wisdom,' said Beleg. 'My heart warns me that we should return to Doriath. Elsewhere a shadow lies before us.'

'Nonetheless, I will not go there,' said Túrin.

'Alas!' said Beleg. 'But as a fond father who grants his son's desire against his own foresight, I yield to your will. At your asking, I will stay.'

'That is well indeed!' said Túrin. Then all at once he fell silent, as if he himself were aware of the shadow, and strove with his pride, which would not let him turn back. For a long while he sat, brooding on the years that lay behind.

Coming suddenly out of thought he looked at Beleg, and said: 'The elf-maiden that you named, though I forget how: I owe her well for her timely witness; yet I cannot recall her. Why did she watch my ways?' Then Beleg looked strangely at him. 'Why indeed?' he said. 'Túrin, have you lived always with your heart and half your mind far away? As a boy you used to walk with Nellas in the woods.'

'That must have been long ago,' said Túrin. 'Or so my childhood now seems, and a mist is over it – save only the memory of my father's house in Dor-lómin. Why would I walk with an elf-maiden?'

'To learn what she could teach, maybe,' said Beleg, 'if no more than a few elven-words of the names of woodland flowers. Their names at least you have not forgotten. Alas! child of Men, there are other griefs in Middle-earth than yours, and wounds made by no weapon. Indeed I begin to think that Elves and Men should not meet or meddle.'

Túrin said nothing, but looked long in Beleg's face, as if he would read in it the riddle of his words. Nellas of

Doriath never saw him again, and his shadow passed from her. Now Beleg and Túrin turned to other matters, debating where they should dwell. 'Let us return to Dimbar, on the north-marches, where once we walked together!' said Beleg eagerly. 'We are needed there. For of late the Orcs have found a way down out of Taur-nu-Fuin, making a road through the Pass of Anach.'

'I do not remember it,' said Túrin.

'No, we never went so far from the borders,' said Beleg. 'But you have seen the peaks of the Crissaegrim far off, and to their east the dark walls of the Gorgoroth. Anach lies between them, above the high springs of Mindeb. A hard and dangerous way; and yet many come by it now, and Dimbar which used to lie in peace is falling under the Dark Hand, and the Men of Brethil are troubled. To Dimbar I call you!'

'Nay, I will not walk backward in life,' said Túrin. 'Nor can I come easily to Dimbar now. Sirion lies between, unbridged and unforded below the Brithiach far northward; it is perilous to cross. Save in Doriath. But I will not pass into Doriath, and make use of Thingol's leave and pardon.'

'A hard man you have called yourself, Túrin. Truly, if by that you meant stubborn. Now the turn is mine. I will go, by your leave, as soon as I may, and bid you farewell. If you wish indeed to have the Strongbow beside you, look for me in Dimbar.' At that time Túrin said no more.

The next day Beleg set out, and Túrin went with him a bowshot from the camp, but said nothing. 'Is it farewell, then, son of Húrin?' said Beleg.

'If you wish indeed to keep your word and stay beside me,' answered Túrin, 'then look for me on Amon Rûdh!' Thus he spoke, being fey and unwitting of what lay before him. 'Else, this is our last farewell.'

'Maybe that is best,' said Beleg, and went his way.

It is said that Beleg went back to Menegroth, and came before Thingol and Melian and told them of all that had happened, save only his evil handling by Túrin's companions. Then Thingol sighed, and he said: 'I took up the fathering of the son of Húrin, and that cannot be laid down for love or hate, unless Húrin the Valiant himself should return. What more would he have me do?'

But Melian said: 'A gift you shall now have of me, Cúthalion, for your help, and your honour, for I have none worthier to give.' And she gave him a store of *lembas*, the waybread of the Elves, wrapped in leaves of silver; and the threads that bound it were sealed at the knots with the seal of the Queen, a wafer of white wax shaped as a single flower of Telperion. For according to the customs of the Eldalië the keeping and the giving of this food belonged to the Queen alone. 'This waybread, Beleg,' she said, 'shall be your help in the wild and the winter, and the help also of those whom you choose. For I commit this now to you, to apportion as you will in my stead.' In nothing did Melian show greater favour to Túrin than in this gift; for the Eldar had never before allowed Men to use this waybread, and seldom did so again.

Then Beleg departed from Menegroth and went back to the north-marches, where he had his lodges, and many friends; but when winter came, and war was stilled, suddenly his companions missed Beleg, and he returned to them no more.

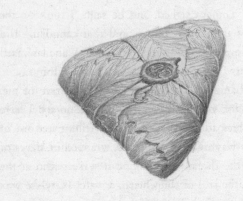

CHAPTER VII

OF MÎM THE DWARF

Now the tale turns to Mîm the Petty-dwarf. The Petty-dwarves are long out of mind, for Mîm was the last. Little was known of them even in days of old. The Nibin-nogrim the Elves of Beleriand called them long ago, but they did not love them; and the Petty-dwarves loved none but themselves. If they hated and feared the Orcs, they hated also the Eldar, and the Exiles most of all; for the Noldor, they said, had stolen their lands and their homes. Nargothrond was first found and its delving begun by the Petty-dwarves, long before Finrod Felagund came over the Sea.

They came, some said, of Dwarves that had been banished from the Dwarf-cities of the east in ancient days. Long before the return of Morgoth they had wandered westward. Being masterless and few in number, they found it hard to come by the ore of metals, and their smith-craft and store of weapons dwindled; and they took to lives of stealth, and became somewhat smaller in stature than their eastern kin, walking with bent shoulders and quick, furtive steps. Nonetheless, as all the Dwarf-kind, they were far stronger than their stature promised, and they could cling to life in great hardship. But now at last they had dwindled and died out of Middle-earth, all save Mîm and his two sons; and Mîm was old even in the reckoning of Dwarves, old and forgotten.

After the departure of Beleg (and that was in the second summer after the flight of Túrin from Doriath) things went ill for the outlaws. There were rains out of season, and Orcs in greater numbers than before came down from the North and along the old South Road over Teiglin, troubling all the woods on the west borders of Doriath. There was little safety or rest, and the company were more often hunted than hunters.

One night as they lay lurking in the fireless dark, Túrin looked on his life, and it seemed to him that it might well be bettered. 'I must find some secure refuge,' he thought, 'and make provision against winter and hunger.' But he did not know whither to turn.

Next day he led his men away southward, further than they had yet come from the Teiglin and the marches of Doriath; and after three days' journeying they halted at the western edge of the woods of Sirion's Vale. There the land was drier and barer, as it began to climb up into the moorlands.

Soon after, it chanced that as the grey light of a day of rain was failing Túrin and his men were sheltering in a holly-thicket; and beyond it was a treeless space, in which there were many great stones, leaning or tumbled together. All was still, save for the drip of rain from the leaves.

Suddenly a watchman gave a call, and leaping up they saw three hooded shapes, grey-clad, going stealthily among the stones. They were burdened each with a great sack, but they went swiftly for all that. Túrin cried to them to halt, and the men ran out on them like hounds; but they held on their way, and though Andróg shot at them two vanished in the dusk. One lagged behind, being slower or more heavily burdened; and he was soon seized and thrown down, and held by many hard hands, though he struggled and bit like a beast. But Túrin came up, and rebuked his men. 'What have you there?' he said. 'What need to be so fierce? It is old and small. What harm is in it?'

'It bites,' said Andróg, nursing a bleeding hand. 'It is an Orc, or of Orc-kin. Kill it!'

'It deserves no less, for cheating our hope,' said another, who had taken the sack. 'There is nothing here but roots and small stones.'

'Nay,' said Túrin, 'it is bearded. It is only a Dwarf, I guess. Let him up, and speak.'

So it was that Mîm came into the Tale of the Children of Húrin. For he stumbled up on his knees before Túrin's feet and begged for his life. 'I am old,' he said, 'and poor. Only a Dwarf, as you say, not an Orc. Mîm is my name. Do not let them slay me, master, for no cause, as Orcs would.'

Then Túrin pitied him in his heart, but he said: 'Poor you seem, Mîm, though that would be strange in a Dwarf; but we are poorer, I think: houseless and friendless Men. If I said that we do not spare for pity's sake only, being in great need, what would you offer for ransom?'

'I do not know what you desire, lord,' said Mîm warily.

'At this time, little enough!' said Túrin, looking about him bitterly with rain in his eyes. 'A safe place to sleep in out of the damp woods. Doubtless you have such for yourself.'

'I have,' said Mîm; 'but I cannot give it in ransom. I am too old to live under the sky.'

'You need grow no older,' said Andróg, stepping up with a knife in his unharmed hand. 'I can spare you that.'

'Lord!' cried Mîm in great fear, clinging to Túrin's knees. 'If I lose my life, you lose the dwelling; for you will not find it without Mîm. I cannot give it, but I will share it. There is more room in it than once there was, so many have gone for ever,' and he began to weep.

'Your life is spared, Mîm,' said Túrin.

'Till we come to his lair, at least,' said Andróg.

But Túrin turned upon him, and said: 'If Mîm brings us to his home without trickery, and it is good, then his life is ransomed; and he shall not be slain by any man who follows me. So I swear.'

Then Mîm kissed Túrin's knees and said: 'Mîm will be your friend, lord. At first he thought you were an Elf, by your speech and your voice. But if you are a Man, that is better. Mîm does not love Elves.'

'Where is this house of yours?' said Andróg. 'It must be good indeed to share it with a Dwarf. For Andróg does not like Dwarves. His people brought few good tales of that race out of the East.'

'They left worse tales of themselves behind them,' said Mîm. 'Judge my home when you see it. But you will need light on your way, you stumbling Men. I will return in good time and lead you.' Then he rose and picked up his sack.

'No, no!' said Andróg. 'You will not allow this, surely, captain? You would never see the old rascal again.'

'It is growing dark,' said Túrin. 'Let him leave us some pledge. Shall we keep your sack and its load, Mîm?'

But at this the Dwarf fell on his knees again in great trouble. 'If Mîm did not mean to return, he would not return for an old sack of roots,' he said. 'I will come back. Let me go!'

'I will not,' said Túrin. 'If you will not part with your sack, you must stay with it. A night under the leaves will make you pity us in your turn, maybe.' But he marked, and others also, that Mîm set more store by the sack and his load than it seemed worth to the eye.

They led the old Dwarf away to their dismal camp, and as he went he muttered in a strange tongue that seemed harsh with ancient hatred; but when they put bonds on his legs he went suddenly quiet. And those who were on the watch saw him sitting on through the night silent and still as a stone, save for his sleepless eyes that glinted as they roved in the dark.

Before morning the rain ceased, and a wind stirred in the trees. Dawn came more brightly than for many days, and light airs from the South opened the sky, pale and clear about the rising of the sun. Mîm sat on without moving, and he seemed as if dead; for now the heavy lids of his eyes were closed, and the morning-light showed him withered and shrunken with age. Túrin stood and looked down on him. 'There is light enough now,' he said.

Then Mîm opened his eyes and pointed to his bonds; and when he was released he spoke fiercely. 'Learn this, fools!' he said. 'Do not put bonds on a Dwarf! He will not forgive it. I do not wish to die, but for what you have done my heart is hot. I repent my promise.'

'But I do not,' said Túrin. 'You will lead me to your home. Till then we will not speak of death. That is *my* will.' He looked steadfastly in the eyes of the Dwarf, and Mîm could not endure it; few indeed could challenge the eyes of Túrin in set will or in wrath. Soon he turned away his head, and rose. 'Follow me, lord!' he said.

'Good!' said Túrin. 'But now I will add this: I understand your pride. You may die, but you shall not be set in bonds again.'

'I will not,' said Mîm. 'But come now!' And with that he led them back to the place where he had been captured, and he pointed westward. 'There is my home!' he said. 'You have often seen it, I guess, for it is tall. Sharbhund we called it, before the Elves changed all the names.' Then they saw that he was pointing to Amon Rûdh, the Bald Hill, whose bare head watched over many leagues of the wild.

'We have seen it, but never nearer,' said Andróg. 'For what safe lair can be there, or water, or any other thing that we need? I guessed that there was some trick. Do men hide on a hill-top?'

'Long sight may be safer than lurking,' said Túrin. 'Amon Rûdh gazes far and wide. Well, Mîm, I will come and see what you have to show. How long will it take us, stumbling Men, to come thither?'

'All this day until dusk, if we start now,' answered Mîm.

Soon the company set out westward, and Túrin went at the head with Mîm at his side. They walked warily when they left the woods, but all the land seemed empty and quiet. They passed over the tumbled stones, and began to climb; for Amon Rûdh stood upon the eastern edge of the high moorlands that rose between the vales of Sirion and Narog, and even above the stony heath at its base its crown was reared up a thousand feet and more. Upon the eastern side a broken land climbed slowly up to the high ridges among knots of birch and rowan, and ancient thorn-trees rooted in rock. Beyond, upon the moors and about the lower slopes of Amon Rûdh, there grew thickets of *aeglos*; but its steep grey head was bare, save for the red *seregon* that mantled the stone.

As the afternoon was waning the outlaws drew near to the roots of the hill. They came now from the north, for so Mîm had led them, and the light of the westering sun fell upon the crown of Amon Rûdh, and the *seregon* was all in flower.

'See! There is blood on the hill-top,' said Andróg.

'Not yet,' said Túrin.

The sun was sinking and light was failing in the hollows. The hill now loomed up before them and above them, and they wondered what need there could be of a guide to so plain a mark. But as Mîm led them on, and they began to climb the last steep slopes, they perceived that he was following some path by secret signs or old custom. Now his course wound to and fro, and if they looked aside they saw that at either hand dark dells and chines opened, or the land ran down into wastes of great stones with falls and holes masked by bramble and thorn. There without a guide they might have laboured and clambered for days to find a way.

At length they came to steeper but smoother ground. They passed under the shadows of ancient rowan-trees, into aisles of long-legged *aeglos*: a gloom filled with a sweet scent. Then suddenly there was a rock-wall before

them, flat-faced and sheer, forty feet high, maybe, but dusk
dimmed the sky above them and guess was uncertain.

'Is this the door of your house?' said Túrin. 'Dwarves
love stone, it is said.' He drew close to Mîm, lest he should
play them some trick at the last.

'Not the door of the house, but the gate of the garth,'
said Mîm. Then he turned to the right along the cliff-foot,
and after twenty paces he halted suddenly; and Túrin saw
that by the work of hands or of weather there was a cleft so
shaped that two faces of the wall overlapped, and an
opening ran back to the left between them. Its entrance was
shrouded by long trailing plants rooted in crevices above,
but within there was a steep stony path going upward in the
dark. Water trickled down it, and it was dank.

One by one they filed up. At the top the path turned
right and south again, and brought them through a thicket
of thorns out upon a green flat, through which it ran on
into the shadows. They had come to Mîm's house, Bar-en-
Nibin-noeg, which only ancient tales in Doriath and Nargothrond remembered, and no Men had seen. But night
was falling, and the east was starlit, and they could not yet
see how this strange place was shaped.

Amon Rûdh had a crown: a great mass like a steep cap
of stone with a bare flattened top. Upon its north side
there stood out from it a shelf, level and almost square,
which could not be seen from below; for behind it stood
the hill-crown like a wall, and west and east from its brink
sheer cliffs fell. Only from the north, as they had come,

could it be reached with ease by those who knew the way. From the 'gate' a path led, and passed soon into a little grove of dwarfed birches growing about a clear pool in a rock-hewn basin. This was fed by a spring at the foot of the wall behind, and through a runnel it spilled like a white thread over the western brink of the shelf. Behind the screen of the trees, near the spring between two tall buttresses of rock, there was a cave. No more than a shallow grot it looked, with a low broken arch; but further in it had been deepened and bored far under the hill by the slow hands of the Petty-dwarves, in the long years that they had dwelt there, untroubled by the Grey-elves of the woods.

Through the deep dusk Mîm led them past the pool, where now the faint stars were mirrored among the shadows of the birch-boughs. At the mouth of the cave he turned and bowed to Túrin. 'Enter, lord!' he said: 'Bar-en-Danwedh, the House of Ransom. For so it shall be called.'

'That may be,' said Túrin. 'I will look at it first.' Then he went in with Mîm, and the others, seeing him unafraid, followed behind, even Andróg, who most misdoubted the Dwarf. They were soon in a black dark; but Mîm clapped his hands, and a little light appeared, coming round a corner: from a passage at the back of the outer grot there stepped another Dwarf bearing a small torch.

'Ha! I missed him, as I feared!' said Andróg. But Mîm spoke quickly with the other in their own harsh tongue, and seeming troubled or angered by what he heard, he darted into the passage and disappeared. Now Andróg was all for going forward. 'Attack first!' he cried. 'There may be a hive of them; but they are small.'

'Three only, I guess,' said Túrin; and he led the way, while behind him the outlaws groped along the passage by the feel of the rough walls. Many times it bent this way and that at sharp angles; but at last a faint light gleamed ahead, and they came into a small but lofty hall, dim-lit by lamps hanging down out of the roof-shadow upon fine chains. Mîm was not there, but his voice could be heard, and led by it Túrin came to the door of a chamber opening at the back of the hall. Looking in, he saw Mîm kneeling on the floor. Beside him stood silent the Dwarf with the torch; but on a stone couch by the far wall lay another. 'Khîm, Khîm, Khîm!' the old Dwarf wailed, tearing at his beard.

'Not all your shots went wild,' said Túrin to Andróg. 'But this may prove an ill hit. You loose shaft too lightly; but you may not live long enough to learn wisdom.'

Leaving the others, Túrin entered softly and stood behind Mîm, and spoke to him. 'What is the trouble, master?' he said. 'I have some healing arts. May I help you?'

Mîm turned his head, and his eyes had a red light. 'Not unless you can turn back time and cut off the cruel hands of your men,' he answered. 'This is my son. An arrow was in his breast. Now he is beyond speech. He died at sunset. Your bonds held me from healing him.'

Again pity long hardened welled in Túrin's heart as water from rock. 'Alas!' he said. 'I would recall that shaft, if I could. Now Bar-en-Danwedh, House of Ransom, shall this be called in truth. For whether we dwell here or no, I will hold myself in your debt; and if ever I come to any wealth, I will pay you a *danwedh* of heavy gold for your son, in token of sorrow, even if it gladdens your heart no more.'

Then Mîm rose and looked long at Túrin. 'I hear you,' he said. 'You speak like a dwarf-lord of old; and at that I marvel. Now my heart is cooled, though it is not glad. My own ransom I will pay, therefore: you may dwell here, if you will. But this I will add: he that loosed the shaft shall break his bow and his arrows and lay them at my son's feet; and he shall never take an arrow nor bear bow again. If he does, he shall die by it. That curse I lay on him.'

Andróg was afraid when he heard of this curse; and though he did so with great grudge, he broke his bow and his arrows and laid them at the dead Dwarf's feet. But as he came out from the chamber, he glanced evilly at Mîm, and muttered: 'The curse of a dwarf never dies, they say; but a Man's too may come home. May he die with a dart in his throat!'

That night they lay in the hall and slept uneasily for the wailing of Mîm and of Ibun, his other son. When that ceased they could not tell; but when they woke at last the Dwarves were gone and the chamber was closed by a stone. The day was fair again, and in the morning sunshine the outlaws washed in the pool and prepared such food as they had; and as they ate Mîm stood before them.

He bowed to Túrin. 'He is gone and all is done,' he said. 'He lies with his fathers. Now we turn to such life as is left, though the days before us may be short. Does Mîm's home please you? Is the ransom paid and accepted?'

'It is,' said Túrin.

'Then all is yours, to order your dwelling here as you will, save this: the chamber that is closed, none shall open it but me.'

'We hear you,' said Túrin. 'But as for our life here, we are secure, or so it seems; but still we must have food, and other things. How shall we go out; or still more, how shall we return?'

To their disquiet Mîm laughed in his throat. 'Do you fear that you have followed a spider to the heart of his web?' he said. 'Nay, Mîm does not eat Men. And a spider could ill deal with thirty wasps at a time. See, you are armed, and I stand here bare. No, we must share, you and I: house, food, and fire, and maybe other winnings. The house, I guess, you will guard and keep secret for your own good, even when you know the ways in and out. You will learn them in time. But in the meantime Mîm must guide you, or Ibun his son, when you go out; and one will go where you go and return when you return – or await you at some point that you know and can find unguided. Ever nearer and nearer home will that be, I guess.'

To this Túrin agreed, and he thanked Mîm, and most of his men were glad; for under the sun of morning, while summer was yet high, it seemed a fair place to dwell in. Andróg alone was ill-content. 'The sooner we are masters of our own goings and comings the better,' he said. 'Never before have we taken a prisoner with a grievance to and fro on our ventures.'

That day they rested, and cleaned their arms and mended their gear; for they had food to last a day or two yet, and Mîm added to what they had. Three great cooking-pots he lent to them, and firing; and he brought out a sack. 'Rubbish,' he said. 'Not worth the stealing. Only wild roots.'

But when they were washed the roots proved white and fleshy with their skins, and when boiled they were good to eat, somewhat like bread; and the outlaws were glad of them, for they had long lacked bread save when they could steal it. 'Wild Elves know them not; Grey-elves have not found them; the proud ones from over the Sea are too proud to delve,' said Mîm.

'What is their name?' said Túrin.

Mîm looked at him sidelong. 'They have no name, save in the dwarf-tongue, which we do not teach,' he said. 'And we do not teach Men to find them, for Men are greedy and thriftless, and would not spare till all the plants had perished; whereas now they pass them by as they go blundering in the wild. No more will you learn of me; but you may have enough of my bounty, as long as you speak fair and do not spy or steal.' Then again he laughed in his throat. 'They are of great worth,' he said. 'More than gold in the hungry winter, for they may be hoarded like the nuts of a squirrel, and already we were building our store from the first that are ripe. But you are fools, if you think that I would not be parted from one small load even for the saving of my life.'

'I hear you,' said Ulrad, who had looked in the sack when Mîm was taken. 'Yet you would not be parted, and your words only make me wonder the more.'

Mîm turned and looked at him darkly. 'You are one of the fools that spring would not mourn if you perished in winter,' he said to him. 'I had spoken my word, and so must have returned, willing or not, with sack or without, let a lawless and faithless man think what he will! But I love not to be parted from my own by force of the wicked, be it no more than a shoe-thong. Do I not remember that your hands were among those that put bonds upon me, and so held me that I did not speak again with my son? Ever when I deal out the earth-bread from my store you will be counted out, and if you eat it, you shall eat by the bounty of your fellows, not of me.'

Then Mîm went away; but Ulrad, who had quailed under his anger, spoke to his back: 'High words! Nonetheless the old rogue had other things in his sack, of like shape but harder and heavier. Maybe there are other things beside earth-bread in the wild which Elves have not found and Men must not know!'

'That may be,' said Túrin. 'Nonetheless the Dwarf spoke the truth in one point at least, calling you a fool. Why must you speak your thoughts? Silence, if fair words stick in your throat, would serve all our ends better.'

The day passed in peace, and none of the outlaws desired to go abroad. Túrin paced much upon the green sward of the shelf, from brink to brink; and he looked out east, and west, and north, and wondered to find how far were the views in the clear air. Northward, and seeming strangely near, he could descry the forest of Brethil climbing green about the Amon Obel. Thither he found that his eyes would stray more often than he wished, though he knew not why; for his heart was set rather to the north-west, where league upon league away on the skirts of the sky it seemed to him that he could glimpse the Mountains of Shadow and the borders of his home. But at evening Túrin looked west into the sunset, as the sun rode down red into the hazes above the far distant coasts, and the Vale of Narog lay deep in the shadows between.

So began the abiding of Túrin son of Húrin in the halls of Mîm, in Bar-en-Danwedh, the House of Ransom.

For a long while the life of the outlaws went well to their liking. Food was not scarce, and they had good shelter, warm and dry, with room enough and to spare; for they found that the caves could have housed a hundred or more at need. There was another smaller hall further in. It had a hearth at one side, above which a smoke-shaft ran up through the rock to a vent cunningly hidden in a crevice on the hillside. There were also many other chambers, opening out of the halls or the passage between them, some for dwelling, some for works or for stores. In storage Mîm had more arts than they, and he had many vessels and chests of stone and wood that looked to be of great age. But most of the chambers were now empty: in the armouries hung axes and other gear rusted and dusty, shelves and aumbries were bare; and the smithies were idle. Save one: a small room that led out of the inner hall and had a hearth which shared the smoke-vent of the hearth in the hall. There Mîm would work at times, but would not allow others to be with him; and he did not tell of a secret hidden stair that led from his house to the flat summit of Amon Rûdh. This Andróg came upon when seeking in hunger to find Mîm's stores of food he became lost in the caves; but he kept this discovery to himself.

During the rest of that year they went on no more raids, and if they stirred abroad for hunting or gathering of food they went for the most part in small parties. But for a long while they found it hard to retrace their road, and beside Túrin not more than six of his men became ever sure of the way. Nonetheless, seeing that those skilled in such things could come to their lair without Mîm's help, they set a watch by day and night near to the cleft in the north-wall. From the south they expected no enemies, nor was there fear of any climbing Amon Rûdh from that quarter; but by day there was at most times a watchman set on the top of the crown, who could look far all about. Steep as were the sides of the crown, the summit could be reached, for to the east of the cave-mouth rough steps had been hewn leading up to slopes where men could clamber unaided.

So the year wore on without hurt or alarm. But as the days drew in, and the pool became grey and cold and the birches bare, and great rains returned, they had to pass more time in shelter. Then they soon grew weary of the dark under hill, or the dim half-light of the halls; and to most it seemed that life would be better if it were not shared with Mîm. Too often he would appear out of some shadowy corner or doorway when they thought him elsewhere; and when Mîm was near unease fell on their talk. They took to speaking ever to one another in whispers.

Yet, and strange it seemed to them, with Túrin it went otherwise; and he became ever more friendly with the old Dwarf, and listened more and more to his counsels. In the winter that followed he would sit for long hours with Mîm, listening to his lore and the tales of his life; nor did Túrin rebuke him if he spoke ill of the Eldar. Mîm seemed well pleased, and showed much favour to Túrin in return; him only would he admit to his smithy at times, and there they would talk softly together.

But when autumn was passed the winter pressed them hard. Before Yule snow came down from the North heavier than they had known it in the river-vales; at that time, and ever the more as the power of Angband grew, the winters worsened in Beleriand. Amon Rûdh was covered deep, and only the hardiest dared stir abroad. Some fell sick, and all were pinched with hunger.

In the dim dusk of a day in midwinter there appeared suddenly among them a Man, as it seemed, of great bulk and girth, cloaked and hooded in white. He had eluded their watchmen, and he walked up to their fire without a word. When men sprang up he laughed and threw back his hood, and they saw that it was Beleg Strongbow. Under his wide cloak he bore a great pack in which he had brought many things for the help of men.

In this way Beleg came back to Túrin, yielding to his love against his wisdom. Túrin was glad indeed, for he had often regretted his stubbornness; and now the desire of his heart was granted without the need to humble himself or to yield his own will. But if Túrin was glad, not so was Andróg, nor some others of his company. It seemed to them that there had been a tryst between Beleg and their captain, which he had kept secret from them; and Andróg watched them jealously as the two sat apart in speech together.

Beleg had brought with him the Helm of Hador; for he hoped that it might lift Túrin's thought again above his life in the wild as the leader of a petty company. 'This is your own which I bring back to you,' he said to Túrin as he took out the helm. 'It was left in my keeping on the north-marches; but was not forgotten, I think.'

'Almost,' said Túrin; 'but it shall not be so again'; and he fell silent, looking far away with the eyes of his thought, until suddenly he caught the gleam of another thing that Beleg held in his hand. It was the gift of Melian; but the silver leaves were red in the firelight, and when Túrin saw the seal his eyes darkened. 'What have you there?' he said.

'The greatest gift that one who loves you still has to give,' answered Beleg. 'Here is *lembas in·Elidh*, the way-bread of the Eldar that no man has yet tasted.'

'The helm of my fathers I take, with good will for your keeping,' said Túrin. 'But I will not receive gifts out of Doriath.'

'Then send back your sword and your arms,' said Beleg. 'Send back also the teaching and fostering of your youth. And let your men, who (you say) have been faithful, die in the desert to please your mood! Nonetheless this waybread was a gift not to you but to me, and I may do with it as I will. Eat it not, if it sticks in your throat; but others may be more hungry and less proud.'

Túrin's eyes glinted, but as he looked in Beleg's face the fire in them died, and they went grey, and he said in a voice hardly to be heard: 'I wonder, friend, that you deign to come back to such a churl. From you I will take whatever you give, even rebuke. Henceforward you shall counsel me in all ways, save the road to Doriath only.'

CHAPTER VIII

THE LAND OF BOW AND HELM

In the days that followed Beleg laboured much for the good of the Company. Those that were hurt or sick he tended, and they were quickly healed. For in those days the Grey-elves were still a high people, possessing great power, and they were wise in the ways of life and of all living things; and though they were less in crafts and lore than the Exiles from Valinor they had many arts beyond the reach of Men. Moreover Beleg the Archer was great among the people of Doriath; he was strong, and enduring, and far-sighted in mind as well as eye, and at need he was valiant in battle, relying not only upon the swift arrows of his long bow, but also upon his great sword Anglachel. And ever the more did hatred grow in the heart of Mîm, who hated all Elves, as has been told, and who looked with a jealous eye on the love that Túrin bore to Beleg.

When winter passed, and the stirring came, and the spring, the outlaws soon had sterner work to do. Morgoth's might was moved; and as the long fingers of a groping hand the forerunners of his armies probed the ways into Beleriand.

Who knows now the counsels of Morgoth? Who can measure the reach of his thought, who had been Melkor, mighty among the Ainur of the Great Song, and sat now, the dark lord upon a dark throne in the North, weighing in his malice all the tidings that came to him, whether by spy or by traitor, seeing in the eyes of his mind and understanding far more of the deeds and purposes of his enemies than even the wisest of them feared, save Melian the Queen. To her often his thought reached out, and there was foiled.

In this year, therefore, he turned his malice towards the lands west of Sirion, where there was still power to oppose him. Gondolin still stood, but it was hidden. Doriath he knew, but could not enter yet. Further still lay Nargothrond, to which none of his servants had yet found the way, a name of fear to them; there the people of Finrod dwelt in hidden strength. And far away from the South, beyond the white woods of the birches of Nimbrethil, from the coast of Arvernien and the mouths of Sirion, came rumour of the Havens of the Ships. Thither he could not reach until all else had fallen.

So now the Orcs came down out of the North in ever greater numbers. Through Anach they came, and Dimbar

was taken, and all the north-marches of Doriath were
infested. Down the ancient road they came that led
through the long defile of Sirion, past the isle where Minas
Tirith of Finrod had stood, and so through the land
between Malduin and Sirion and then on through the
eaves of Brethil to the Crossings of Teiglin. Thence of old
the road passed on into the Guarded Plain, and then,
along the feet of the highlands watched over by Amon
Rûdh, it ran down into the vale of Narog and came at last
to Nargothrond. But the Orcs did not go far upon that
road as yet; for there dwelt now in the wild a terror that
was hidden, and upon the red hill were watchful eyes of
which they had not been warned.

In that spring Túrin put on again the Helm of Hador,
and Beleg was glad. At first their company had less than
fifty men, but the woodcraft of Beleg and the valour of
Túrin made them seem to their enemies as a host. The
scouts of the Orcs were hunted, their camps were espied,
and if they gathered to march in force in some narrow
place, out of the rocks or from the shadow of the trees
there leaped the Dragon-helm and his men, tall and fierce.
Soon at the very sound of his horn in the hills their captains would quail and the Orcs would turn to flight before
any arrow whined or sword was drawn.

It has been told that when Mîm surrendered his hidden
dwelling on Amon Rûdh to Túrin and his company, he
demanded that he who had loosed the arrow that slew his

son should break his bow and his arrows and lay them at the feet of Khîm; and that man was Andróg. Then with great ill-will Andróg did as Mîm bade. Moreover Mîm declared that Andróg must never again bear bow and arrow, and he laid a curse on him, that if nevertheless he should do so, then would he meet his own death by that means.

Now in the spring of that year Andróg defied the curse of Mîm and took up a bow again in a foray from Bar-en-Danwedh; and in that foray he was struck by a poisoned orc-arrow, and was brought back dying in pain. But Beleg healed him of his wound. And now the hatred that Mîm bore to Beleg was increased still more, for he had thus undone his curse; but 'it will bite again,' he said.

In that year far and wide in Beleriand the whisper went, under wood and over stream and through the passes of the hills, saying that the Bow and Helm that had fallen in Dimbar (as was thought) had arisen again beyond hope. Then many, both Elves and Men, who went leaderless, dispossessed but undaunted, remnants of battle and defeat and lands laid waste, took heart again, and came to seek the Two Captains, though where they had their stronghold none yet knew. Túrin received gladly all who came to him, but by the counsel of Beleg he admitted no newcomer to his refuge upon Amon Rûdh (and that was now named Echad i Sedryn, Camp of the Faithful); the way thither only those of the Old Company knew and no others were admitted. But other guarded camps and forts were established round about: in the forest eastward, or in the highlands, or in the south-ward fens, from Methed-en-glad ('the End of the Wood') south of the Crossings of Teiglin to Bar-erib some leagues south of Amon Rûdh in the once fertile land between Narog and the Meres of Sirion. From all these places men could see the summit of Amon Rûdh, and by signals receive tidings and commands.

In this way, before the summer had passed, the follow-ing of Túrin had swelled to a great force, and the power of Angband was thrown back. Word of this came even to Nargothrond, and many there grew restless, saying that if an outlaw could do such hurt to the Enemy, what might not the Lord of Narog do. But Orodreth King of Nar-gothrond would not change his counsels. In all things he followed Thingol, with whom he exchanged messengers by secret ways; and he was a wise lord, according to the wisdom of those who considered first their own people, and how long they might preserve their life and wealth against the lust of the North. Therefore he allowed none of his people to go to Túrin, and he sent messengers to say to him that in all that he might do or devise in his war he should not set foot in the land of Nargothrond, nor drive Orcs thither. But help other than in arms he offered to the Two Captains, should they have need (and in this, it is thought, he was moved by Thingol and Melian).

Then Morgoth withheld his hand; though he made fre-quent feint of attack, so that by easy victory the confidence of these rebels might become overweening. As it proved indeed. For Túrin now gave the name of Dor-Cúarthol to all the land between Teiglin and the west march of Doriath; and claiming the lordship of it he named himself anew, Gorthol, the Dread Helm; and his heart was high. But to Beleg it seemed now that the Helm had wrought otherwise with Túrin than he had hoped; and looking into the days to come he was troubled in mind.

One day as summer was wearing on he and Túrin were sitting in the Echad resting after a long affray and march. Túrin said then to Beleg: 'Why are you sad, and thoughtful? Does not all go well, since you returned to me? Has not my purpose proved good?'

'All is well now,' said Beleg. 'Our enemies are still surprised and afraid. And still good days lie before us – for a while.'

'And what then?' said Túrin.

'Winter,' said Beleg. 'And after that another year, for those who live to see it.'

'And what then?'

'The wrath of Angband. We have burned the fingertips of the Black Hand – no more. It will not withdraw.'

'But is not the wrath of Angband our purpose and delight?' said Túrin. 'What else would you have me do?'

'You know full well,' said Beleg. 'But of that road you have forbidden me to speak. But hear me now. A king or the lord of a great host has many needs. He must have a secure refuge; and he must have wealth, and many whose work is

not in war. With numbers comes the need of food, more than
the wild will furnish to hunters. And there comes the passing
of secrecy. Amon Rûdh is a good place for a few – it has eyes
and ears. But it stands alone, and is seen far off; and no great
force is needed to surround it – unless a host defends it,
greater far than ours is yet or than it is likely ever to be.'

'Nonetheless, I will be the captain of my own host,'
said Túrin; 'and if I fall, then I fall. Here I stand in the path
of Morgoth, and while I so stand he cannot use the southward road.'

Report of the Dragon-helm in the land west of Sirion
came swiftly to the ear of Morgoth, and he laughed, for
now Túrin was revealed to him again, who had long been
lost in the shadows and under the veils of Melian. Yet he
began to fear that Túrin would grow to such a power that
the curse that he had laid upon him would become void,
and he would escape the doom that had been designed for
him, or else that he might retreat to Doriath and be lost to
his sight again. Now therefore he had a mind to seize
Túrin and afflict him even as his father, to torment him
and enslave him.

Beleg had spoken truly when he said to Túrin that they
had but scorched the fingers of the Black Hand, and that
it would not withdraw. But Morgoth concealed his
designs, and for that time contented himself with the
sending out of his most skilled scouts; and ere long Amon
Rûdh was surrounded by spies, lurking unobserved in the

wilderness and making no move against the parties of men that went in and out.

But Mîm was aware of the presence of Orcs in the lands about Amon Rûdh, and the hatred that he bore to Beleg led him now in his darkened heart to an evil resolve. One day in the waning of the year he told the men in Bar-en-Danwedh that he was going with his son Ibun to search for roots for their winter store; but his true purpose was to seek out the servants of Morgoth, and to lead them to Túrin's hiding-place.[*]

Nevertheless he attempted to impose certain conditions on the Orcs, who laughed at him, but Mîm said that they knew little if they believed that they could gain anything from a Petty-dwarf by torture. Then they asked him what these conditions might be, and Mîm declared his demands: that they pay him the weight in iron of each man whom they caught or slew, but of Túrin and Beleg in gold; that Mîm's house, when rid of Túrin and his company, be left to him, and himself unmolested; that Beleg be left behind, bound, for Mîm to deal with; and that Túrin be let go free.

To these conditions the emissaries of Morgoth readily agreed, with no intention of fulfilling either the first or the second. The Orc-captain thought that the fate of Beleg

---

[*]   But another tale is told, which has it that Mîm did not encounter the Orcs with deliberate intent. It was the capture of his son and their threat to torture him that led Mîm to his treachery.

might well be left to Mîm; but as to letting Túrin go free, 'alive to Angband' were his orders. While agreeing to the conditions he insisted that they keep Ibun as hostage; and then Mîm became afraid, and tried to back out of his undertaking, or else to escape. But the Orcs had his son, and so Mîm was obliged to guide them to Bar-en-Danwedh. Thus was the House of Ransom betrayed.

It has been told that the stony mass that was the crown or cap of Amon Rûdh had a bare or flattened top, but that steep as were its sides men could reach the summit by climbing a stair cut into the rock, leading up from the shelf or terrace before the entrance to Mîm's house. On the summit watchmen were set, and they gave warning of the approach of the enemies. But these, guided by Mîm, came onto the level shelf before the doors, and Túrin and Beleg were driven back to the entrance of Bar-en-Danwedh. Some of the men who tried to climb up the steps cut in the rock were shot down by the arrows of the Orcs.

Túrin and Beleg retreated into the cave, and rolled a great stone across the passage. In these straits Andróg revealed to them the hidden stair leading to the flat summit of Amon Rûdh which he had found when lost in the caves, as has been told. Then Túrin and Beleg with many of their men went up by this stair and came out on the summit, surprising those few of the Orcs who had already come there by the outer path, and driving them over the edge. For a little while they held off the Orcs climbing up the rock, but they had no shelter on the bare summit, and many were shot from below. Most valiant of these was Andróg, who fell mortally wounded by an arrow at the head of the outside stair.

Then Túrin and Beleg with the ten men left to them drew back to the centre of the summit, where there was a standing stone, and making a ring about it they defended themselves until all were slain save Beleg and Túrin, for over them the Orcs cast nets. Túrin was bound and carried off; Beleg who was wounded was bound likewise, but he was laid on the ground with wrists and ankles tied to iron pins driven in to the rock.

Now the Orcs, finding the issue of the secret stair, left the summit and entered Bar-en-Danwedh, which they defiled and ravaged. They did not find Mîm, lurking in his caves, and when they had departed from Amon Rûdh Mîm appeared on the summit, and going to where Beleg lay prostrate and unmoving he gloated over him while he sharpened a knife.

But Mîm and Beleg were not the only living beings on that stony height. Andróg, though himself wounded to the death, crawled among the dead bodies towards them, and seizing a sword he thrust it at the Dwarf. Shrieking in fear Mîm ran to the brink of the cliff and disappeared: he fled down a steep and difficult goat's path that was known to him. But Andróg putting forth his last strength cut through the wristbands and fetters that bound Beleg, and so released him; but dying he said: 'My hurts are too deep even for your healing.'

CHAPTER IX

THE DEATH OF BELEG

Beleg sought among the dead for Túrin, to bury him; but he could not discover his body. He knew then that Húrin's son was still alive, and taken to Angband; but he remained perforce in Bar-en-Danwedh until his wounds were healed. He set out then with little hope to try to find the trail of the Orcs, and he came upon their tracks near the Crossings of Teiglin. There they divided, some passing along the eaves of the Forest of Brethil towards the Ford of Brithiach, while others turned away westwards; and it seemed plain to Beleg that he must follow those that went direct with greatest speed to Angband, making for the Pass of Anach. Therefore he journeyed on through Dimbar, and up to the Pass of Anach in Ered Gorgoroth, the Mountains of Terror, and so to the highlands of Taur-nu-Fuin, the Forest under

Night, a region of dread and dark enchantment, of wandering and despair.

Benighted in that evil land, it chanced that Beleg saw a small light among the trees, and going towards it he found an Elf, lying asleep beneath a great dead tree: beside his head was a lamp, from which the covering had slipped off. Then Beleg woke the sleeper, and gave him *lembas*, and asked him what fate had brought him to this terrible place; and he named himself Gwindor, son of Guilin.

Grieving Beleg looked at him, for Gwindor was but a bent and timid shadow of his former shape and mood, when in the Battle of Unnumbered Tears that lord of Nargothrond rode to the very doors of Angband, and there was taken. For few of the Noldor whom Morgoth took captive were put to death, because of their skill in mining for metals and gems; and Gwindor was not slain, but put to labour in the mines of the North. These Noldor possessed many of the Fëanorian lamps, which were crystals hung in a fine chain net, the crystals being ever-shining with an inner blue radiance marvellous for finding the way in the darkness of night or in tunnels; of these lamps they themselves did not know the secret. Many of the mining Elves thus escaped from the darkness of the mines, for they were able to bore their way out; but Gwindor received a small sword from one who worked in the forges, and when working in a stone-gang turned suddenly on the guards. He escaped, but with one hand cut off; and now he lay exhausted under the great pines of Taur-nu-Fuin.

From Gwindor Beleg learned that the small company of Orcs ahead of them, from whom he had hidden, had no captives, and were going with speed: an advance guard, perhaps, bearing report to Angband. At this news Beleg despaired: for he guessed that the tracks that he had seen turning away westwards after the Crossings of Teiglin were those of a greater host, who had in orc-fashion gone marauding in the lands seeking food and plunder, and might now be returning to Angband by way of 'the Narrow Land', the long defile of Sirion, much further to the west. If this were so, his sole hope lay in returning to the Ford of Brithiach, and then going north to Tol Sirion. But scarcely had he determined on this than they heard the noise of a great host approaching through the forest from the south; and hiding in the boughs of a tree they watched the servants of Morgoth pass, moving slowly, laden with booty and captives, surrounded by wolves. And they saw Túrin with chained hands being driven on with whips.

Then Beleg told him of his own errand in Taur-nu-Fuin; and Gwindor sought to dissuade him from his quest, saying that he would but join Túrin in the anguish that awaited him. But Beleg would not abandon Túrin, and despairing himself he aroused hope again in Gwindor's heart; and together they went on, following the Orcs until they came out of the forest on the high slopes that ran down to the barren dunes of the Anfauglith. There within sight of the peaks of Thangorodrim the Orcs made their encampment in a bare dale, and set wolf-sentinels all about its rim. There they fell to carousing and feasting on their booty; and after tormenting their prisoners most fell drunkenly asleep. By that time day was failing and it became very dark. A great storm rode up out of the West, and thunder rumbled far off as Beleg and Gwindor crept towards the camp.

When all in the camp were sleeping Beleg took up his bow and in the darkness shot four of the wolf-sentinels on the south side, one by one and silently. Then in great peril they entered in, and they found Túrin fettered hand and foot and tied to a tree. All about knives that had been cast at him by his tormentors were embedded in the trunk, but he was not hurt; and he was senseless in a drugged stupor or swooned in a sleep of utter weariness. Then Beleg and Gwindor cut the bonds from the tree, and bore Túrin out of the camp. But he was too heavy to carry far, and they could go no further than to a thicket of thorn trees high on the slopes above the camp. There they laid him down; and now the storm drew nearer, and lightning flashed on Thangorodrim. Beleg drew his sword Anglachel, and with it he cut the fetters that bound Túrin; but fate was that day more strong, for the blade of Eöl the Dark Elf slipped in his hand, and pricked Túrin's foot.

Then Túrin was roused into a sudden wakefulness of rage and fear, and seeing a form bending over him in the gloom with a naked blade in hand he leapt up with a great cry, believing that Orcs were come again to torment him; and grappling with him in the darkness he seized Anglachel, and slew Beleg Cúthalion thinking him a foe.

But as he stood, finding himself free, and ready to sell his life dearly against imagined foes, there came a great flash of lightning above them, and in its light he looked down on Beleg's face. Then Túrin stood stonestill and silent, staring on that dreadful death, knowing what he had done; and so terrible was his face, lit by the lightning that flickered all about them, that Gwindor cowered down upon the ground and dared not raise his eyes.

But now in the camp beneath the Orcs were roused, both by the storm and by Túrin's cry, and discovered that Túrin was gone; but no search was made for him, for they were filled with terror by the thunder that came out of the West, believing that it was sent against them by the great Enemies beyond the Sea. Then a wind arose, and great rains fell, and torrents swept down from the heights of Taur-nu-Fuin; and though Gwindor cried out to Túrin, warning him of their utmost peril, he made no answer, but sat unmoving and unweeping beside the body of Beleg Cúthalion, lying in the dark forest slain by his hand even as he cut the bonds of thraldom from him.

When morning came the storm was passed away eastward over Lothlann, and the sun of autumn rose hot and bright; but the Orcs hating this almost as much as the thunder, and believing that Túrin would have fled far from that place and all trace of his flight be washed away, they departed in haste, eager to return to Angband. Far off Gwindor saw them marching northward over the steaming sands of Anfauglith. Thus it came to pass that they returned to Morgoth empty-handed, and left behind them the son of Húrin, who sat crazed and unwitting on the slopes of Taur-nu-Fuin, bearing a burden heavier than their bonds.

Then Gwindor roused Túrin to aid him in the burial of Beleg, and he rose as one that walked in sleep; and together they laid Beleg in a shallow grave, and placed beside him Belthronding his great bow, that was made of black yew-wood. But the dread sword Anglachel Gwindor took, saying that it were better that it should take vengeance on the servants of Morgoth than lie useless in the earth; and he took also the *lembas* of Melian to strengthen them in the wild.

Thus ended Beleg Strongbow, truest of friends, greatest in skill of all that harboured in the woods of Beleriand in the Elder Days, at the hand of him whom he most loved; and that grief was graven on the face of Túrin and never faded.

But courage and strength were renewed in the Elf of Nargothrond, and departing from Taur-nu-Fuin he led Túrin far away. Never once as they wandered together on long and grievous paths did Túrin speak, and he walked as one without wish or purpose, while the year waned and winter drew on over the northern lands. But Gwindor was ever beside him to guard him and guide him; and thus they passed westward over Sirion and came at length to the Beautiful Mere and Eithel Ivrin, the springs whence Narog rose beneath the Mountains of Shadow. There Gwindor spoke to Túrin, saying: 'Awake, Túrin son of Húrin! On Ivrin's lake is endless laughter. She is fed from crystal fountains unfailing, and guarded from defilement by Ulmo, Lord of Waters, who wrought her beauty in ancient days.' Then Túrin knelt and drank from that water; and suddenly he cast himself down, and his tears were unloosed at last, and he was healed of his madness.

There he made a song for Beleg, and he named it *Laer Cú Beleg*, the Song of the Great Bow, singing it aloud heedless of peril. And Gwindor gave the sword Anglachel into his hands, and Túrin knew that it was heavy and strong and had great power; but its blade was black and dull and its edges blunt. Then Gwindor said: 'This is a strange blade, and unlike any that I have seen in Middle-earth. It mourns for Beleg even as you do. But be comforted; for I return to Nargothrond of the House of Finarfin, where I was born and dwelt before my grief. You shall come with me, and be healed and renewed.'

'Who are you?' said Túrin.

'A wandering Elf, a thrall escaped, whom Beleg met and comforted,' said Gwindor. 'Yet once I was Gwindor son of Guilin, a lord of Nargothrond, until I went to the Nirnaeth Arnoediad, and was enslaved in Angband.'

'Then have you seen Húrin son of Galdor, the warrior of Dor-lómin?' said Túrin.

'I have not seen him,' said Gwindor. 'But the rumour

runs through Angband that he still defies Morgoth; and Morgoth has laid a curse upon him and all his kin.'

'That I do believe,' said Túrin.

And now they arose, and departing from Eithel Ivrin they journeyed southward along the banks of Narog, until they were taken by scouts of the Elves and brought as prisoners to the hidden stronghold.

Thus did Túrin come to Nargothrond.

CHAPTER X

TÚRIN IN NARGOTHROND

At first his own people did not know Gwindor, who went out young and strong, and returned now seeming as one of the aged among mortal Men, because of his torments and his labours; and now also he was maimed. But Finduilas daughter of Orodreth the King knew him and welcomed him, for she had loved him, and indeed they were betrothed, before the Nirnaeth, and so greatly did Gwindor love her beauty that he named her Faelivrin, which is the sheen of the sun upon the pools of Ivrin.

Thus Gwindor came home, and for his sake Túrin was admitted with him; for Gwindor said that he was a valiant man, dear friend of Beleg Cúthalion of Doriath. But when Gwindor would tell his name Túrin checked him, saying: 'I am Agarwaen, the son of Úmarth (which is the Blood-stained, son of Ill-fate), a hunter in the woods.' But though the Elves guessed that he took these names because of the slaying of his friend (not knowing other reasons), they questioned him no more.

The sword Anglachel was forged anew for him by the cunning smiths of Nargothrond, and though ever black its edges shone with pale fire. Then Túrin himself became known in Nargothrond as Mormegil, the Black Sword, for the rumour of his deeds with that weapon; but he named the sword Gurthang, Iron of Death.

Because of his prowess and his skill in warfare with Orcs Túrin found favour with Orodreth, and was admitted to his council. Now Túrin had no liking for the manner of fighting of the Elves of Nargothrond, of ambush and stealth and secret arrow, and he urged that it be abandoned, and that they should use their strength to attack the servants of the Enemy, to open battle and pursuit. But Gwindor spoke ever against Túrin in this matter in the council of the King, saying that he had been in Angband and had had a glimpse of the power of Morgoth, and had some inkling of his designs. 'Petty victories will prove profitless at the last,' he said; 'for thus Morgoth learns where the boldest of his enemies are to be found, and gathers strength great enough to destroy them. All the might of the Elves and Edain united sufficed only to contain him, and to gain the peace of a siege; long indeed, but only so long as Morgoth bided his time before he broke the leaguer; and never again can such a union be made. Only in secrecy lies hope of survival. Until the Valar come.'

'The Valar!' said Túrin. 'They have forsaken you, and they hold Men in scorn. What use to look westward across the endless Sea to a dying sunset in the West? There is but one Vala with whom we have to do, and that is Morgoth; and if in the end we cannot overcome him, at least we can hurt him and hinder him. For victory is victory, however small, nor is its worth only from what follows from it. But it is expedient also. Secrecy is not finally possible: arms are the only wall against Morgoth. If you do nothing to halt him, all Beleriand will fall under his shadow before many years are passed, and then one by one he will smoke you out of your earths. And what then? A pitiable remnant will fly south and west, to cower on the shores of the Sea, caught between Morgoth and Ossë. Better then to win a time of glory, though it be shortlived; for the end will be no worse. You speak of secrecy, and say that therein lies the only hope; but could you ambush and waylay every scout and spy of Morgoth to the last and least, so that none came ever back with tidings to Angband, yet from that he would learn that you lived and guess where. And this also I say: though mortal Men have little life beside the span of the Elves, they would rather spend it in battle than fly or submit. The defiance of Húrin Thalion is a great deed; and though Morgoth slay the doer he cannot make the deed not to have been. Even the Lords of the West will honour it; and is it not written into the history of Arda, which neither Morgoth nor Manwë can unwrite?'

'You speak of high things,' Gwindor answered, 'and plain it is that you have lived among the Eldar. But a darkness is on you if you set Morgoth and Manwë together, or speak of the Valar as the foes of Elves and Men; for the Valar scorn nothing, and least of all the Children of Ilúvatar. Nor do you know all the hopes of the Eldar. It is a prophecy among us that one day a messenger from Middle-earth will come through the shadows to Valinor, and Manwë will hear, and Mandos relent. For that time shall we not attempt to preserve the seed of the Noldor, and of the Edain also? And Círdan dwells now in the South, and there is building of ships; but what know you of ships, or of the Sea? You think of yourself and of your own glory, and bid us each do likewise; but we must think of others beside ourselves, for not all can fight and fall, and those we must keep from war and ruin, while we can.'

'Then send them to your ships, while there is yet time,' said Túrin.

'They will not be parted from us,' said Gwindor, 'even could Círdan sustain them. We must abide together as long as we may, and not court death.'

'All this I have answered,' said Túrin. 'Valiant defence of the borders and hard blows ere the enemy gathers; in that course lies the best hope of your long abiding together. And do those that you speak of love such skulkers in the woods, hunting strays like a wolf, better than one who puts on his helm and figured shield, and drives away the foe, be they far greater than all his host? At least the women of the Edain do not. They did not hold back the men from the Nirnaeth Arnoediad.'

'But they suffered greater woe than if that field had not been fought,' said Gwindor.

But Túrin advanced greatly in the favour of Orodreth, and he became the chief counsellor of the King, who submitted all things to his advice. In that time the Elves of Nargothrond forsook their secrecy, and great store of weapons were made; and by the counsel of Túrin the Noldor built a mighty bridge over the Narog from the Doors of Felagund for the swifter passage of their arms, since war was now chiefly east of Narog in the Guarded Plain. As its north-march Nargothrond now held the 'Debatable Land' about the sources of Ginglith, Narog, and the fringes of the Woods of Núath. Between Nenning and Narog no Orc came; and east of Narog their realm went to the Teiglin and the borders of the Moors of the Nibin-noeg.

Gwindor fell into dishonour, for he was no longer forward in arms, and his strength was small; and the pain of his maimed left arm was often upon him. But Túrin was young, and only now reached his full manhood; and he was in truth the son of Morwen Eledhwen to look upon: tall, dark-haired and pale-skinned, with grey eyes, and his face more beautiful than any other among mortal men, in the Elder Days. His speech and bearing were those of the ancient kingdom of Doriath, and even among the Elves he might be taken at first meeting for one from the great houses of the Noldor. So valiant was Túrin, and so exceedingly skilled in arms, especially with sword and shield, that the Elves said that he could not be slain, save by mischance, or an evil arrow from afar. Therefore they gave him dwarf-mail, to guard him; and in a grim mood he found in the armouries a dwarf-mask all gilded, and he put it on before battle, and his enemies fled before his face.

Now that he had his way, and all went well, and he had work to do after his heart, and had honour in it, he was courteous to all, and less grim than of old, so that well nigh all hearts were turned to him; and many called him Adanedhel, the Elf-man. But most of all Finduilas the daughter of Orodreth found her heart moved whenever he came near, or was in hall. She was golden-haired after the manner of the house of Finarfin, and Túrin began to take pleasure in the sight of her and in her company; for she reminded him of his kindred and the women of Dor-lómin in his father's house.

At first he met her only when Gwindor was by; but after a while she sought him out, so that they met at times alone, though it seemed to be by chance. Then she would question him about the Edain, of whom she had seen few and seldom, and about his country and his kin.

Then Túrin spoke freely to her concerning these things, though he did not name the land of his birth, nor any of his kindred; and on a time he said to her: 'I had a sister, Lalaith, or so I named her; and of her you put me in mind. But Lalaith was a child, a yellow flower in the green grass of spring; and had she lived she would now, maybe, have become dimmed with grief. But you are queenly, and as a golden tree; I would I had a sister so fair.'

'But you are kingly,' said she, 'even as the lords of the people of Fingolfin; I would I had a brother so valiant. And I do not think that Agarwaen is your name, nor is it fit for you, Adanedhel. I call you Thurin, the Secret.'

At this Túrin started, but he said: 'That is not my name; and I am not a king, for our kings are of the Eldar, as I am not.'

Now Túrin marked that Gwindor's friendship grew cooler towards him; and he wondered also that whereas at first the woe and horror of Angband had begun to be lifted from him, now he seemed to slip back into care and sorrow. And he thought, it may be that he is grieved that I oppose his counsels, and have overcome him; I would it were not so. For he loved Gwindor as his guide and healer, and was filled with pity for him. But in those days the radiance of Finduilas also became dimmed, her footsteps slow and her face grave, and she grew wan and thin; and Túrin perceiving this surmised that the words of Gwindor had set fear in her heart of what might come to pass.

In truth Finduilas was torn in mind. For she honoured Gwindor and pitied him, and wished not to add one tear to his suffering; but against her will her love for Túrin grew day by day, and she thought of Beren and Lúthien. But Túrin was not like Beren! He did not scorn her, and was glad in her company; yet she knew that he had no love of the kind she wished. His mind and heart were elsewhere, by rivers in springs long past.

Then Túrin spoke to Finduilas, and said: 'Do not let the words of Gwindor affright you. He has suffered in the darkness of Angband; and it is hard for one so valiant to be thus crippled and backward perforce. He needs all solace, and a longer time for healing.'

'I know it well,' she said.

'But we will win that time for him!' said Túrin. 'Nargothrond shall stand! Never again will Morgoth the Craven come forth from Angband, and all his reliance must be on his servants; thus says Melian of Doriath. They are the fingers of his hands; and we will smite them, and cut them off, till he draws back his claws. Nargothrond shall stand!'

'Perhaps,' said she. 'It shall stand, if you can achieve it. But have a care, Thurin; my heart is heavy when you go out to battle, lest Nargothrond be bereaved.'

Afterwards Túrin sought out Gwindor, and said to him: 'Gwindor, dear friend, you are falling back into sadness; do not so! For your healing will come in the houses of your kin, and in the light of Finduilas.'

Then Gwindor stared at Túrin, but he said nothing, and his face was clouded.

'Why do you look upon me so?' said Túrin. 'Often your eyes have gazed at me strangely of late. How have I grieved you? I have opposed your counsels; but a man must speak as he sees, nor hide the truth that he believes, for any private cause. I would that we were one in mind; for to you I owe a great debt, and I shall not forget it.'

'Will you not?' said Gwindor. 'Nonetheless your deeds and your counsels have changed my home and my kin. Your shadow lies upon them. Why should I be glad, who have lost all to you?'

Túrin did not understand these words, and did but guess that Gwindor begrudged him his place in the heart and counsels of the King.

But Gwindor, when Túrin had gone, sat alone in dark thought, and he cursed Morgoth who could thus pursue his enemies with woe, whithersoever they might run. 'And now at last,' he said, 'I believe the rumour of Angband that Morgoth has cursed Húrin and all his kin.' And going to find Finduilas he said to her: 'A sadness and doubt is upon you; and too often now I miss you, and begin to guess that you are avoiding me. Since you tell me not the cause, I must guess. Daughter of the house of Finarfin, let no grief lie between us; for though Morgoth has laid my life in ruin, you still I love. But go whither love leads you; for I am become unfit to wed you; and neither my prowess nor my counsel have any honour more.'

Then Finduilas wept. 'Weep not yet!' said Gwindor. 'But beware lest you have cause. Not fitting is it that the Elder Children of Ilúvatar should wed the Younger; nor is it wise, for they are brief, and soon pass, to leave us in widowhood while the world lasts. Neither will fate suffer it, unless it be once or twice only, for some high cause of doom that we do not perceive.

'But this man is not Beren, even if he be both as fair and as brave. A doom lies on him; a dark doom. Enter not into it! And if you will, your love shall betray you to bitterness and death. For hearken to me! Though he be indeed *agarwaen* son of *úmarth*, his right name is Túrin son of Húrin, whom Morgoth holds in Angband, and has cursed all his kin. Doubt not the power of Morgoth Bauglir! Is it not written in me?'

Then Finduilas rose, and queenly indeed she looked. 'Your eyes are dimmed, Gwindor,' she said. 'You do not see or understand what has here come to pass. Must I now be put to double shame to reveal the truth to you? For I love you, Gwindor, and I am ashamed that I love you not more, but have taken a love even greater, from which I cannot escape. I did not seek it, and long I put it aside. But if I have pity for your hurts, have pity on mine. Túrin loves me not, nor will.'

'You say this,' said Gwindor, 'to take the blame from him whom you love. Why does he seek you out, and sit long with you, and come ever more glad away?'

'Because he also needs solace,' said Finduilas, 'and is bereaved of his kin. You both have your needs. But what of Finduilas? Now is it not enough that I must confess myself to you unloved, but that you should say that I speak so to deceive?'

'Nay, a woman is not easily deceived in such a case,' said Gwindor. 'Nor will you find many who will deny that they are loved, if that is true.'

'If any of us three be faithless, it is I: but not in will. But what of your doom and rumours of Angband? What of death and destruction? The Adanedhel is mighty in the tale of the World, and his stature shall reach yet to Morgoth in some far day to come.'

'He is proud,' said Gwindor.

'But also he is merciful,' said Finduilas. 'He is not yet awake, but still pity can ever pierce his heart, and he will never deny it. Pity maybe shall be ever the only entry. But he does not pity me. He holds me in awe, as were I both his mother and a queen.'

Maybe Finduilas spoke truly, seeing with the keen eyes of the Eldar. And now Túrin, not knowing what had passed between Gwindor and Finduilas, was ever gentler towards her as she seemed more sad. But on a time Finduilas said to him: 'Thurin Adanedhel, why did you hide your name from me? Had I known who you were I should not have honoured you less, but I should better have understood your grief.'

'What do you mean?' he said. 'Whom do you make me?'

'Túrin son of Húrin Thalion, captain of the North.'

Now when Túrin learned from Finduilas of what had passed, he was wrathful, and he said to Gwindor: 'In love I hold you for rescue and safe-keeping. But now you have done ill to me, friend, to betray my right name, and call down my doom upon me, from which I would lie hid.'

But Gwindor answered: 'The doom lies in yourself, not in your name.'

In that time of respite and hope, when because of the deeds of the Mormegil the power of Morgoth was stemmed west of Sirion, and all the woods had peace, Morwen fled at last from Dor-lómin with Niënor her daughter, and adventured the long journey to Thingol's halls. There new grief awaited her, for she found Túrin gone, and to Doriath there had come no tidings since the Dragon-helm had vanished from the lands west of Sirion; but Morwen remained in Doriath with Niënor as guests of Thingol and Melian, and were treated with honour.

CHAPTER XI

THE FALL OF NARGOTHROND

When five years had passed since Túrin came to Nargothrond, in the spring of the year, there came two Elves, and they named themselves Gelmir and Arminas, of the people of Finarfin; and they said that they had an errand to the Lord of Nargothrond. Túrin now commanded all the forces of Nargothrond, and ruled all matters of war; indeed he was become stern and proud, and would order all things as he wished or thought good. They were brought therefore before Túrin; but Gelmir said: 'It is to Orodreth, Finarfin's son, that we would speak.'

And when Orodreth came, Gelmir said to him: 'Lord, we were of Angrod's people, and we have wandered far since the Nirnaeth; but of late we have dwelt among Círdan's following by the Mouths of Sirion. And on a day he called us, and bade us go to you; for Ulmo himself, the

Lord of Waters, had appeared to him and warned him of great peril that draws near to Nargothrond.'

But Orodreth was wary, and he answered: 'Why then do you come hither out of the North? Or perhaps you had other errands also?'

Then Arminas said: 'Yes, lord. Ever since the Nirnaeth I have sought for the hidden kingdom of Turgon, and I have found it not; and in this search I fear now that I have delayed our errand hither over long. For Círdan sent us along the coast by ship, for secrecy and speed, and we were put ashore in Drengist. But among the sea-folk were some that came south in past years as messengers from Turgon, and it seemed to me from their guarded speech that maybe Turgon dwells still in the North, and not in the South as most believe. But we have found neither sign nor rumour of what we sought.'

'Why do you seek Turgon?' said Orodreth.

'Because it is said that his kingdom shall stand longest against Morgoth,' answered Arminas. And these words seemed to Orodreth ill-omened, and he was displeased.

'Then tarry not in Nargothrond,' said he; 'for here you will hear no news of Turgon. And I need none to teach me that Nargothrond stands in peril.'

'Be not angered, lord,' said Gelmir, 'if we answer your questions with truth. And our wandering from the straight path hither has not been fruitless, for we have passed beyond the reach of your furthest scouts; we have traversed Dor-lómin and all the lands under the eaves of

Ered Wethrin, and we have explored the Pass of Sirion spying out the ways of the Enemy. There is a great gathering of Orcs and evil creatures in those regions, and a host is mustering about Sauron's Isle.'

'I know it,' said Túrin. 'Your news is stale. If the message of Círdan was to any purpose, it should have come sooner.'

'At least, lord, you shall hear the message now,' said Gelmir to Orodreth. 'Hear then the words of the Lord of Waters! Thus he spoke to Círdan: "The Evil of the North has defiled the springs of Sirion, and my power withdraws from the fingers of the flowing waters. But a worse thing is yet to come forth. Say therefore to the Lord of Nargothrond: Shut the doors of the fortress, and go not abroad. Cast the stones of your pride into the loud river, that the creeping evil may not find the gate."'

These words seemed dark to Orodreth, and he turned as ever to Túrin for counsel. But Túrin mistrusted the messengers, and he said in scorn: 'What does Círdan know of our wars, who dwell nigh to the Enemy? Let the mariner look to his ships! But if in truth the Lord of Waters would send us counsel, let him speak more plainly. Otherwise to one trained in war it will still seem better in our case to muster our strength, and go boldly to meet our foes, ere they come too nigh.'

Then Gelmir bowed before Orodreth, and said: 'I have spoken as I was bidden, lord'; and he turned away. But Arminas said to Túrin: 'Are you indeed of the House of Hador, as I have heard said?'

'Here I am named Agarwaen, the Black Sword of Nargothrond,' answered Túrin. 'You deal much, it seems, in guarded speech, friend Arminas. It is well that Turgon's secret is hid from you, or soon it would be heard in Angband. A man's name is his own, and should the son of Húrin learn that you have betrayed him when he would be hid, then may Morgoth take you and burn out your tongue!'

Arminas was dismayed by the black wrath of Túrin; but Gelmir said: 'He shall not be betrayed by us, Agarwaen. Are we not in council behind closed doors, where speech may be plainer? And Arminas, I deem, questioned you, since it is known to all that dwell by the Sea that Ulmo has great love for the House of Hador, and some say that Húrin and Huor his brother came once into the Hidden Realm.'

'If that were so, then he would speak of it to none, neither the great nor the less, and least of all to his son in childhood,' answered Túrin. 'Therefore I do not believe that Arminas asked this of me in order to learn aught of Turgon. I mistrust such messengers of mischief.'

'Save your mistrust!' said Arminas in anger. 'Gelmir mistakes me. I asked because I doubted what here seems believed; for little indeed do you resemble the kin of Hador, whatever your name.'

'And what do you know of them?' said Túrin.

'Húrin I have seen,' answered Arminas, 'and his fathers before him. And in the wastes of Dor-lómin I met with Tuor, son of Huor, Húrin's brother; and he is like his fathers, as you are not.'

'That may be,' said Túrin, 'though of Tuor I have heard no word ere now. But if my head be dark and not golden, of that I am not ashamed. For I am not the first of sons in the likeness of his mother; and I come through Morwen Eledhwen of the House of Bëor and the kindred of Beren Camlost.'

'I spoke not of the difference between the black and the gold,' said Arminas. 'But others of the House of Hador bear themselves otherwise, and Tuor among them. For they use courtesy, and they listen to good counsel, holding the Lords of the West in awe. But you, it seems, will take counsel with your own wisdom, or with your sword only; and you speak haughtily. And I say to you, Agarwaen Mormegil, that if you do so, other shall be your doom than one of the Houses of Hador and Bëor might look for.'

'Other it has ever been,' answered Túrin. 'And if, as it seems, I must bear the hate of Morgoth because of the valour of my father, shall I also endure the taunts and ill-boding of a runagate from war, though he claim the kinship of kings? Get you back to the safe shores of the Sea!'

Then Gelmir and Arminas departed, and went back to the South; but despite Túrin's taunts they would gladly have awaited battle beside their kin, and they went only because Círdan had bidden them under the command of Ulmo to bring back word to him of Nargothrond and of the speeding of their errand there. And Orodreth was much troubled by the words of the messengers; but all the more fell became the mood of Túrin, and he would by no means listen to their counsels, and least of all would he suffer the great bridge to be cast down. For so much at least of the words of Ulmo were read aright.

Soon after the departure of the messengers Handir Lord of Brethil was slain; for the Orcs invaded his land, seeking to secure the Crossings of Teiglin for their further advance. Handir gave them battle, but the Men of Brethil were worsted and driven back into their woods. The Orcs did not pursue them, for they had achieved their purpose for that time; and they continued to muster their strength in the Pass of Sirion.

In the autumn of the year, biding his hour, Morgoth loosed upon the people of Narog the great host that he had long prepared; and Glaurung the Father of Dragons passed over Anfauglith, and came thence into the north vales of Sirion and there did great evil. Under the shadows of Ered Wethrin, leading a great army of Orcs in his train, he defiled the Eithel Ivrin, and thence he passed into the realm of Nargothrond, burning the Talath Dirnen, the Guarded Plain, between Narog and Teiglin.

Then the warriors of Nargothrond went forth, and tall and terrible on that day looked Túrin, and the heart of the host was uplifted as he rode on the right hand of Orodreth. But greater far was the host of Morgoth than any scouts had told, and none but Túrin defended by his dwarf-mask could withstand the approach of Glaurung.

The Elves were driven back and defeated on the field of Tumhalad; and there all the pride and host of Nargothrond withered away. Orodreth the King was slain in the forefront of the battle, and Gwindor son of Guilin was wounded to the death. But Túrin came to his aid, and all fled before him; and he bore Gwindor out of the rout, and escaping to a wood there laid him on the grass.

Then Gwindor said to Túrin: 'Let bearing pay for bearing! But ill-fated was mine, and vain is yours; for my body is marred beyond healing, and I must leave Middle-earth. And though I love you, son of Húrin, yet I rue the day that I took you from the Orcs. But for your prowess and your pride, still I should have love and life, and Nargothrond should yet stand a while. Now if you love me, leave me! Haste you to Nargothrond, and save Finduilas. And this last I say to you: she alone stands between you and your doom. If you fail her, it shall not fail to find you. Farewell!'

Then Túrin sped back to Nargothrond, mustering such of the rout as he met with on the way; and the leaves fell from the trees in a great wind as they went, for the autumn was passing to a dire winter. But Glaurung and his host of Orcs were there before him, because of his rescue of Gwindor, and they came suddenly, ere those that were left on guard were aware of what had befallen on the field of Tumhalad. In that day the bridge that Túrin had caused to be built over Narog proved an evil; for it was great and mightily made and could not swiftly be destroyed, and thus the enemy came readily over the deep river, and Glaurung came in full fire against the Doors of Felagund, and overthrew them, and passed within.

And even as Túrin came up the ghastly sack of Nargothrond was well-nigh achieved. The Orcs had slain or driven off all that remained in arms, and they were even then ransacking the great halls and chambers, plundering and destroying; but those of the women and maidens that were not burned or slain they had herded on the terrace before the doors, as slaves to be taken to Angband. Upon this ruin and woe Túrin came, and none could withstand him; or would not, though he struck down all before him, and passed over the bridge, and hewed his way towards the captives.

And now he stood alone, for the few that had followed him had fled into hiding. But in that moment Glaurung the fell issued from the gaping Doors of Felagund, and lay behind, between Túrin and the bridge. Then suddenly he spoke by the evil spirit that was in him, saying: 'Hail, son of Húrin. Well met!'

Then Túrin sprang about, and strode against him, and fire was in his eyes, and the edges of Gurthang shone as with flame. But Glaurung withheld his blast, and opened wide his serpent-eyes and gazed upon Túrin. Without fear Túrin looked in those eyes as he raised up his sword; and straightway he fell under the dreadful spell of the dragon, and was as one turned to stone. Thus long they stood unmoving, silent before the great Doors of Felagund. Then

Glaurung spoke again, taunting Túrin. 'Evil have been all your ways, son of Húrin,' said he. 'Thankless fosterling, outlaw, slayer of your friend, thief of love, usurper of Nargothrond, captain foolhardy, and deserter of your kin. As thralls your mother and your sister live in Dor-lómin, in misery and want. You are arrayed as a prince, but they go in rags. For you they yearn, but you care not for that. Glad may your father be to learn that he has such a son: as learn he shall.' And Túrin being under the spell of Glaurung hearkened to his words, and he saw himself as in a mirror misshapen by malice, and he loathed what he saw.

And while he was yet held by the eyes of Glaurung in torment of mind, and could not stir, at a sign from the Dragon the Orcs drove away the herded captives, and they passed nigh to Túrin and went over the bridge. And among them was Finduilas, and she held out her arms to Túrin, and called him by name. But not until her cries and the wailing of the captives was lost upon the northward road did Glaurung release Túrin, and he might not stop his ears against that voice that haunted him after.

Then suddenly Glaurung withdrew his glance, and waited; and Túrin stirred slowly as one waking from a hideous dream. Then coming to himself with a loud cry he sprang upon the Dragon. But Glaurung laughed, saying: 'If you wish to be slain, I will slay you gladly. But small help will that be to Morwen and Niënor. No heed did you give to the cries of the Elf-woman. Will you deny also the bond of your blood?'

But Túrin drawing back his sword stabbed at his eyes; and Glaurung coiling back swiftly towered above him, and said: 'Nay! At least you are valiant. Beyond all whom I have met. And they lie who say that we of our part do not honour the valour of foes. See now! I offer you freedom. Go to your kin, if you can. Get you gone! And if Elf or Man be left to make tale of these days, then surely in scorn they will name you, if you spurn this gift.'

Then Túrin, being yet bemused by the eyes of the dragon, as if he were treating with a foe that could know pity, believed the words of Glaurung, and turning away he sped over the bridge. But as he went, Glaurung spoke behind him, saying in a fell voice: 'Haste you now, son of Húrin, to Dor-lómin! Or perhaps the Orcs shall come before you, once again. And if you tarry for Finduilas, then never shall you see Morwen or Niënor again; and they will curse you.'

But Túrin passed away on the northward road, and Glaurung laughed once more, for he had accomplished the errand of his Master. Then he turned to his own pleasure, and sent forth his blast, and burned all about him. But all the Orcs that were busy in the sack he routed forth, and drove them away, and denied them their plunder even to the last thing of worth. The bridge then he broke down and cast into the foam of Narog; and being thus secure he gathered all the hoard and riches of Felagund and heaped them, and lay upon them in the innermost hall, and rested a while.

And Túrin hastened along the ways to the North, through the lands now desolate between Narog and Teiglin, and the Fell Winter came down to meet him; for that year snow fell ere autumn was passed, and spring came late and cold. Ever it seemed to him as he went that he heard the cries of Finduilas, calling his name by wood and hill, and great was his anguish; but his heart being hot with the lies of Glaurung, and seeing ever in his mind the Orcs burning the house of Húrin or putting Morwen and Niënor to torment, he held on his way, turning never aside.

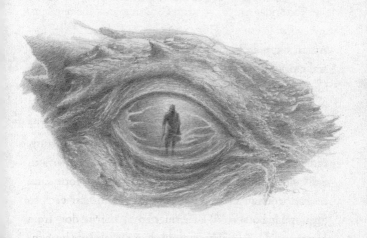

CHAPTER XII

THE RETURN OF TÚRIN TO DOR-LÓMIN

At last worn by haste and the long road (for forty leagues and more had he journeyed without rest) he came with the first ice of winter to the pools of Ivrin, where before he had been healed. But they were now only a frozen mire, and he could drink there no more.

Thence he came to the passes into Dor-lómin, and snow came bitterly from the North, and the ways were perilous and cold. Though three and twenty years were gone since he had trodden that path, it was graven in his heart, so great was the sorrow of each step at the parting from Morwen. Thus at last he came back to the land of his childhood. It was bleak and bare; and the people there were few and churlish, and they spoke the harsh tongue of the Easterlings, and the old tongue was become the language of serfs, or of foes. Therefore Túrin walked warily, hooded and silent, and he came at last to the house that he sought. It stood empty and dark, and no living thing dwelt near it; for Morwen was gone, and Brodda the Incomer (he that took by force Aerin, Húrin's kinswoman, to wife) had plundered her house, and taken all that was left to her of goods or of servants. Brodda's house stood nearest to the old house of Húrin, and thither Túrin came, spent with wandering and grief, begging for shelter; and it was granted to him, for some of the kindlier manners of old were still kept there by Aerin. He was given a seat by the fire by the servants, and a few vagabonds as grim and wayworn as he; and he asked news of the land.

At that the company fell silent, and some drew away, looking askance at the stranger. But one old vagabond man, with a crutch, said: 'If you must speak the old tongue, master, speak it softer, and ask for no tidings. Would you be beaten for a rogue, or hung for a spy? For both you may well be by the looks of you. Which is but to say,' he said, coming near and speaking low in Túrin's ear, 'one of the kindly folk of old that came with Hador in the days of gold, before heads wore wolf-hair. Some here are of like sort, though now made beggars and slaves, and but for the Lady Aerin would get neither this fire nor this broth. Whence are you, and what news would you have?'

'There was a lady called Morwen,' answered Túrin, 'and long ago I lived in her house. Thither after far wandering I came to seek welcome, but neither fire nor folk are there now.'

'Nor have been this long year and more,' answered the old man. 'But scant were both fire and folk in that house since the deadly war; for she was of the old people — as doubtless you know, the widow of our lord, Húrin Galdor's son. They dared not touch her, though, for they feared her; proud and fair as a queen, before sorrow marred her. Witchwife they called her, and shunned her. Witchwife: it is but "elf-friend" in the new language. Yet they robbed her. Often would she and her daughter have gone hungry, but for the Lady Aerin. She aided them in secret, it is said, and was often beaten for it by the churl Brodda, her husband by need.'

'And this long year and more?' said Túrin. 'Are they dead, or made thralls? Or have the Orcs assailed her?'

'It is not known for sure,' said the old man. 'But she is gone with her daughter; and this Brodda has plundered her and stripped what remained. Not a dog is left, and her few folk made his slaves; save some that have gone begging, as have I. I served her many a year, and the great master before, Sador Onefoot: a cursed axe in the woods long ago, or I would be lying in the Great Mound now. Well I remember the day when Húrin's boy was sent away, and how he wept; and she, when he was gone. To the Hidden Kingdom he went, it was said.'

With that the old man stayed his tongue, and eyed Túrin doubtfully. 'I am old and I babble, master,' he said. 'Mind me not! But though it be pleasant to speak the old tongue with one that speaks it fair as in time past, the days are ill, and one must be wary. Not all that speak the fair tongue are fair at heart.'

'Truly,' said Túrin. 'My heart is grim. But if you fear that I am a spy of the North or the East, then you have learned little more wisdom than you had long ago, Sador Labadal.'

The old man eyed him agape; then trembling he spoke. 'Come outside! It is colder, but safer. You speak too loud, and I too much, for an Easterling's hall.'

When they were come into the court he clutched at Túrin's cloak. 'Long ago you dwelt in that house, you say. Lord Túrin, why have you come back? My eyes are opened, and my ears at last: you have the voice of your father. But young Túrin alone ever gave me that name, Labadal. He meant no ill: we were merry friends in those days. What does he seek here now? Few are we left; and we are old and weaponless. Happier are those in the Great Mound.'

'I did not come with thought of battle,' said Túrin, 'though your words have waked the thought in me now, Labadal. But it must wait. I came seeking the Lady Morwen and Niënor. What can you tell me, and swiftly?'

'Little, lord,' said Sador. 'They went away secretly. It was whispered among us that they were summoned by the Lord Túrin; for we did not doubt that he had grown great in the years, a king or a lord in some south country. But it seems this is not so.'

'It is not,' answered Túrin. 'A lord I was in a south country, though now I am a vagabond. But I did not summon them.'

'Then I know not what to tell you,' said Sador. 'But the Lady Aerin will know, I doubt not. She knew all the counsel of your mother.'

'How can I come to her?'

'That I know not. It would cost her much pain were she caught whispering at a door with a wandering wretch of the downtrod people, even could any message call her forth. And such a beggarman as you are will not walk far up the hall towards the high board before the Easterlings seize him and beat him, or worse.'

Then in anger Túrin cried: 'May I not walk up Brodda's hall, and will they beat me? Come, and see!'

Thereupon he went into the hall, and cast back his hood, and thrusting aside all in his path he strode towards the board where sat the master of the house and his wife, and other Easterling lords. Then some rose to seize him, but he flung them to the ground, and cried: 'Does no one rule this house, or is it an Orc-hold rather? Where is the master?'

Then Brodda rose in wrath. 'I rule this house,' said he. But before he could say more, Túrin said: 'Then you have not yet learned the courtesy that was in this land before you. Is it now the manner of men to let lackeys mishandle the kinsmen of their wives? Such am I, and I have an errand to the Lady Aerin. Shall I come freely, or shall I come as I will?'

'Come,' said Brodda, scowling; but Aerin turned pale.

Then Túrin strode to the high board and stood before it, and bowed. 'Your pardon, Lady Aerin,' he said, 'that I break in upon you thus; but my errand is urgent and has brought me far. I seek Morwen, Lady of Dor-lómin, and Niënor her daughter. But her house is empty and plundered. What can you tell me?'

'Nothing,' said Aerin in great fear, for Brodda watched her narrowly.

'That I do not believe,' said Túrin.

Then Brodda sprang forth, and he was red with drunken rage. 'No more!' he cried. 'Shall my wife be gainsaid before me, by a beggar that speaks the serf-tongue? There is no Lady of Dor-lómin. But as for Morwen, she was of the thrall-folk, and has fled as thralls will. Do you likewise, and swiftly, or I will have you hung on a tree!'

Then Túrin leapt at him, and drew his black sword, and seized Brodda by the hair and laid back his head. 'Let no one stir,' said he, 'or this head will leave its shoulders! Lady Aerin, I would beg your pardon once more, if I thought that this churl had ever done you anything but wrong. But speak now, and do not deny me! Am I not Túrin, Lord of Dor-lómin? Shall I command you?'

'Command me,' she said.

'Who plundered the house of Morwen?'

'Brodda,' she answered.

'When did she flee, and whither?'

'A year and three months gone,' said Aerin. 'Master Brodda and others of the Incomers of the East hereabout oppressed her sorely. Long ago she was bidden to the

Hidden Kingdom; and she went forth at last. For the lands between were then free of evil for a while, because of the prowess of the Blacksword of the south country, it is said; but that is now ended. She looked to find her son there awaiting her. But if you are he, then I fear that all has gone awry.'

Then Túrin laughed bitterly. 'Awry, awry?' he cried. 'Yes, ever awry: as crooked as Morgoth!' And suddenly a black wrath shook him; for his eyes were opened, and the spell of Glaurung loosed its last threads, and he knew the lies with which he had been cheated. 'Have I been cozened, that I might come and die here dishonoured, who might at least have ended valiantly before the Doors of Nargothrond?' And out of the night about the hall it seemed to him that he heard the cries of Finduilas.

'Not first will I die here!' he cried. And he seized Brodda, and with the strength of his great anguish and wrath he lifted him on high and shook him, as if he were a dog. 'Morwen of the thrall-folk, did you say? You son of dastards, thief, slave of slaves!' Thereupon he flung Brodda head foremost across his own table, full in the face of an Easterling that rose to assail Túrin. In that fall Brodda's neck was broken; and Túrin leapt after his cast and slew three more that cowered there, for they were caught weaponless. There was tumult in the hall. The Easterlings that sat there would have come against Túrin, but many others were gathered there who were of the elder people of Dor-lómin: long had they been tame servants, but now they rose with shouts of rebellion. Soon there was great fighting in the hall, and though the thralls had but meat-knives and such things as they could snatch up against daggers and swords, many were quickly slain on either hand, before Túrin leapt down among them and slew the last of the Easterlings that remained in the hall.

Then he rested, leaning against a pillar, and the fire of his rage was as ashes. But old Sador crept up to him and clutched him about the knees, for he was wounded to the death. 'Thrice seven years and more, it was long to wait for this hour,' he said. 'But now go, go, lord! Go, and do not come back, unless with greater strength. They will raise the land against you. Many have run from the hall. Go, or you will end here. Farewell!' Then he slipped down and died.

'He speaks with the truth of death,' said Aerin. 'You have learned what you would. Now go swiftly! But go first to Morwen and comfort her, or I will hold all the wrack you have wrought here hard to forgive. For ill though my life was, you have brought death to me with your violence. The Incomers will avenge this night on all that were here. Rash are your deeds, son of Húrin, as if you were still but the child that I knew.'

'And faint heart is yours, Aerin Indor's daughter, as it was when I called you aunt, and a rough dog frightened you,' said Túrin. 'You were made for a kinder world. But come away! I will bring you to Morwen.'

'The snow lies on the land, but deeper upon my head,' she answered. 'I should die as soon in the wild with you, as with the brute Easterlings. You cannot mend what you have done. Go! To stay will make all the worse, and rob Morwen to no purpose. Go, I beg you!'

Then Túrin bowed low to her, and turned, and left the hall of Brodda; but all the rebels that had the strength followed him. They fled towards the mountains, for some among them knew well the ways of the wild, and they blessed the snow that fell behind them and covered their trail. Thus though soon the hunt was up, with many men and dogs and braying of horses, they escaped south into the hills. Then looking back they saw a red light far off in the land they had left.

'They have fired the hall,' said Túrin. 'To what purpose is that?'

'They? No, lord: she, I guess,' said one, Asgon by name. 'Many a man of arms misreads patience and quiet. She did much good among us at much cost. Her heart was not faint, and patience will break at the last.'

Now some of the hardiest that could endure the winter stayed with Túrin and led him by strange paths to a refuge in the mountains, a cave known to outlaws and runagates; and some store of food was hidden there. There they waited until the snow ceased, and they gave him food and took him to a pass little used that led south to Sirion's Vale, where the snow had not come. On the downward path they parted.

'Farewell now, Lord of Dor-lómin,' said Asgon. 'But do not forget us. We shall be hunted men now; and the Wolf-folk will be crueller because of your coming. Therefore go, and do not return, unless you come with strength to deliver us. Farewell!'

CHAPTER XIII

THE COMING OF TÚRIN INTO BRETHIL

Now Túrin went down towards Sirion, and he was torn in mind. For it seemed to him that whereas before he had two bitter choices, now there were three, and his oppressed people called him, upon whom he had brought only increase of woe. This comfort only he had: that beyond doubt Morwen and Niënor had come long since to Doriath, and only by the prowess of the Blacksword of Nargothrond had their road been made safe. And he said in his thought: 'Where else better might I have bestowed them, had I come indeed sooner? If the Girdle of Melian be broken, then all is ended. Nay, it is better as things be; for by my wrath and rash deeds I cast a shadow wherever I dwell. Let Melian keep them! And I will leave them in peace unshadowed for a while.'

But too late now Túrin sought for Finduilas, roaming the

woods under the eaves of Ered Wethrin, wild and wary as a beast; and he waylaid all the roads that went north to the Pass of Sirion. Too late. For all trails had been washed away by the rains and the snows. But thus it was that Túrin passing down Teiglin came upon some of the People of Haleth from the Forest of Brethil. They were dwindled now by war to a small people, and dwelt for the most part secretly within a stockade upon Amon Obel deep in the forest. Ephel Brandir that place was named; for Brandir son of Handir was now their lord, since his father was slain. And Brandir was no man of war, being lamed by a leg broken in a misadventure in childhood; and he was moreover gentle in mood, loving wood rather than metal, and the knowledge of things that grow in the earth rather than other lore.

But some of the woodmen still hunted the Orcs on their borders; and thus it was that as Túrin came thither he heard the sound of an affray. He hastened towards it, and coming warily through the trees he saw a small band of men surrounded by Orcs. They defended themselves desperately, with their backs to a knot of trees that grew apart in a glade; but the Orcs were in great number, and they had little hope of escape, unless help came. Therefore, out of sight in the underwood, Túrin made a great noise of stamping and crashing, and then he cried in a loud voice, as if leading many men: 'Ha! Here we find them! Follow me all! Out now, and slay!'

At that many of the Orcs looked back in dismay, and then out came Túrin leaping, waving as if to men behind, and the edges of Gurthang flickered like flame in his hand. Too well was that blade known to the Orcs, and even before he sprang among them many scattered and fled. Then the woodmen ran to join him, and together they hunted their foes into the river: few came across. At last they halted on the bank, and Dorlas, leader of the woodmen, said: 'You are swift in the hunt, lord; but your men are slow to follow.'

'Nay,' said Túrin, 'we all run together as one man, and will not be parted.'

Then the Men of Brethil laughed, and said: 'Well, one such is worth many. And we owe you great thanks. But who are you, and what do you here?'

'I do but follow my trade, which is Orc-slaying,' said Túrin. 'And I dwell where my trade is. I am Wildman of the Woods.'

'Then come and dwell with us,' said they. 'For we dwell in the woods, and we have need of such craftsmen. You would be welcome!'

Then Túrin looked at them strangely, and said: 'Are there then any left who will suffer me to darken their doors? But, friends, I have still a grievous errand: to find Finduilas, daughter of Orodreth of Nargothrond, or at least to learn news of her. Alas! Many weeks is it since she was taken from Nargothrond, but still I must go seeking.'

Then they looked on him with pity, and Dorlas said: 'Seek no more. For an Orc-host came up from Nargothrond towards the Crossings of Teiglin, and we had long warning of it: it marched very slow, because of the number of captives that were led. Then we thought to deal our small stroke in the war, and we ambushed the Orcs with all the bowmen we could muster, and hoped to save some of the prisoners. But alas! as soon as they were assailed the foul Orcs slew first the women among their captives; and the daughter of Orodreth they fastened to a tree with a spear.'

Túrin stood as one mortally stricken. 'How do you know this?' he said.

'Because she spoke to me, before she died,' said Dorlas. 'She looked upon us as though seeking one whom she had expected, and she said: "Mormegil. Tell the Mormegil that Finduilas is here." She said no more. But because of her latest words we laid her where she died. She lies in a mound beside Teiglin. Yes, it is a month now ago.'

'Bring me there,' said Túrin; and they led him to a hillock by the Crossings of Teiglin. There he laid himself down, and a darkness fell on him, so that they thought he was dead. But Dorlas looked down at him as he lay, and then he turned to his men and said: 'Too late! This is a piteous chance. But see: here lies the Mormegil himself, the great captain of Nargothrond. By his sword we should have known him, as did the Orcs.' For the fame of the Black Sword of the South had gone far and wide, even into the deeps of the wood.

Now therefore they lifted him with reverence and bore him to Ephel Brandir; and Brandir coming to meet them wondered at the bier that they bore. Then drawing back the coverlet he looked on the face of Túrin son of Húrin; and a dark shadow fell on his heart. 'O cruel Men of Haleth!' he cried. 'Why did you hold back death from this man? With great labour you have brought hither the last bane of our people.'

But the woodmen said: 'Nay, it is the Mormegil of Nargothrond, a mighty Orc-slayer, and he shall be a great help to us, if he lives. And were it not so, should we leave a man woe-stricken to lie as carrion by the way?'

'You should not indeed,' said Brandir. 'Doom willed it not so.' And he took Túrin into his house and tended him with care.

But when at last Túrin shook off the darkness, spring was returning; and he awoke and saw sun on the green buds. Then the courage of the House of Hador awoke in him also, and he arose and said in his heart: 'All my deeds and past days were dark and full of evil. But a new day is come. Here I will stay at peace, and renounce name and kin; and so I will put my shadow behind me, or at the least not lay it upon those that I love.'

Therefore he took a new name, calling himself Turambar, which in the High-elven speech signified Master of Doom; and he dwelt among the woodmen, and was loved by them, and he charged them to forget his name of old, and to count him as one born in Brethil. Yet with the change of a name he could not change wholly his temper, nor forget his old griefs against the servants of Morgoth;

and he would go hunting the Orcs with a few of the same mind, though this was displeasing to Brandir. For he hoped rather to preserve his people by silence and secrecy.

'The Mormegil is no more,' said he, 'yet have a care lest the valour of Turambar bring a like vengeance on Brethil!'

Therefore Turambar laid his black sword by, and took it no more to battle, and wielded rather the bow and the spear. But he would not suffer the Orcs to use the Crossings of Teiglin or draw near the mound where Finduilas was laid. Haudh-en-Elleth it was named, the Mound of the Elf-maid, and soon the Orcs learned to dread that place, and shunned it. And Dorlas said to Turambar: 'You have renounced the name, but the Blacksword you are still; and does not rumour say truly that he was the son of Húrin of Dor-lómin, lord of the House of Hador?'

And Turambar answered: 'So I have heard. But publish it not, I beg you, as you are my friend.'

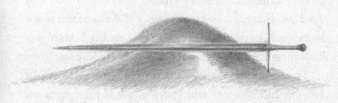

CHAPTER XIV

THE JOURNEY OF MORWEN AND NIËNOR TO NARGOTHROND

When the Fell Winter withdrew new tidings of Nargothrond came to Doriath. For some that escaped from the sack, and had survived the winter in the wild, came at last seeking refuge with Thingol, and the march-wards brought them to the King. And some said that all the enemy had withdrawn northwards, and others that Glaurung abode still in the halls of Felagund; and some said that the Mormegil was slain, and others that he was cast under a spell by the Dragon and dwelt there yet, as one changed to stone. But all declared that it was known in Nargothrond ere the end that the Blacksword was none other than Túrin son of Húrin of Dor-lómin.

Then great was the fear and sorrow of Morwen and of Niënor; and Morwen said: 'Such doubt is the very work of Morgoth! May we not learn the truth, and know surely the worst that we must endure?'

Now Thingol himself desired greatly to know more of the fate of Nargothrond, and had in mind already the sending out of some that might go warily thither, but he believed that Túrin was indeed slain or beyond rescue, and he was loath to see the hour when Morwen should know this clearly. Therefore he said to her: 'This is a perilous matter, Lady of Dor-lómin, and must be pondered. Such doubt may in truth be the work of Morgoth, to draw us on to some rashness.'

But Morwen being distraught cried: 'Rashness, lord! If my son lurks in the woods hungry, if he lingers in bonds, if his body lies unburied, then I would be rash. I would lose no hour to go to seek him.'

'Lady of Dor-lómin,' said Thingol, 'that surely the son of Húrin would not desire. Here would he think you better bestowed than in any other land that remains: in the keeping of Melian. For Húrin's sake and Túrin's I would not have you wander abroad in the black peril of these days.'

'You did not hold Túrin from peril, but me you will hold from him,' cried Morwen. 'In the keeping of Melian! Yes, a prisoner of the Girdle! Long did I hold back before I entered it, and now I rue it.'

'Nay, if you speak so, Lady of Dor-lómin,' said Thingol, 'know this: the Girdle is open. Free you came hither: free you shall stay – or go.'

Then Melian, who had remained silent, spoke: 'Go not hence, Morwen. A true word you said: this doubt is of Morgoth. If you go, you go at his will.'

'Fear of Morgoth will not withhold me from the call of my kin,' Morwen answered. 'But if you fear for me, lord, then lend me some of your people.'

'I command you not,' said Thingol. 'But my people are my own to command. I will send them at my own advice.'

Then Morwen said no more, but wept; and she left the presence of the King. Thingol was heavy-hearted, for it seemed to him that the mood of Morwen was fey; and he asked Melian whether she would not restrain her by her power. 'Against the coming in of evil I may do much,' she answered. 'But against the going out of those who will go, nothing. That is your part. If she is to be held here, you must hold her with strength. Yet maybe thus you will overthrow her mind.'

Now Morwen went to Niënor, and said: 'Farewell, daughter of Húrin. I go to seek my son, or true tidings of him, since none here will do aught, but tarry till too late. Await me here until haply I return.' Then Niënor in dread and distress would restrain her, but Morwen answered nothing, and went to her chamber; and when morning came she had taken horse and gone.

Now Thingol had commanded that none should stay her, or seem to waylay her. But as soon as she went forth, he gathered a company of the hardiest and most skilled of his march-wards, and he set Mablung in charge.

'Follow now speedily,' he said, 'yet let her not be aware of you. But when she is come into the wild, if danger threatens, then show yourselves; and if she will not return, then guard her as you may. But some of you I would have go forward as far as you can, and learn all that you may.'

Thus it was that Thingol sent out a larger company than he had at first intended, and there were ten riders among them with spare horses. They followed after Morwen; and she went south through Region, and so came to the shores of Sirion above the Twilit Meres; and there she halted, for Sirion was wide and swift, and she did not know the way. Therefore now the guards must needs reveal themselves; and Morwen said: 'Will Thingol stay me? Or late does he send me the help he denied?'

'Both,' answered Mablung. 'Will you not return?'

'No,' she said.

'Then I must help you,' said Mablung, 'though it is against my own will. Wide and deep here is Sirion, and perilous to swim for beast or man.'

'Then bring me over by whatever way the Elven-folk are used to cross,' said Morwen; 'or else I will try the swimming.'

Therefore Mablung led her to the Twilit Meres. There amid creeks and reeds ferries were kept hidden and guarded on the east shore; for by that way messengers would pass to and fro between Thingol and his kin in Nargothrond. Now they waited until the starlit night was late, and they passed over in the white mists before the dawn. And even as the sun rose red beyond the Blue Mountains, and a strong morning-wind blew and scattered the mists, the guards went up onto the west shore, and left the Girdle of Melian. Tall Elves of Doriath they were, grey-clad, and cloaked over their mail. Morwen from the ferry watched them as they passed silently, and then suddenly she gave a cry, and pointed to the last of the company that went by.

'Whence came he?' she said. 'Thrice ten you came to me. Thrice ten and one you go ashore!'

Then the others turned, and saw that the sun shone upon a head of gold: for it was Niënor, and her hood was blown back by the wind. Thus it was revealed that she had followed the company, and joined them in the dark before they crossed the river. They were dismayed, and none more than Morwen. 'Go back! Go back! I command you!' she cried.

'If the wife of Húrin can go forth against all counsel at the call of kindred,' said Niënor, 'then so also can Húrin's daughter. Mourning you named me, but I will not mourn alone, for father, brother, and mother. But of these you only have I known, and above all do I love. And nothing that you fear not do I fear.'

In truth little fear was seen in her face or her bearing. Tall and strong she seemed; for of great stature were those of Hador's house, and thus clad in Elvish raiment she matched well with the guards, being smaller only than the greatest among them.

'What would you do?' said Morwen.

'Go where you go,' said Niënor. 'This choice indeed I bring. To lead me back and bestow me safely in the keeping of Melian; for it is not wise to refuse her counsel.

Or to know that I shall go into peril, if you go.' For in truth Niënor had come most in hope that for fear and love of her her mother would turn back; and Morwen was indeed torn in mind.

'It is one thing to refuse counsel,' said she. 'It is another to refuse the command of your mother. Go now back!'

'No,' said Niënor. 'It is long since I was a child. I have a will and wisdom of my own, though until now it has not crossed yours. I go with you. Rather to Doriath, for reverence of those that rule it; but if not, then westward. Indeed, if either of us should go on, it is I rather, in the fullness of strength.'

Then Morwen saw in the grey eyes of Niënor the steadfastness of Húrin; and she wavered, but she could not overcome her pride, and would not (save the fair words) seem thus to be led back by her daughter, as one old and doting. 'I go on, as I have purposed,' she said. 'Come you also, but against my will.'

'Let it be so,' said Niënor.

Then Mablung said to his company: 'Truly, it is by lack of counsel not of courage that Húrin's kin bring woe to others! Even so with Túrin; yet not so with his fathers. But now they are all fey, and I like it not. More do I dread this errand of the King than the hunting of the Wolf. What is to be done?'

But Morwen, who had come ashore and now drew near, heard the last of his words. 'Do as you are bidden by the King,' said she. 'Seek for tidings of Nargothrond, and of Túrin. For this end are we all come together.'

'It is yet a long way and dangerous,' said Mablung. 'If you go further, you shall both be horsed and go among the riders, and stray no foot from them.'

Thus it was that with the full day they set forth, and passed slowly and warily out of the country of reeds and low willows, and came to the grey woods that covered much of the southern plain before Nargothrond. All day they went due west, and saw nothing but desolation, and heard nothing; for the lands were silent, and it seemed to Mablung that a present fear lay upon them. That same way had Beren trodden years before, and then the woods were filled with the hidden eyes of the hunters; but now all the people of Narog were gone, and the Orcs, it seemed, were not yet roaming so far southward. That night they encamped in the grey wood without fire or light.

The next two days they went on, and by evening of the third day from Sirion they were come across the plain and were drawing near to the east shores of Narog. Then so great an unease came upon Mablung that he begged Morwen to go no further. But she laughed, and said: 'You will be glad soon to be rid of us, as is likely enough. But you must endure us a little longer. We are come too near now to turn back in fear.'

Then Mablung cried: 'Fey are you both, and foolhardy. You help not but hinder any gathering of news. Now hear me! I was bidden not to stay you with strength; but I was bidden also to guard you, as I might. In this pass, one only can I do. And I will guard you. Tomorrow I will lead you to Amon Ethir, the Spyhill, which is near; and there you shall sit under guard, and go no further while I command here.' Now Amon Ethir was a mound as great as a hill that long ago Felagund had caused to be raised with great labour in the plain before his Doors, a league east of Narog. It was tree-grown, save on the summit, whence a wide view might be had all ways of the roads that led to the great bridge of Nargothrond and of the lands round about. To this hill they came late in the morning and climbed up from the east. Then looking out towards the High Faroth, brown and bare beyond the river, Mablung saw with elven-sight the terraces of Nargothrond on the steep west bank, and as a small black hole in the hill-wall the gaping Doors of Felagund. But he could hear no sound, and he could see no sign of any foe, nor any token of the Dragon, save the burning about the Doors that he had wrought in the day of the sack. All lay quiet under a pale sun.

Now therefore Mablung, as he had said, commanded his ten riders to keep Morwen and Niënor on the hill-top, and not to stir thence until he returned, unless some great peril arose: and if that befell, the riders should set Morwen and Niënor in their midst and flee as swiftly as they might, east-away towards Doriath, sending one ahead to bring news and seek aid.

Then Mablung took the other score of his company, and they crept down from the hill; and then passing into the fields westward, where trees were few, they scattered and made each his way, daring but stealthy, to the banks of Narog. Mablung himself took the middle way, going towards the bridge, and so came to its hither end and found it all broken down; and the deep-cloven river, running wild after rains far away northward, was foaming and roaring among the fallen stones.

But Glaurung lay there, just within the shadow of the great passage that led inward from the ruined Doors, and he had long been aware of the spies, though few other eyes in Middle-earth would have discerned them. But the glance of his fell eyes was keener than that of the eagles, and outreached the far sight of the Elves; and indeed he knew also that some remained behind and sat upon the bare top of Amon Ethir.

Thus, even as Mablung crept among the rocks, seeking whether he could ford the wild river upon the fallen stones of the bridge, suddenly Glaurung came forth with a great blast of fire, and crawled down into the stream. Then straightway there was a vast hissing and huge vapours arose, and Mablung and his followers that lurked near were engulfed in a blinding steam and foul stench; and the most fled as best they could guess towards the Spyhill. But as Glaurung was passing over Narog, Mablung drew aside and lay under a rock, and remained; for it seemed to him that he had an errand yet to do. He knew now indeed that Glaurung abode in Nargothrond, but he was bidden also to learn the truth concerning Húrin's son, if he might; and in the stoutness of his heart, therefore, he purposed to cross the river, as soon as Glaurung was gone, and search the halls of Felagund. For he thought that all had been done that could be for the keeping of Morwen and Niënor: the coming of Glaurung would be marked, and even now the riders should be speeding towards Doriath.

Glaurung therefore passed Mablung by, a vast shape in the mist; and he went swiftly, for he was a mighty Worm, and yet lithe. Then Mablung behind him forded Narog in great peril; but the watchers upon Amon Ethir beheld the issuing of the Dragon, and were dismayed. At once they bade Morwen and Niënor mount, without debate, and prepared to flee eastward as they were bidden. But even as they came down from the hill into the plain, an ill wind blew the great vapours upon them, bringing a stench that no horses would endure. Then, blinded by the fog and in mad terror of the dragon-reek, the horses soon became ungovernable, and went wildly this way and that; and the guards were dispersed, and were dashed against trees to great hurt, or sought vainly one for another. The neighing of the horses and the cries of the riders came to the ears of Glaurung; and he was well pleased.

One of the Elf-riders, striving with his horse in the fog, saw suddenly the Lady Morwen passing near, a grey wraith upon a mad steed, but she vanished in the mist, crying *Niënor*, and they saw her no more.

But when the blind terror came upon the riders, Niënor's horse, running wild, stumbled, and she was thrown. Falling softly into grass she was unhurt; but when she got to her feet she was alone: lost in the mist without horse or companion.

Her heart did not fail her, and she took thought; and it seemed to her vain to go towards this cry or that, for cries were all about her, but growing ever fainter. Better it seemed to her in such case to seek again for the hill: thither doubtless Mablung would come before he went away, if only to be sure that none of his company had remained there.

Therefore walking at guess she found the hill, which was indeed close at hand, by the rising of the ground before her feet; and slowly she climbed the path that led up from the east. And as she climbed so the fog grew thinner, until she came at last out into the sunlight on the bare summit. Then she stepped forward and looked westward. And there right before her was the great head of Glaurung, who had even then crept up from the other side; and before she was aware her eyes had looked in the fell spirit of his eyes, and they were terrible, being filled with the fell spirit of Morgoth, his master.

Strong was the will and heart of Niënor, and she strove against Glaurung; but he put forth his power against her. 'What seek you here?' he said.

And constrained to answer she said: 'I do but seek one Túrin that dwelt here a while. But he is dead, maybe.'

'I know not,' said Glaurung. 'He was left here to defend the women and weaklings; but when I came he deserted them and fled. A boaster but a craven, it seems. Why seek you such a one?'

'You lie,' said Niënor. 'The children of Húrin at least are not craven. We fear you not.'

Then Glaurung laughed, for so was Húrin's daughter revealed to his malice. 'Then you are fools, both you and your brother,' said he. 'And your boast shall be made vain. For I am Glaurung!'

Then he drew her eyes into his, and her will swooned. And it seemed to her that the sun sickened and all became dim about her; and slowly a great darkness drew down on her and in that darkness there was emptiness; she knew nothing, and heard nothing, and remembered nothing.

Long Mablung explored the halls of Nargothrond, as well he might for the darkness and the stench; but he found no living thing there: nothing stirred among the bones, and none answered his cries. At last, being oppressed by the horror of the place, and fearing the return of Glaurung, he came back to the Doors. The sun was sinking west, and the shadows of the Faroth behind lay dark on the terraces and the wild river below; but away beneath Amon Ethir he descried, as it seemed, the evil shape of the Dragon. Harder and more perilous was the return over Narog in such haste and fear; and scarcely had he reached the east shore and crept aside under the bank when Glaurung drew nigh. But he was slow now and stealthy; for all the fires in him were burned low: great power had gone out of him, and he would rest and sleep in the dark. Thus he writhed through the water and slunk up to the Doors like a huge snake, ashen-grey, sliming the ground with his belly.

But he turned before he went in and looked back eastward, and there came from him the laughter of Morgoth, dim but horrible, as an echo of malice out of the black depths far away. And this voice, cold and low, came after: 'There you lie like a vole under the bank, Mablung the mighty! Ill do you run the errands of Thingol. Haste you now to the hill and see what is become of your charge!'

Then Glaurung passed into his lair, and the sun went down and grey evening came chill over the land. But Mablung hastened back to Amon Ethir, and as he climbed to the top the stars came out in the east. Against them he saw there standing, dark and still, a figure as it were an image of stone. Thus Niënor stood, and heard nothing that he said, and made him no answer. But when at last he took her hand, she stirred, and suffered him to lead her away; and while he held her she followed, but if he loosed her, she stood still.

Then great was Mablung's grief and bewilderment; but no other choice had he but to lead Niënor so upon the long eastward way, without help or company. Thus they passed away, walking like dreamers, out into the night-shadowed plain. And when morning returned Niënor stumbled and fell, and lay still; and Mablung sat beside her in despair.

'Not for nothing did I dread this errand,' he said. 'For it will be my last, it seems. With this unlucky child of Men I shall perish in the wilderness, and my name shall be held in scorn in Doriath: if any tidings indeed are ever heard of our fate. All else doubtless are slain, and she alone spared, but not in mercy.'

Thus they were found by three of the company that had fled from Narog at the coming of Glaurung, and after much wandering, when the mist had passed, went back to the hill; and finding it empty they had begun to seek their way home. Hope then returned to Mablung; and they went on now together steering northward and eastward, for there was no road back into Doriath in the south, and since the fall of Nargothrond the ferry-wards were forbidden to set any across save those that came from within.

Slow was their journey, as for those that lead a weary child. But ever as they passed further from Nargothrond and drew nearer to Doriath, so little by little strength returned to Niënor, and she would walk hour by hour obediently, led by the hand. Yet her wide eyes saw nothing, and her ears heard no words, and her lips spoke no words.

And now at length after many days they came nigh to the west border of Doriath, somewhat south of the Teiglin; for they intended to pass the fences of the little land of Thingol beyond Sirion and so come to the guarded bridge near the inflowing of Esgalduin. There a while they halted; and they laid Niënor on a couch of grass, and she closed her eyes, as she had not yet done, and it seemed that she slept. Then the Elves rested also, and for very weariness were unheedful. Thus they were assailed at unawares by a band of orc-hunters, such as now roamed much in that region, as nigh to the fences of Doriath as they dared to go. In the midst of the affray suddenly Niënor leapt up from her couch, as one waking out of sleep to an alarm by night, and with a cry she sped away into the forest. Then the Orcs turned and gave chase, and the Elves after them. But a strange change had come upon Niënor and now she outran them all, flying like a deer among the trees with her hair streaming in the wind of her speed. The Orcs indeed Mablung and his companions swiftly overtook, and they slew them one and all, and hastened on. But by then Niënor had passed away like a wraith; and neither sight nor slot of her could they find, though they hunted far northward and searched for many days.

Then at last Mablung returned to Doriath bowed with grief and with shame. 'Choose you a new master of your hunters, lord,' he said to the King. 'For I am dishonoured.'

But Melian said: 'It is not so, Mablung. You did all that you could, and none other among the King's servants would have done so much. But by ill chance you were matched against a power too great for you, too great indeed for all that now dwell in Middle-earth.'

'I sent you to win tidings, and that you have done,' said Thingol. 'It is no fault of yours that those whom your tidings touch nearest are now beyond hearing. Grievous indeed is this end of all Húrin's kin, but it lies not at your door.'

For not only was Niënor now run witless into the wild, but Morwen also was lost. Neither then nor after did any certain news of her fate come to Doriath or to Dorlómin. Nonetheless Mablung would not rest, and with a small company he went into the wild and for three years wandered far, from Ered Wethrin even to the Mouths of Sirion, seeking for sign or tidings of the lost.

CHAPTER XV

NIËNOR IN BRETHIL

But as for Niënor, she ran on into the wood, hearing the shouts of pursuit come behind; and her clothing she tore off, casting away her garments one by one as she fled, until she went naked; and all that day still she ran, as a beast that is hunted to heart-bursting, and dare not stay or draw breath. But at evening suddenly her madness passed. She stood still a moment as in wonder, and then, in a swoon of utter weariness, she fell as one stricken down into a deep brake of fern. And there amid the old bracken and the swift fronds of spring she lay and slept, heedless of all.

In the morning she woke, and rejoiced in the light as one first called to life; and all things that she saw seemed to her new and strange, and she had no names for them. For behind her lay only an empty darkness, through which came no memory of anything she had ever known, nor any echo of any word. A shadow of fear only she remembered, and so she was wary, and sought ever for hidings: she would climb into trees or slip into thickets, swift as a squirrel or fox, if any sound or shadow frightened her; and thence she would peer long through the leaves with shy eyes, before she went on again.

Thus going forward in the way she first ran, she came to the river Teiglin, and stayed her thirst; but no food she found, nor knew how to seek it, and she was famished and cold. And since the trees across the water seemed closer and darker (as indeed they were, being the eaves of Brethil forest) she crossed over at last, and came to a green mound and there cast herself down: for she was spent, and it seemed to her that the darkness that lay behind her was overtaking her again, and the sun going dark.

But indeed it was a black storm that came up out of the South, laden with lightning and great rain; and she lay there cowering in terror of the thunder, and the dark rain smote her nakedness, and she watched without words as a wild thing that is trapped.

Now it chanced that some of the woodmen of Brethil came by in that hour from a foray against Orcs, hastening over the Crossings of Teiglin to a shelter that was near; and there came a great flash of lightning, so that the Haudh-en-Elleth was lit as with a white flame. Then Turambar who led the men started back and covered his eyes, and trembled; for it seemed that he saw the wraith of a slain maiden that lay on the grave of Finduilas.

But one of the men ran to the mound, and called to him: 'Hither, lord! Here is a young woman lying, and she lives!' and Turambar coming lifted her, and the water dripped from her drenched hair, but she closed her eyes and quivered and strove no more. Then marvelling that she lay thus naked Turambar cast his cloak about her and bore her away to the hunters' lodge in the woods. There they lit a fire and wrapped coverlets about her, and she opened her eyes and looked upon them; and when her glance fell on Turambar a light came in her face and she put out a hand towards him, for it seemed to her that she had found at last something that she had sought in the darkness, and she was comforted. But Turambar took her hand, and smiled, and said: 'Now, lady, will you not tell us your name and your kin, and what evil has befallen you?'

Then she shook her head, and said nothing, but began to weep; and they troubled her no more, until she had eaten hungrily of what food they could give her. And when she had eaten she sighed, and laid her hand again in Turambar's; and he said: 'With us you are safe. Here you may rest this night, and in the morning we will lead you to our homes up in the high forest. But we would know your name and your kin, so that we may find them, maybe, and bring them news of you. Will you not tell us?' But again she made no answer, and wept.

'Do not be troubled!' said Turambar. 'Maybe the tale is too sad yet to tell. But I will give you a name, and call you

Níniel, Maid of Tears.' And at that name she looked up, and she shook her head, but said: 'Níniel.' And that was the first word that she spoke after her darkness, and it was her name among the woodmen ever after.

In the morning they bore Níniel towards Ephel Brandir, and the road went steeply up until it came to a place where it must cross the tumbling stream of Celebros. There a bridge of wood had been built, and below it the stream went over a lip of worn stone, and fell down by many foaming steps into a rocky bowl far below; and all the air was filled with spray like rain. There was a wide green sward at the head of the falls, and birches grew about it, but over the bridge there was a wide view towards the ravines of Teiglin some two miles to the west. There the air was ever cool, and there wayfarers in summer would rest and drink of the cold water. Dimrost, the Rainy Stair, those falls were called, but after that day Nen Girith, the Shuddering Water; for Turambar and his men halted there, but as soon as Níniel came to that place she grew cold and shivered, and they could not warm her or comfort her. Therefore they hastened on their way; but before they came to Ephel Brandir Níniel was wandering in a fever.

Long she lay in her sickness, and Brandir used all his skill in her healing, and the wives of the woodmen watched over her by night and by day. But only when Turambar stayed near her would she lie at peace, or sleep without moaning; and this thing all marked that watched her:

throughout all her fever, though often she was much troubled, she murmured never a word in any tongue of Elves
or of Men. And when health slowly returned to her, and
she waked, and began to eat again, then as with a child the
women of Brethil must teach her to speak, word by word.
But in this learning she was quick and took great delight,
as one that finds again treasures, great and small, that were
mislaid; and when at length she had learned enough to
speak with her friends she would say: 'What is the name of
this thing? For in my darkness I lost it.' And when she was
able to go about again, she would seek the house of
Brandir; for she was most eager to learn the names of all
living things, and he knew much of such matters; and they
would walk together in the gardens and the glades.

Then Brandir grew to love her; and when she grew
strong she would lend him her arm for his lameness, and
she called him her brother. But to Turambar her heart was
given, and only at his coming would she smile, and only
when he spoke gaily would she laugh.

One evening of the golden autumn they sat together,
and the sun set the hillside and the houses of Ephel
Brandir aglow, and there was a deep quiet. Then Níniel
said to him: 'Of all things I have now asked the name, save
you. What are you called?'

'Turambar,' he answered.

Then she paused as if listening for some echo; but she
said: 'And what does that say, or is it just the name for you
alone?'

'It means,' said he, 'Master of the Dark Shadow. For I also, Níniel, had my darkness, in which dear things were lost; but now I have overcome it, I deem.'

'And did you also flee from it, running, until you came to these fair woods?' she said. 'And when did you escape, Turambar?'

'Yes,' he answered. 'I fled for many years. And I escaped when you did so. For it was dark when you came, Níniel, but ever since it has been light. And it seems to me that what I long sought in vain has come to me.' And as he went back to his house in the twilight, he said to himself: 'Haudh-en-Elleth! From the green mound she came. Is that a sign, and how shall I read it?'

Now that golden year waned and passed to a gentle winter, and there came another bright year. There was peace in Brethil, and the woodmen held themselves quiet and went not abroad, and they heard no tidings of the lands that lay about them. For the Orcs that at that time came southward to the dark reign of Glaurung, or were sent to spy on the borders of Doriath, shunned the Crossings of Teiglin, and passed westward far beyond the river.

And now Níniel was fully healed, and was grown fair and strong, and Turambar restrained himself no longer, but asked her in marriage. Then Níniel was glad; but when Brandir heard of it his heart was sick within him, and he said to her: 'Be not in haste! Think me not unkindly, if I counsel you to wait.'

'Nothing that you do is done unkindly,' she said. 'But why then do you give me such counsel, wise brother?'

'Wise brother?' he answered. 'Lame brother, rather, unloved and unlovely. And I scarce know why. Yet there lies a shadow on this man, and I am afraid.'

'There was a shadow,' said Níniel, 'for so he told me. But he has escaped from it, even as I. And is he not worthy of love? Though he now holds himself at peace, was he not once the greatest captain, from whom all our enemies would flee, if they saw him?'

'Who told you this?' said Brandir.

'It was Dorlas,' she said. 'Does he not speak truth?'

'Truth indeed,' said Brandir, but he was ill pleased, for Dorlas was chief of that party that wished for war on the Orcs. And yet he sought still for reasons to delay Níniel; and he said therefore: 'The truth, but not the whole truth; for he was the Captain of Nargothrond, and came before out of the North, and was (it is said) son of Húrin of Dor-lómin of the warlike House of Hador.' And Brandir, seeing the shadow that passed over her face at that name, misread her, and said more: 'Indeed, Níniel, well may you think that such a one is likely ere long to go back to war, far from this land, maybe. And if so, how long will you endure it? Have a care, for I forebode that if Turambar goes again to battle, then not he but the Shadow shall have the mastery.'

'Ill would I endure it,' she answered; 'but unwedded no better than wedded. And a wife, maybe, would better restrain him, and hold off the shadow.' Nonetheless she was troubled by the words of Brandir, and she bade Turambar wait yet a while. And he wondered and was downcast; but when he learned from Níniel that Brandir had counselled her to wait he was ill pleased.

But when the next spring came he said to Níniel: 'Time passes. We have waited, and now I will wait no longer. Do as your heart bids you, Níniel most dear, but see: this is the choice before me. I will go back now to war in the wild; or I will wed you, and go never to war again – save only to defend you, if some evil assails our home.'

Then she was glad indeed, and she plighted her troth, and at the mid-summer they were wedded; and the woodmen made a great feast, and they gave them a fair house which they had built for them upon Amon Obel. There they dwelt in happiness, but Brandir was troubled, and the shadow on his heart grew deeper.

CHAPTER XVI

THE COMING OF GLAURUNG

Now the power and malice of Glaurung grew apace, and he waxed fat, and he gathered Orcs to him, and ruled as a dragon-king, and all the realm of Nargothrond that had been was laid under him. And before this year ended, the third of Turambar's dwelling among the woodmen, he began to assail their land, which for a while had had peace; for indeed it was well known to Glaurung and to his Master that in Brethil there abode a remnant of free men, the last of the Three Houses to defy the power of the North. And this they would not brook; for it was the purpose of Morgoth to subdue all Beleriand and to search out its every corner, so that none in any hole or hiding might live that were not thrall to him. Thus, whether Glaurung guessed where Túrin was hidden, or whether (as some hold) he had indeed for that time escaped from the eye of Evil that pursued him, is of little matter. For in the end the counsels of Brandir must prove vain, and at the last two choices only could there be for Turambar: to sit deedless until he was found, driven forth like a rat; or to go forth soon to battle, and be revealed.

But when tidings of the coming of the Orcs were first brought to Ephel Brandir, he did not go forth and yielded to the prayers of Níniel. For she said: 'Our homes are not yet assailed, as your word was. It is said that the Orcs are not many. And Dorlas told me that before you came such affrays were not seldom, and the woodmen held them off.'

But the woodmen were worsted, for these Orcs were of a fell breed, fierce and cunning; and indeed they came with a purpose to invade the Forest of Brethil, not as before passing through its eaves on other errands, or hunting in small bands. Therefore Dorlas and his men were driven back with loss, and the Orcs came over Teiglin and roamed far into the woods. And Dorlas came to Turambar and showed his wounds, and he said: 'See, lord, now is the time of our need come upon us, after a false peace, even as I foreboded. Did you not ask to be counted one of our people, and no stranger? Is this peril not yours also? For our homes will not remain hidden, if the Orcs come further into our land.'

Therefore Turambar arose, and took up again his sword Gurthang, and he went to battle; and when the woodmen learned this they were greatly heartened, and they gathered to him, till he had a force of many hundreds. Then they hunted through the forest and slew all the Orcs that crept there, and hung them on the trees near the Crossings of Teiglin. And when a new host came against them, they trapped it, and being surprised both by the numbers of the woodmen and by the terror of the Black Sword that had returned, the Orcs were routed and slain in great number. Then the woodmen made great pyres and burned the bodies of the soldiers of Morgoth in heaps, and the smoke of their vengeance rose black into heaven, and the wind bore it away westward. But few living went back to Nargothrond with these tidings.

Then Glaurung was wrathful indeed; but for a while he lay still and pondered what he had heard. Thus the winter passed in peace, and men said: 'Great is the Black Sword of Brethil, for all our enemies are overcome.' And Níniel was comforted, and she rejoiced in the renown of Turambar; but he sat in thought, and he said in his heart: 'The die is cast. Now comes the test, in which my boast shall be made good, or fail utterly. I will flee no more. Turambar indeed I will be, and by my own will and prowess I will surmount my doom – or fall. But falling or riding, Glaurung at least I will slay.'

Nonetheless he was unquiet, and he sent out men of daring as scouts far afield. For indeed, though no word was said, he now ordered things as he would, as if he were lord of Brethil, and no man heeded Brandir.

Spring came hopefully, and men sang at their work. But in that spring Níniel conceived, and she became pale and wan, and all her happiness was dimmed. And soon after there came strange tidings, from the men that had gone abroad beyond Teiglin, that there was a great burning far out in the woods of the plain towards Nargothrond, and men wondered what it might be.

But before long there came more reports: that the fires drew ever northward, and that indeed Glaurung himself made them. For he had left Nargothrond, and was abroad again on some errand. Then the more foolish or more hopeful said: 'His army is destroyed, and now at last he sees wisdom, and is going back whence he came.' And others said: 'Let us hope that he will pass us by.' But Turambar had no such hope, and knew that Glaurung was coming to seek him. Therefore though he masked his mind because of Níniel, he pondered ever by day and by night what counsel he should take; and spring turned towards summer.

A day came when two men returned to Ephel Brandir in terror, for they had seen the Great Worm himself. 'In truth, lord,' they said, 'he draws now near to Teiglin, and turns not aside. He lay in the midst of a great burning, and the trees smoked about him. The stench of him is scarce to be endured. And all the long leagues back to Nargothrond his foul swath lies, we deem, in a line that swerves not, but points straight to us. What is to be done?'

'Little,' said Turambar, 'but to that little I have already given thought. The tidings you bring give me hope rather than dread; for if indeed he goes straight, as you say, and does not swerve, then I have some counsel for hardy hearts.'

The men wondered, for he said no more at that time; but they took heart from his steadfast bearing.

Now the river Teiglin ran in this manner. It flowed down from Ered Wethrin swift as Narog, but at first between low shores, until after the Crossings, gathering power from other streams, it clove a way through the feet of the highlands upon which stood the Forest of Brethil. Thereafter it ran in deep ravines, whose great sides were like walls of rock, but pent at the bottom the waters flowed with great force and noise. And right in the path of Glaurung there lay now one of these gorges, by no means the deepest, but the narrowest, just north of the inflow of Celebros. Therefore Turambar sent out three hardy men to keep watch from the brink on the movements of the Dragon; but he himself would ride to the high fall of Nen Girith, where news could find him swiftly, and whence he himself could look far across the lands.

But first he gathered the woodmen together in Ephel Brandir and spoke to them, saying: 'Men of Brethil, a deadly peril has come upon us, which only great hardihood shall turn aside. But in this matter numbers will avail little; we must use cunning, and hope for good fortune. If we went up against the Dragon with all our strength, as against an army of Orcs, we should but offer ourselves all to death, and so leave our wives and kin defenceless. Therefore I say that you should stay here, and prepare for

flight. For if Glaurung comes, then you must abandon this
place, and scatter far and wide; and so may some escape
and live. For certainly, if he can, he will destroy it, and all
that he espies; but afterwards he will not abide here. In
Nargothrond lies all his treasure, and there are the deep
halls in which he can lie safe, and grow.'

Then the men were dismayed, and were utterly downcast, for they trusted in Turambar, and had looked for more
hopeful words. But he said: 'Nay, that is the worst. And it
shall not come to pass, if my counsel and fortune are good.
For I do not believe that this Dragon is unconquerable,
though he grows greater in strength and malice with the
years. I know somewhat of him. His power is rather in the
evil spirit that dwells within him than in the might of his
body, great though that be. For hear now this tale that I was
told by some that fought in the year of the Nirnaeth, when
I and most that hear me were children. In that field the
Dwarves withstood him and Azaghâl of Belegost pricked
him so deep that he fled back to Angband. But here is a
thorn sharper and longer than the knife of Azaghâl.'

And Turambar swept Gurthang from its sheath and
stabbed with it up above his head, and it seemed to those
that looked on that a flame leapt from Turambar's hand
many feet into the air. Then they gave a great cry: 'The
Black Thorn of Brethil!'

'The Black Thorn of Brethil,' said Turambar: 'well may
he fear it. For know this: it is the doom of this Dragon
(and all his brood, it is said) that how great so ever be his

armour of horn, harder than iron, below he must go with the belly of a snake. Therefore, Men of Brethil, I go now to seek the belly of Glaurung, by what means I may. Who will come with me? I need but a few with strong arms and stronger hearts.'

Then Dorlas stood forth and said: 'I will go with you, lord: for I would ever go forward rather than wait for a foe.'

But no others were so swift to the call, for the dread of Glaurung lay on them, and the tale of the scouts that had seen him had gone about and grown in the telling. Then Dorlas cried out: 'Hearken, Men of Brethil, it is now well seen that for the evil of our times the counsels of Brandir were vain. There is no escape by hiding. Will none of you take the place of the son of Handir, that the house of Haleth be not put to shame?' Thus Brandir, who sat indeed in the high-seat of the lord of the assembly, but unheeded, was scorned, and he was bitter in his heart; for Turambar did not rebuke Dorlas. But one Hunthor, Brandir's kinsman, arose and said: 'You do evilly, Dorlas, to speak thus to the shame of your lord, whose limbs by ill hazard cannot do as his heart would. Beware lest the contrary be seen in you at some turn! And how can it be said that his counsels were vain, when they were never taken? You, his liege, have ever set them at naught. I say to you that Glaurung comes now to us, as to Nargothrond before, because our deeds have betrayed us, as he feared. But since this woe is now come, with your leave, son of Handir, I will go on behalf of Haleth's house.'

Then Turambar said: 'Three is enough! You twain will I take. But, lord, I do not scorn you. See! We must go in great haste, and our task will need strong limbs. I deem that your place is with your people. For you are wise, and are a healer; and it may be that there will be great need of wisdom and healing ere long.' But these words, though fair spoken, did but embitter Brandir the more, and he said to Hunthor: 'Go then, but not with my leave. For a shadow lies on this man, and it will lead you to evil.'

Now Turambar was in haste to go; but when he came to Níniel to bid her farewell, she clung to him, weeping grievously. 'Go not forth, Turambar, I beg!' she said. 'Challenge not the shadow that you have fled from! Nay, nay, flee still, and take me with you, far away!'

'Níniel most dear,' he answered, 'we cannot flee further, you and I. We are hemmed in this land. And even should I go, deserting the people that befriended us, I could but take you forth into the houseless wild, to your death and the death of our child. A hundred leagues lie between us and any land that is yet beyond the reach of the Shadow. But take heart, Níniel. For I say to you: neither you nor I shall be slain by this Dragon, nor by any foes of the North.' Then Níniel ceased to weep and fell silent, but her kiss was cold as they parted.

Then Turambar with Dorlas and Hunthor went away hotfoot to Nen Girith, and when they came there the sun was westering and shadows were long; and the last two of the scouts were there awaiting them.

'You come not too soon, lord,' said they. 'For the Dragon has come on, and already when we left he had reached the brink of the Teiglin, and glared across the water. He moves ever by night, and we may look then for some stroke before tomorrow's dawn.'

Turambar looked out over the falls of Celebros and saw the sun going down to its setting, and black spires of smoke rising by the borders of the river. 'There is no time to lose,' he said; 'yet these tidings are good. For my fear was that he would seek about; and if he passed northward and came to the Crossings and so to the old road in the lowland, then hope would be dead. But now some fury of pride and malice drives him headlong.' But even as he spoke, he wondered, and mused in his mind: 'Or can it be that one so evil and fell shuns the Crossings, even as the Orcs? Haudh-en-Elleth! Does Finduilas lie still between me and my doom?'

Then he turned to his companions and said: 'This task now lies before us. We must wait yet a little, for too soon in this case were as ill as too late. When dusk falls, we must creep down, with all stealth, to Teiglin. But beware! For the ears of Glaurung are as keen as his eyes, and they are deadly. If we reach the river unmarked, we must then climb down into the ravine, and cross the water, and so come in the path that he will take when he stirs.'

'But how can he come forward so?' said Dorlas. 'Lithe he may be, but he is a great Dragon, and how shall he climb down the one cliff and up the other, when part must again be climbing before the hinder part is yet descended? And if he can so, what will it avail us to be in the wild water below?'

'Maybe he can so,' answered Turambar, 'and indeed if he does, it will go ill with us. But it is my hope from what we learn of him, and from the place where he now lies, that his purpose is otherwise. He is come to the brink of Cabed-en-Aras, over which, as you tell, a deer once leaped from the huntsmen of Haleth. So great is he now that I think he will seek to cast himself across there. That is all our hope, and we may trust to it.'

Dorlas' heart sank at these words; for he knew better than any all the land of Brethil, and Cabed-en-Aras was a grim place indeed. On the east side was a sheer cliff of some forty feet, bare but tree-grown at the crown; on the other side was a bank somewhat less sheer and less high, shrouded with hanging trees and bushes, but between them the water ran fiercely between rocks, and though a man bold and sure-footed might ford it by day, it was perilous to dare it at night. But this was the counsel of Turambar, and it was useless to gainsay him.

They set out therefore at dusk, and they did not go straight towards the Dragon, but took first the path towards the Crossings; then, before they came so far, they turned southward by a narrow track and passed into the twilight of the woods above Teiglin. And as they drew near to Cabed-en-Aras, step by step, halting often to listen, the reek of burning came to them, and a stench that sickened them. But all was deadly still, and there was no stir of air. The first stars glimmered in the east before them, and faint spires of smoke rose straight and unwavering against the last light in the west.

Now when Turambar was gone Níniel stood silent as a stone; but Brandir came to her and said: 'Níniel, fear not the worst until you must. But did I not counsel you to wait?'

'You did so,' she answered. 'Yet how would that profit me now? For love may abide and suffer unwedded.'

'That I know,' said Brandir. 'Yet wedding is not for nothing.'

'No,' said Níniel. 'For now I am two months gone with his child. But it does not seem to me that my fear of loss is the more heavy to bear. I understand you not.'

'Nor I myself,' said he. 'And yet I am afraid.'

'What a comforter you are!' she cried. 'But Brandir, friend: wedded or unwedded, mother or maid, my dread is beyond enduring. The Master of Doom is gone to challenge his doom far hence, and how shall I stay here and wait for the slow coming of tidings, good or ill? This night, it may be, he will meet with the Dragon, and how shall I stand or sit, or pass the dreadful hours?'

'I know not,' said he, 'but somehow the hours must pass, for you and for the wives of those that went with him.'

'Let them do as their hearts bid!' she cried. 'But for me, I shall go. The miles shall not lie between me and my lord's peril. I will go to meet the tidings!'

Then Brandir's dread grew black at her words, and he cried: 'That you shall not do, if I may hinder it. For thus will you endanger all counsel. The miles that lie between may give time for escape, if ill befall.'

'If ill befall, I shall not wish to escape,' she said. 'And now your wisdom is vain, and you shall not hinder me.' And she stood forth before the people that were still gathered in the open place of the Ephel, and she cried: 'Men of Brethil! I will not wait here. If my lord fails, then all hope is false. Your land and woods shall be burned utterly, and all your houses laid in ashes, and none, none, shall escape. Therefore why tarry here? Now I go to meet the tidings and whatever doom may send. Let all those of like mind come with me!'

Then many were willing to go with her: the wives of Dorlas and Hunthor because those whom they loved were gone with Turambar; others for pity of Níniel and desire to befriend her; and many more that were lured by the very rumour of the Dragon, in their hardihood or their folly (knowing little of evil) thinking to see strange and glorious deeds. For indeed so great in their minds had the Black Sword become that few could believe that even Glaurung would conquer him. Therefore they set forth soon in haste, a great company, towards a peril that they did not understand; and going with little rest they came wearily at last, just at nightfall, to Nen Girith but a little while after Turambar had departed. But night is a cold counsellor, and many were now amazed at their own rashness; and when they heard from the scouts that remained there how near Glaurung was come, and the desperate purpose of Turambar, their hearts were chilled, and they dared go no further. Some looked out towards Cabed-en-Aras with anxious eyes, but nothing could they see, and nothing hear save the cold voice of the falls. And Níniel sat apart, and a great shuddering seized her.

When Níniel and her company had gone, Brandir said to those that remained: 'Behold how I am scorned, and all my counsel disdained! Choose you another to lead you: for here I renounce both lordship and people. Let Turambar be your lord in name, since already he has taken all my authority. Let none seek of me ever again either counsel or healing!' And he broke his staff. To himself he thought: 'Now nothing is left to me, save only my love of Níniel: therefore where she goes, in wisdom or folly, I must go. In this dark hour nothing can be foreseen; but it may well chance that even I could ward off some evil from her, if I were nigh.'

He girt himself therefore with a short sword, as seldom before, and took his crutch, and went with what speed he might out of the gate of the Ephel, limping after the others down the long path to the west march of Brethil.

CHAPTER XVII

THE DEATH OF GLAURUNG

At last, even as full night closed over the land, Turambar and his companions came to Cabed-en-Aras, and they were glad of the great noise of the water; for though it promised peril below, it covered all other sounds. Then Dorlas led them a little aside, southwards, and they climbed down by a cleft to the cliff-foot; but there his heart quailed, for many rocks and great stones lay in the river, and the water ran wild about them, grinding its teeth. 'This is a sure way to death,' said Dorlas.

'It is the only way, to death or to life,' said Turambar, 'and delay will not make it seem more hopeful. Therefore follow me!' And he went on before them, and by skill and hardihood, or by fate, he came across, and in the deep dark he turned to see who came after. A dark form stood beside him. 'Dorlas?' he said.

'No, it is I,' said Hunthor. 'Dorlas failed at the crossing, I think. For a man may love war, and yet dread many
things. He sits shivering on the shore, I guess; and may
shame take him for his words to my kinsman.'

Now Turambar and Hunthor rested a little, but soon
the night chilled them, for they were both drenched with
water, and they began to seek a way along the stream
northwards towards the lodgement of Glaurung. There
the chasm grew darker and narrower, and as they felt their
way forward they could see a flicker above them as of
smouldering fire, and they heard the snarling of the Great
Worm in his watchful sleep. Then they groped for a way
up, to come nigh under the brink; for in that lay all their
hope to come at their enemy beneath his guard. But so
foul now was the reek that their heads were dizzy, and
they slipped as they clambered, and clung to the tree-
stems, and retched, forgetting in their misery all fear save
the dread of falling into the teeth of Teiglin.

Then Turambar said to Hunthor: 'We spend our
waning strength to no avail. For till we be sure where the
Dragon will pass, it is vain to climb.'

'But when we know,' said Hunthor, 'then there will be
no time to seek a way up out of the chasm.'

'Truly,' said Turambar. 'But where all lies on chance, to
chance we must trust.' They halted therefore and waited,
and out of the dark ravine they watched a white star far
above creep across the faint strip of sky; and then slowly
Turambar sank into a dream, in which all his will was

given to clinging, though a black tide sucked and gnawed at his limbs.

Suddenly there was a great noise and the walls of the chasm quivered and echoed. Turambar roused himself, and said to Hunthor: 'He stirs. The hour is upon us. Strike deep, for two must strike now for three!'

And with that Glaurung began his assault upon Brethil; and all passed much as Turambar had hoped. For now the Dragon crawled with slow weight to the edge of the cliff, and he did not turn aside, but made ready to spring over the chasm with his great forelegs and then draw his bulk after. Terror came with him; for he did not begin his passage right above, but a little to the northward, and the watchers from beneath could see the huge shadow of his head against the stars; and his jaws gaped, and he had seven tongues of fire. Then he sent forth a blast, so that all the ravine was filled with a red light, and black shadows flying among the rocks; but the trees before him withered and went up in smoke, and stones crashed down into the river. And thereupon he hurled himself forward, and grappled the further cliff with his mighty claws, and began to heave himself across.

Now there was need to be bold and swift, for though Turambar and Hunthor had escaped the blast, since they were not right in Glaurung's path, they yet had to come at him, before he passed over, or all their hope failed. Heedless of peril therefore Turambar clambered along the cliff to come beneath him; but there so deadly was the heat and the stench that he tottered and would have fallen if Hunthor, following stoutly behind, had not seized his arm and steadied him.

'Great heart!' said Turambar. 'Happy was the choice that took you for a helper!' But even as he spoke, a great stone hurtled from above and smote Hunthor on the head, and he fell into the water, and so ended: not the least valiant of the House of Haleth. Then Turambar cried: 'Alas! It is ill to walk in my shadow! Why did I seek aid? For now you are alone, O Master of Doom, as you should have known it must be. Now conquer alone!'

Then he summoned to him all his will, and all his hatred of the Dragon and his Master, and it seemed to him that suddenly he found a strength of heart and of body that he had not known before; and he climbed the cliff, from stone to stone, and root to root, until he seized at last a slender tree that grew a little beneath the lip of the chasm, and though its top was blasted it still held fast by its roots. And even as he steadied himself in a fork of its boughs, the midmost parts of the Dragon came above him, and swayed down with their weight almost upon his head, ere Glaurung could heave them up. Pale and wrinkled was their underside, and all dank with a grey slime, to which clung all manner of dropping filth; and it stank of death. Then Turambar drew the Black Sword of Beleg and stabbed upwards with all the might of his arm, and of his hate, and the deadly blade, long and greedy, went into the belly even to its hilts.

Then Glaurung, feeling his death-pang, gave forth a scream, whereat all the woods were shaken, and the watchers at Nen Girith were aghast. Turambar reeled as from a blow, and slipped down, and his sword was torn from his grasp, and clave to the belly of the Dragon. For Glaurung in a great spasm bent up all his shuddering bulk and hurled it over the ravine, and there upon the further shore he writhed, screaming, lashing and coiling himself in his agony, until he had broken a great space all about him, and lay there at last in a smoke and a ruin, and was still.

Now Turambar clung to the roots of the tree, stunned and well-nigh overcome. But he strove against himself and drove himself on, and half sliding and half climbing he came down to the river, and dared again the perilous crossing, crawling now on hands and feet, clinging, blinded with spray, until he came over at last, and climbed wearily up the cleft by which they had descended. Thus he came at length to the place of the dying Dragon, and he looked on his stricken enemy without pity, and was glad.

There now Glaurung lay, with jaws agape; but all his fires were burned out, and his evil eyes were closed. He was stretched out in his length, and had rolled upon one side, and the hilts of Gurthang stood in his belly. Then the heart of Turambar rose high within him, and though the Dragon still breathed he would recover his sword, which if he prized it before was now worth to him all the treasure of Nargothrond. True proved the words spoken at its forging that nothing, great or small, should live that once it had bitten.

Therefore going up to his foe he set foot upon his belly, and seizing the hilts of Gurthang he put forth his strength to withdraw it. And he cried in mockery of Glaurung's words at Nargothrond: 'Hail, Worm of Morgoth! Well met again! Die now and the darkness have you! Thus is Túrin son of Húrin avenged.' Then he wrenched out the sword, and even as he did so a spout of black blood followed it, and fell upon his hand, and his flesh was burned by the venom, so that he cried aloud at the pain. Thereat Glaurung stirred and opened his baleful eyes and looked upon Turambar with such malice that it seemed to him that he was smitten by an arrow; and for that and for the anguish of his hand he fell in a swoon, and lay as one dead beside the Dragon, and his sword was beneath him.

Now the screams of Glaurung came to the people at Nen Girith, and they were filled with terror; and when the watchers beheld from afar the great breaking and burning that the Dragon made in his throes, they believed that he was trampling and destroying those that had assailed him. Then indeed they wished the miles longer that lay between them; but they dared not leave the high place where they were gathered, for they remembered the words of Turambar that, if Glaurung conquered, he would go first to Ephel Brandir. Therefore they watched in fear for any sign of his movement, but none were so hardy as to go down and seek for tidings in the place of the battle. And Níniel sat, and did not move, save that she shuddered and could not still her limbs; for when she heard the voice of Glaurung her heart died within her, and she felt her darkness creeping upon her again.

Thus Brandir found her. For he came at last to the bridge over Celebros, slow and weary; all the long way alone he had limped on his crutch, and it was five leagues at the least from his home. Fear for Níniel had driven him on, and now the tidings that he learned were no worse than he had dreaded. 'The Dragon has crossed the river,' men told him, 'and the Black Sword is surely dead, and those that went with him.' Then Brandir stood by Níniel, and guessed her misery, and he yearned to her; but he thought nonetheless: 'The Black Sword is dead, and Níniel lives.' And he shuddered, for suddenly it seemed cold by the waters of Nen Girith; and he cast his cloak about Níniel. But he found no words to say; and she did not speak.

Time passed, and still Brandir stood silent beside her, peering into the night and listening; but he could see nothing, and could hear no sound but the falling of the waters of Nen Girith, and he thought: 'Now surely Glaurung has gone and has passed into Brethil.' But he pitied his people no more, fools that had flouted his counsel, and had scorned him. 'Let the Dragon go to Amon Obel, and there will be time then to escape, and to lead Níniel away.' Whither, he scarce knew, for he had never journeyed beyond Brethil.

At last he bent down and touched Níniel on the arm, and said to her: 'Time passes, Níniel! Come! It is time to go. If you will let me, I will lead you.' Then silently she arose, and took his hand, and they passed over the bridge and went down the path to the Crossings of Teiglin. But those that saw them moving as shadows in the dark knew not who they were, and cared not. And when they had gone some little way through the silent trees, the moon rose beyond Amon Obel, and the glades of the forest were filled with a grey light. Then Níniel halted and said to Brandir: 'Is this the way?'

And he answered: 'What is the way? For all our hope in Brethil is ended. We have no way, save to escape the Dragon, and flee far from him while there is yet time.'

Níniel looked at him in wonder and said: 'Did you not offer to lead me to him? Or would you deceive me? The Black Sword was my beloved and my husband, and only to find him do I go. What else could you think? Now do as you will, but I must hasten.'

And even as Brandir stood a moment amazed, she sped from him; and he called after her, crying: 'Wait, Níniel! Go not alone! You know not what you will find. I will come with you!' But she paid no heed to him, and went now as though her blood burned her, which before had been cold; and though he followed as he could she passed soon out of his sight. Then he cursed his fate and his weakness; but he would not turn back.

Now the moon rose white in the sky, and was near the full, and as Níniel came down from the upland towards the land near the river, it seemed to her that she remembered it, and feared it. For she was come to the Crossings of Teiglin, and Haudh-en-Elleth stood there before her, pale in the moonlight, with a black shadow cast athwart it; and out of the mound came a great dread.

Then she turned with a cry and fled south along the river, and cast her cloak as she ran, as though casting off a darkness that clung to her; and beneath she was all clad in white, and she shone in the moon as she flitted among the trees. Thus Brandir above on the hill-side saw her, and turned to cross her course, if he could; and finding by fortune the narrow path that Turambar had used, for it left the more beaten road and went steeply down southward to the river, he came at last close behind her again. But though he called, she did not heed, or did not hear, and soon once more she passed on ahead; and so they drew near to the woods beside Cabed-en-Aras and the place of the agony of Glaurung.

The moon was then riding in the south unclouded, and the light was cold and clear. Coming to the edge of the ruin that Glaurung had wrought, Níniel saw his body lying there, and his belly grey in the moon-sheen; but beside him lay a man. Then forgetting her fear she ran on amid the smouldering wrack and so came to Turambar. He was fallen on his side, and his sword lay beneath him, but his face was wan as death in the white light. Then she threw herself down by him weeping, and kissed him; and it seemed to her that he breathed faintly, but she thought it but a trickery of false hope, for he was cold, and did not move, nor did he answer her. And as she caressed him she found that his hand was blackened as if it had been scorched, and she washed it with her tears, and tearing a strip from her raiment she bound it about. But still he did not move at her touch, and she kissed him again, and cried aloud: 'Turambar, Turambar, come back! Hear me! Awake! For it is Níniel. The Dragon is dead, dead, and I alone am here by you.' But he answered nothing. Her cry Brandir heard, for he had come to the edge of the ruin; but even as he stepped forward towards Níniel he was halted, and stood still. For at the cry of Níniel Glaurung stirred for the last time, and a quiver ran through all his body; and he opened his baleful eyes a slit, and the moon gleamed in them, as gasping he spoke:

'Hail, Niënor, daughter of Húrin. We meet again ere we end. I give you joy that you have found your brother at last. And now you shall know him: a stabber in the dark, treacherous to foes, faithless to friends, and a curse unto his kin, Túrin son of Húrin! But the worst of all his deeds you shall feel in yourself.'

Then Niënor sat as one stunned, but Glaurung died; and with his death the veil of his malice fell from her, and all her memory grew clearer before her, from day unto day, neither did she forget any of those things that had befallen her since she lay on Haudh-en-Elleth. And her whole body shook with horror and anguish. But Brandir, who had heard all, was stricken, and leaned against a tree.

Then suddenly Niënor started to her feet, and stood pale as a wraith in the moon, and looked down on Túrin, and cried: 'Farewell, O twice beloved! *A Túrin Turambar turún*' *ambartanen*: master of doom by doom mastered! O happy to be dead!' Then distraught with woe and the horror that had overtaken her she fled wildly from that place; and Brandir stumbled after her, crying: 'Wait! Wait, Níniel!'

One moment she paused, looking back with staring eyes. 'Wait?' she cried. 'Wait? That was ever your counsel. Would that I had heeded! But now it is too late. And now I will wait no more upon Middle-earth.' And she sped on before him.

Swiftly she came to the brink of Cabed-en-Aras, and there stood and looked on the loud water crying: 'Water, water! Take now Níniel Niënor daughter of Húrin; Mourning, Mourning daughter of Morwen! Take me and bear me down to the Sea!'

With that she cast herself over the brink: a flash of white swallowed in the dark chasm, a cry lost in the roaring of the river.

The waters of Teiglin flowed on, but Cabed-en-Aras was no more: Cabed Naeramarth, the Leap of Dreadful Doom, thereafter it was named by men; for no deer would ever leap there again, and all living things shunned it, and no man would walk upon its shore. Last of men to look down into its darkness was Brandir son of Handir; and he turned away in horror, for his heart quailed, and though he hated now his life, he could not there take the death that he desired. Then his thought turned to Túrin Turambar, and he cried: 'Do I hate you, or do I pity you? But you are dead. I owe you no thanks, taker of all that I had or would have. But my people owe you a debt. It is fitting that from me they should learn it.'

And so he began to limp back to Nen Girith, avoiding the place of the Dragon with a shudder; and as he climbed the steep path again he came on a man that peered through the trees, and seeing him drew back. But he had marked his face in a gleam of the sinking moon.

'Ha, Dorlas!' he cried. 'What news can you tell? How came you off alive? And what of my kinsman?'

'I know not,' answered Dorlas sullenly.

'Then that is strange,' said Brandir.

'If you will know,' said Dorlas, 'the Black Sword would have us ford the races of Teiglin in the dark. Is it strange that I could not? I am a better man with an axe than some, but I am not goat-footed.'

'So they went on without you to come at the Dragon?' said Brandir. 'But how when he passed over? At the least you would stay near, and would see what befell.'

But Dorlas made no answer, and stared only at Brandir with hatred in his eyes. Then Brandir understood, perceiving suddenly that this man had deserted his companions, and unmanned by shame had then hidden in the woods. 'Shame on you, Dorlas!' he said. 'You are the begetter of our woes: egging on the Black Sword, bringing the Dragon upon us, putting me to scorn, drawing Hunthor to his death, and then you flee to skulk in the woods!' And as he spoke another thought entered his mind, and he said in great anger: 'Why did you not bring tidings? It was the least penance that you could do. Had you done so, the Lady Níniel would have had no need to seek them herself. She need never have seen the Dragon. She might have lived. Dorlas, I hate you!'

'Keep your hate!' said Dorlas. 'It is as feeble as all your counsels. But for me the Orcs would have come and hung you as a scarecrow in your garden. Take the name skulker to yourself!' And with that, being for his shame the readier to wrath, he aimed a blow at Brandir with his great fist, and so ended his life, before the look of amazement left his eyes: for Brandir drew his sword and hewed him his death-blow. Then for a moment he stood trembling, sickened by the blood; and casting down his sword he turned, and went on his way, bowed upon his crutch.

As Brandir came to Nen Girith the pallid moon was gone down, and the night was fading; morning was opening in the east. The people that cowered there still by the bridge saw him come like a grey shadow in the dawn, and some called to him in wonder: 'Where have you been? Have you seen her? For the Lady Níniel is gone.'

'Yes,' said Brandir, 'she is gone. Gone, gone, never to return! But I am come to bring you tidings. Hear now, people of Brethil, and say if there was ever such a tale as the tale that I bear! The Dragon is dead, but dead also is Turambar at his side. And those are good tidings: yes, both are good indeed.'

Then the people murmured, wondering at his speech, and some said that he was mad; but Brandir cried: 'Hear me to the end! Níniel too is dead, Níniel the fair whom you loved, whom I loved dearest of all. She leaped from the brink of the Deer's Leap, and the teeth of Teiglin have taken her. She is gone, hating the light of day. For this she learned before she fled: Húrin's children were they both, sister and brother. The Mormegil he was called, Turambar he named himself, hiding his past: Túrin son of Húrin. Níniel we named her, not knowing her past: Niënor she was, daughter of Húrin. To Brethil they brought their dark doom's shadow. Here their doom has fallen, and of grief this land shall never again be free. Call it not Brethil, not the land of the Halethrim, but *Sarch nia Chîn Húrin*, Grave of the Children of Húrin!'

Then though they did not understand yet how this evil had come to pass, the people wept as they stood, and some said: 'A grave there is in Teiglin for Níniel the beloved, a grave shall there be for Turambar, most valiant of men. Our deliverer shall not be left to lie under the sky. Let us go to him.'

CHAPTER XVIII

THE DEATH OF TÚRIN

Now even as Níniel fled away, Túrin stirred, and it seemed to him that out of his deep darkness he heard her call to him far away; but as Glaurung died, the black swoon left him, and he breathed deep again, and sighed, and passed into a slumber of great weariness. But before dawn it grew bitter cold, and he turned in his sleep, and the hilts of Gurthang drove into his side, and suddenly he awoke. Night was going, and there was a breath of morning in the air; and he sprang to his feet, remembering his victory, and the burning venom on his hand. He raised it up, and looked at it, and marvelled. For it was bound about with a strip of white cloth, yet moist, and it was at ease; and he said to himself: 'Why should one tend me so, and yet leave me here to lie cold amid the wrack and the dragon-stench? What strange things have chanced?'

Then he called aloud, but there was no answer. All was black and drear about him, and there was a reek of death. He stooped and lifted his sword, and it was whole, and the light of its edges was undimmed. 'Foul was the venom of Glaurung,' he said, 'but you are stronger than I, Gurthang. All blood will you drink. Yours is the victory. But come! I must go seek for aid. My body is weary, and there is a chill in my bones.'

Then he turned his back upon Glaurung and left him to rot; but as he passed from that place each step seemed more heavy, and he thought: 'At Nen Girith, maybe, I will find one of the scouts awaiting me. But would I were soon in my own house, and might feel the gentle hands of Níniel, and the good skill of Brandir!' And so at last, walking wearily, leaning on Gurthang, through the grey light of early day he came to Nen Girith, and even as men were setting forth to seek his dead body, he stood before the people.

Then they gave back in terror, believing that it was his unquiet spirit, and the women wailed and covered their eyes. But he said: 'Nay, do not weep, but be glad! See! Do I not live? And have I not slain the Dragon that you feared?'

Then they turned upon Brandir, and cried: 'Fool, with your false tales, saying that he lay dead. Did we not say that you were mad?' Then Brandir was aghast, and stared at Túrin with fear in his eyes, and he could say nothing.

But Túrin said to him: 'It was you then that were there, and tended my hand? I thank you. But your skill is failing, if you cannot tell swoon from death.' Then he turned to the people: 'Speak not so to him, fools all of you. Which of you would have done better? At least he had the heart to come down to the place of battle, while you sit wailing!

'But now, son of Handir, come! There is more that I would learn. Why are you here, and all this people, whom I left at the Ephel? If I may go into the peril of death for your sakes, may I not be obeyed when I am gone? And where is Níniel? At the least I may hope that you did not bring her hither, but left her where I bestowed her, in my house, with true men to guard it?'

And when no one answered him, 'Come, say where is Níniel?' he cried. 'For her first I would see; and to her first will I tell the tale of the deeds in the night.'

But they turned their faces from him, and Brandir said at last: 'Níniel is not here.'

'That is well then,' said Túrin. 'Then I will go to my home. Is there a horse to bear me? Or a bier would be better. I faint with my labours.'

'Nay, nay!' said Brandir in anguish of heart. 'Your house is empty. Níniel is not there. She is dead.'

But one of the women – the wife of Dorlas, who loved Brandir little – cried shrilly: 'Pay no heed to him, lord! For he is crazed. He came crying that you were dead, and called it good tidings. But you live. Why then should his tale of Níniel be true: that she is dead, and yet worse?'

Then Túrin strode towards Brandir: 'So my death was good tidings?' he cried. 'Yes, ever you did begrudge her to me, that I knew. Now she is dead, you say. And yet worse? What lie have you begotten in your malice, Club-foot? Would you slay us then with foul words, since you can wield no other weapon?'

Then anger drove pity from Brandir's heart, and he cried: 'Crazed? Nay, crazed are you, Black Sword of black doom! And all this dotard people. I do not lie! Níniel is dead, dead, dead! Seek her in Teiglin!'

Then Túrin stood still and cold. 'How do you know?' he said softly. 'How did you contrive it?'

'I know because I saw her leap,' answered Brandir. 'But the contriving was yours. She fled from you, Túrin son of Húrin, and in Cabed-en-Aras she cast herself, that she might never see you again. Níniel! Níniel? Nay, Niënor daughter of Húrin.'

Then Túrin seized him and shook him; for in those words he heard the feet of his doom overtaking him, but in horror and fury his heart would not receive them, as a beast hurt to death that will wound ere it dies all that are near it.

'Yes, I am Túrin son of Húrin,' he cried. 'So long ago you guessed. But nothing do you know of Niënor my sister. Nothing! She dwells in the Hidden Kingdom, and is safe. It is a lie of your own vile mind, to drive my wife witless, and now me. You limping evil – would you dog us both to death?'

But Brandir shook him off. 'Touch me not!' he said. 'Stay your raving. She that you name wife came to you and tended you, and you did not answer her call. But one answered for you. Glaurung the Dragon, who I deem bewitched you both to your doom. So he spoke, before he ended: "Niënor daughter of Húrin, here is your brother: treacherous to foes, faithless to friends, a curse unto his kin, Túrin son of Húrin."' Then suddenly a fey laughter seized on Brandir. 'On their deathbed men will speak true, they say,' he cackled. 'And even a Dragon too, it seems. Túrin son of Húrin, a curse unto your kin and unto all that harbour you!'

Then Túrin grasped Gurthang and a fell light was in his eyes. 'And what shall be said of you, Club-foot?' he said slowly. 'Who told her secretly behind my back my right name? Who brought her to the malice of the Dragon? Who stood by and let her die? Who came hither to publish this horror at the swiftest? Who would now gloat upon me? Do men speak true before death? Then speak it now quickly.'

Then Brandir, seeing his death in Túrin's face, stood still and did not quail, though he had no weapon but his crutch; and he said: 'All that has chanced is a long tale to tell, and I am weary of you. But you slander me, son of Húrin. Did Glaurung slander you? If you slay me, then all shall see that he did not. Yet I do not fear to die, for then I will go to seek Níniel whom I loved, and perhaps I may find her again beyond the Sea.'

'Seek Níniel!' cried Túrin. 'Nay, Glaurung you shall find, and breed lies together. You shall sleep with the

Worm, your soul's mate, and rot in one darkness!' Then he lifted up Gurthang and hewed Brandir, and smote him to death. But the people hid their eyes from that deed, and as he turned and went from Nen Girith they fled from him in terror.

Then Túrin went as one witless through the wild woods, now cursing Middle-earth and all the life of Men, now calling upon Níniel. But when at last the madness of his grief left him he sat awhile and pondered all his deeds, and he heard himself crying: 'She dwells in the Hidden Kingdom, and is safe!' And he thought that now, though all his life was in ruin, he must go thither; for all the lies of Glaurung had ever led him astray. Therefore he arose and went to the Crossings of Teiglin, and as he passed by Haudh-en-Elleth he cried: 'Bitterly have I paid, O Finduilas! that ever I gave heed to the Dragon. Send me now counsel!'

But even as he cried out he saw twelve huntsmen well-armed that came over the Crossings, and they were Elves; and as they drew near he knew one, for it was Mablung, chief huntsman of Thingol. And Mablung hailed him, crying: 'Túrin! Well met at last. I seek you, and glad I am to see you living, though the years have been heavy on you.'

'Heavy!' said Túrin. 'Yes, as the feet of Morgoth. But if you are glad to see me living, you are the last in Middle-earth. Why so?'

'Because you were held in honour among us,' answered Mablung; 'and though you have escaped many perils, I feared for you at the last. I watched the coming forth of Glaurung, and I thought that he had fulfilled his wicked purpose and was returning to his Master. But he turned towards Brethil, and at the same time I learned from wanderers in the land that the Black Sword of Nargothrond had appeared there again, and the Orcs shunned its borders as death. Then I was filled with dread, and I said: "Alas! Glaurung goes where his Orcs dare not, to seek out Túrin." Therefore I came hither as swift as might be, to warn you and aid you.'

'Swift, but not swift enough,' said Túrin. 'Glaurung is dead.'

Then the Elves looked at him in wonder, and said: 'You have slain the Great Worm! Praised for ever shall your name be among Elves and Men!'

'I care not,' said Túrin. 'For my heart also is slain. But since you come from Doriath, give me news of my kin. For I was told in Dor-lómin that they had fled to the Hidden Kingdom.'

The Elves made no answer, but at length Mablung spoke: 'They did so indeed, in the year before the coming of the Dragon. But they are not there now, alas!' Then Túrin's heart stood still, hearing the feet of doom that would pursue him to the end. 'Say on!' he cried. 'And be swift!'

'They went out into the wild seeking you,' said Mablung. 'It was against all counsel; but they would go to Nargothrond, when it was known that you were the Black Sword; and Glaurung came forth, and all their guard were scattered. Morwen none have seen since that day; but Niënor had a spell of dumbness upon her, and fled north into the woods like a wild deer, and was lost.' Then to the wonder of the Elves Túrin laughed loud and shrill. 'Is not that a jest?' he cried. 'O the fair Niënor! So she ran from Doriath to the Dragon, and from the Dragon to me. What a sweet grace of fortune! Brown as a berry she was, dark was her hair; small and slim as an Elf-child, none could mistake her!'

Then Mablung was amazed, and he said: 'But some mistake is here. Not such was your sister. She was tall, and her eyes were blue, her hair fine gold, the very likeness in woman's form of Húrin her father. You cannot have seen her!'

'Can I not, can I not, Mablung?' cried Túrin. 'But why no! For see, I am blind! Did you not know? Blind, blind, groping since childhood in a dark mist of Morgoth! Therefore leave me! Go, go! Go back to Doriath, and may winter shrivel it! A curse upon Menegroth! And a curse on your errand! This only was wanting. Now comes the night!'

Then he fled from them, like the wind, and they were filled with wonder and fear. But Mablung said: 'Some strange and dreadful thing has chanced that we know not. Let us follow him and aid him if we may: for now he is fey and witless.'

But Túrin sped far before them, and came to Cabed-en-Aras, and stood still; and he heard the roaring of the

water, and saw that all the trees near and far were withered, and their sere leaves fell mournfully, as though
winter had come in the first days of summer.

'Cabed-en-Aras, Cabed Naeramarth!' he cried. 'I will
not defile your waters where Níniel was washed. For all
my deeds have been ill, and the latest the worst.'

Then he drew forth his sword, and said: 'Hail
Gurthang, iron of death, you alone now remain! But what
lord or loyalty do you know, save the hand that wields
you? From no blood will you shrink. Will you take Túrin
Turambar? Will you slay me swiftly?'

And from the blade rang a cold voice in answer: 'Yes, I
will drink your blood, that I may forget the blood of
Beleg my master, and the blood of Brandir slain unjustly.
I will slay you swiftly.'

Then Túrin set the hilts upon the ground, and cast
himself upon the point of Gurthang, and the black blade
took his life.

But Mablung came and looked on the hideous shape of
Glaurung lying dead, and he looked upon Túrin and was
grieved, thinking of Húrin as he had seen him in the Nirnaeth Arnoediad, and the dreadful doom of his kin. As the
Elves stood there, men came down from Nen Girith to
look upon the Dragon, and when they saw to what end
the life of Túrin Turambar had come they wept; and the
Elves learning at last the reason of Túrin's words to them
were aghast. Then Mablung said bitterly: 'I also have been

meshed in the doom of the Children of Húrin, and thus with words have slain one that I loved.'

Then they lifted up Túrin, and saw that his sword was broken asunder. So passed all that he possessed.

With toil of many hands they gathered wood and piled it high and made a great burning and destroyed the body of the Dragon, until he was but black ash and his bones beaten to dust, and the place of that burning was ever bare and barren thereafter. But Túrin they laid in a high mound where he had fallen, and the shards of Gurthang were set beside him. And when all was done, and the minstrels of Elves and Men had made lament, telling of the valour of Turambar and the beauty of Níniel, a great grey stone was brought and set upon the mound; and thereon the Elves carved in the Runes of Doriath:

TÚRIN TURAMBAR DAGNIR GLAURUNGA

and beneath they wrote also:

NIËNOR NÍNIEL

But she was not there, nor was it ever known whither the cold waters of Teiglin had taken her.

Here ends the Tale of the Children of Húrin, longest of all the lays of Beleriand.

After the deaths of Túrin and Niënor Morgoth released
Húrin from bondage in furtherance of his evil purpose.
In the course of his wanderings he reached the Forest of
Brethil, and came up in the evening from the Crossings of
Teiglin to the place of the burning of Glaurung and the
great stone standing on the brink of Cabed Naeramarth.
Of what befell there this is told.

But Húrin did not look at the stone, for he knew what
was written there; and his eyes had seen that he was not
alone. Sitting in the shadow of the stone there was a figure
bent over its knees. Some homeless wanderer broken with
age it seemed, too wayworn to heed his coming; but its rags
were the remnants of a woman's garb. At length as Húrin
stood there silent she cast back her tattered hood and lifted
up her face slowly, haggard and hungry as a long-hunted
wolf. Grey she was, sharp-nosed with broken teeth, and
with a lean hand she clawed at the cloak upon her breast.
But suddenly her eyes looked into his, and then Húrin
knew her; for though they were wild now and full of fear, a
light still gleamed in them hard to endure: the elven-light
that long ago had earned her her name, Eledhwen, proudest of mortal women in the days of old.

'Eledhwen! Eledhwen!' Húrin cried; and she rose and
stumbled forward, and he caught her in his arms.

'You come at last,' she said. 'I have waited too long.'

'It was a dark road. I have come as I could,' he answered.

'But you are late,' she said, 'too late. They are lost.'

'I know,' he said. 'But you are not.'

'Almost,' she said. 'I am spent utterly. I shall go with the sun. They are lost.' She clutched at his cloak. 'Little time is left,' she said. 'If you know, tell me! How did she find him?'

But Húrin did not answer, and he sat beside the stone with Morwen in his arms; and they did not speak again. The sun went down, and Morwen sighed and clasped his hand and was still; and Húrin knew that she had died.

GENEALOGIES

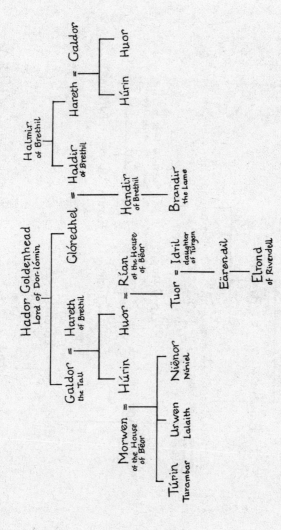

The House of Hador & the People of Haleth

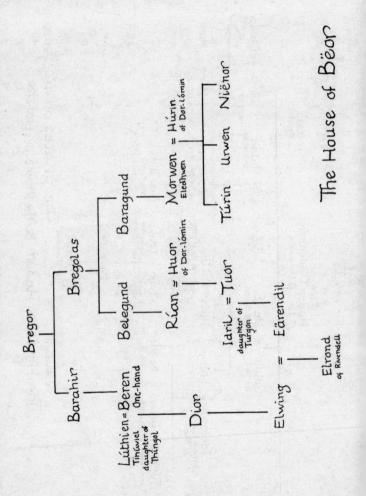

The House of Bëor

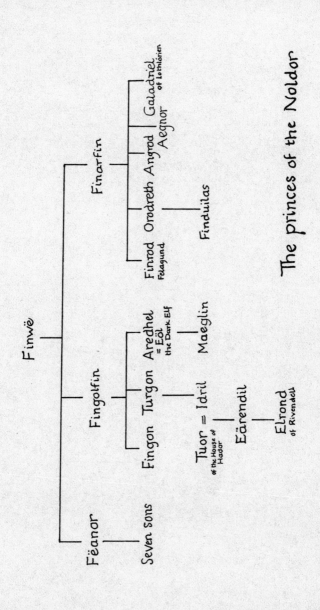

The princes of the Noldor

APPENDIX

(1)

THE EVOLUTION OF
THE GREAT TALES

These interrelated but independent stories had from far back stood out from the long and complex history of Valar, Elves and Men in Valinor and the Great Lands; and in the years that followed his abandonment of the *Lost Tales* before they were completed my father turned away from prose composition and began work on a long poem with the title *Túrin son of Húrin and Glórund the Dragon*, later changed in a revised version to *The Children of Húrin*. This was in the earlier 1920s, when he held appointments at the University of Leeds. For this poem he employed the ancient English alliterative metre (the verse form of *Beowulf* and other Anglo-Saxon poetry), imposing on modern English the demanding patterns of stress and 'initial rhyme' observed by the old poets: a skill in which he achieved great mastery, in very different modes, from the dramatic dialogue of *The Homecoming of Beorhtnoth* to the elegy for the men who died in the battle of the Pelennor Fields. The alliterative *Children of Húrin* was by far the longest of his poems in this metre, running to well over two thousand lines; yet he conceived it on so lavish a scale that even so he had reached no further in the narrative than the assault of the Dragon on Nargothrond when he abandoned it. With so much more of the *Lost Tale* still to come it would have needed on this scale many more thousands of lines; while a second version, abandoned at an earlier point in the narrative, is about double the length of the first version to that same point.

In that part of the legend of the Children of Húrin that my father achieved in the alliterative poem the old story in *The Book of Lost Tales* was substantially extended and elaborated. Most notably, it was now that the great underground fortress-city of Nargothrond emerged, and the wide lands of its dominion (a central element not only in the legend of Túrin and Niënor but in the history of the Elder Days of Middle-earth), with a description of the farmlands of the Elves of Nargothrond that gives a rare suggestion of the 'arts of peace' in the ancient world, such glimpses being few and far between. Coming south along the river Narog Túrin and his companion (Gwindor in the text in this book) found the lands near the entrance to Nargothrond to all appearance deserted:

> . . . they came to a country   kindly tended;
> through flowery frith   and fair acres
> they fared, and found   of folk empty
> the leas and leasows   and the lawns of Narog,
> the teeming tilth   by trees enfolded
> twixt hills and river.   The hoes unrecked
> in the fields were flung,   and fallen ladders
> in the long grass lay   of the lush orchards;

> *every tree there turned   its tangled head*
> *and eyed them secretly,   and the ears listened*
> *of the nodding grasses;   though noontide glowed*
> *on land and leaf,   their limbs were chilled.*

And so the two travellers came to the doors of Nargothrond, in the gorge of the Narog:

> *there steeply stood   the strong shoulders*
> *of the hills, o'erhanging   the hurrying water;*
> *there shrouded in trees   a sheer terrace,*
> *wide and winding,   worn to smoothness,*
> *was fashioned in the face   of the falling slope.*
> *Doors there darkly   dim gigantic*
> *were hewn in the hillside;   huge their timbers,*
> *and their posts and lintels   of ponderous stone.*

Seized by Elves they were haled through the portal, which
closed behind them:

> *Ground and grumbled   on its great hinges*
> *the door gigantic;   with din ponderous*
> *it clanged and closed   like clap of thunder,*
> *and echoes awful   in empty corridors*
> *there ran and rumbled   under roofs unseen;*
> *the light was lost.   Then led them on*
> *down long and winding   lanes of darkness*
> *their guards guiding   their groping feet,*

till the faint flicker   of fiery torches
flared before them;   fitful murmur
as of many voices   in meeting thronged
they heard as they hastened.   High sprang the roof.
Round a sudden turning   they swung amazed,
and saw a solemn   silent conclave,
where hundreds hushed   in huge twilight
neath distant domes   darkly vaulted
them wordless waited.

But in the text of *The Children of Húrin* given in this book we are told no more than this (p. 158):

> And now they arose, and departing from Eithel Ivrin they journeyed southward along the banks of Narog, until they were taken by scouts of the Elves and brought as prisoners to the hidden stronghold.
>
> Thus did Túrin come to Nargothrond.

How did this come about? In what follows I shall try to answer that question.

It seems virtually certain that all that my father wrote of his alliterative poem on Túrin was accomplished at Leeds, and that he abandoned it at the end of 1924 or early in 1925; but why he did so must remain unknown. What he then turned to is however not mysterious: in the summer of 1925 he embarked on a new poem in a wholly different metre, octosyllabic rhyming couplets, entitled *The Lay of Leithian* 'Release from Bondage'. Thus he took up now another of the tales that he described years later, in 1951, as I have already noted, as full in treatment, independent, and yet linked to 'the general history'; for the subject of *The Lay of Leithian* is the legend of Beren and Lúthien. He worked on this second long poem for six years, and in its turn abandoned it, in September 1931, having written more than 4000 lines. As does the alliterative *Children of Húrin* which it succeeded and supplanted, this poem represents a substantial advance in the evolution of the legend from the original *Lost Tale* of Beren and Lúthien.

While *The Lay of Leithian* was in progress, in 1926, he wrote a 'Sketch of the Mythology', expressly intended for R.W. Reynolds, who had been his teacher at King Edward's school in Birmingham, 'to explain the background of the alliterative version of Túrin and the Dragon'. This brief manuscript, which would run to some twenty printed pages, was avowedly written as a synopsis, in the present tense and in a succinct style; and yet it was the starting-point of the subsequent 'Silmarillion' versions (though that name was not yet given). But while the entire mythological conception was set out in this text, the tale of Túrin has very evidently pride of place – and indeed the title in the manuscript is 'Sketch of the mythology with especial reference to the "Children of Húrin"', in keeping with his purpose in writing it.

In 1930 there followed a much more substantial work, the *Quenta Noldorinwa* (the History of the Noldor: for the history of the Noldorin Elves is the central theme of

'The Silmarillion'). This was directly derived from the 'Sketch', and while much enlarging the earlier text and writing in a more finished manner, my father nonetheless still saw the *Quenta* very much as a *summarising* work, an epitome of far richer narrative conceptions: as is in any case clearly shown by the sub-title that he gave to it, in which he declared that it was 'a *brief history* [of the Noldor] drawn from the Book of Lost Tales'.

It is to be borne in mind that at that time the *Quenta* represented (if only in a somewhat bare structure) the full extent of my father's 'imagined world'. It was not the history of the First Age, as it afterwards became, for there was as yet no Second Age, nor Third Age; there was no Númenor, no hobbits, and of course no Ring. The history ended with the Great Battle, in which Morgoth was finally defeated by the other Gods (the Valar), and by them 'thrust through the Door of Timeless Night into the Void, beyond the Walls of the World'; and my father wrote at the end of the *Quenta*: 'Such is *the end of the tales* of the days before the days in the Northern regions of the Western world.'

Thus it will seem strange indeed that the *Quenta* of 1930 was nonetheless the only completed text (after the 'Sketch') of 'The Silmarillion' that he ever made; but as was so often the case, external pressures governed the evolution of his work. The *Quenta* was followed later in the 1930s by a new version in a beautiful manuscript, bearing at last the title *Quenta Silmarillion, History of the Silmarilli.* This was, or was to be, much longer than the preceding *Quenta Noldorinwa*, but the conception of the work as essentially a *summarising* of myths and legends (themselves of an altogether different nature and scope if fully told) was by no means lost, and is again defined in the title: 'The *Quenta Silmarillion* . . . . This is a *history in brief* drawn from many older tales; for all the matters that it contains were of old, and still are among the Eldar of the West, recounted more fully in other histories and songs.'

It seems at least probable that my father's view of *The Silmarillion* did actually arise from the fact that what may be called the '*Quenta* phase' of the work in the 1930s began in a condensed synopsis serving a particular purpose, but then underwent expansion and refinement in successive stages until it lost the appearance of a synopsis, but nonetheless retaining, from the form of its origin, a characteristic 'evenness' of tone. I have written elsewhere that 'the compendious or epitomising form and manner of *The Silmarillion*, with its suggestion of ages of poetry and "lore" behind it, strongly evokes a sense of "untold tales", even in the telling of them; "distance" is never lost. There is no narrative urgency, the pressure and fear of the immediate and unknown event. We do not actually see the Silmarils as we see the Ring.'

However, the *Quenta Silmarillion* in this form came to an abrupt and, as it turned out, a decisive end in 1937. *The Hobbit* was published by George Allen and Unwin on 21 September of that year, and not long afterwards, at the invitation of the publisher, my father sent in a number of his manuscripts, which were delivered in London on 15 November 1937. Among these was the *Quenta Silmarillion*, so far as it then went, ending in the middle of a sentence at the foot of a page. But while it was gone he continued the narrative in draft form as far as Túrin's flight from Doriath and his taking up the life of an outlaw:

> passing the borders of the realm he gathered to himself a company of such houseless and desperate folk as could be found in those evil days lurking in the wild; and their hands were turned against all who came in their path, Elves, Men, or Orcs.

This is the forerunner of the passage, in the text in this book p. 98, at the beginning of *Túrin among the Outlaws*.

My father had reached these words when the *Quenta Silmarillion* and the other manuscripts were returned to him; and three days later, on 19 December 1937, he wrote to Allen and Unwin saying: 'I have written the first chapter of a new story about Hobbits – "A long expected party".'

It was at this point that the continuous and evolving tradition of *The Silmarillion* in the summarising, *Quenta* mode came to an end, brought down in full flight, at Túrin's departure from Doriath. The further history from that point remained during the years that followed in the simple, compressed, and undeveloped form of the *Quenta* of 1930, frozen, as it were, while the great structures of the Second and Third Ages arose with the writing of *The Lord of the Rings*. But that further history was of cardinal importance in the ancient legends, for the concluding stories (deriving from the original *Book of Lost Tales*) told of the disastrous history of Húrin, father of Túrin, after Morgoth released him, and of the ruin of the Elvish kingdoms of Nargothrond, Doriath, and Gondolin, of which Gimli chanted in the mines of Moria many thousands of years afterwards.

> *The world was fair, the mountains tall,*
> *In Elder Days before the fall*
> *Of mighty kings in Nargothrond*
> *And Gondolin, who now beyond*
> *The Western Seas have passed away. . . .*

And this was to be the crown and completion of the whole: the doom of the Noldorin Elves in their long struggle against the power of Morgoth, and the parts that Húrin and Túrin played in that history; ending with the tale of Eärendil, who escaped from the burning ruin of Gondolin.

When, many years later, early in 1950, *The Lord of the Rings* was finished, my father turned with energy and confidence to 'the Matter of the Elder Days', now become 'the First Age'; and in the years immediately following he took out many old manuscripts from where they had long lain. Turning to *The Silmarillion*, he covered at this time the beautiful manuscript of the *Quenta Silmarillion* with corrections and expansions; but that revision ceased in 1951 before he reached the story of Túrin, where the *Quenta Silmarillion* was abandoned in 1937 with the advent of 'the new story about Hobbits'.

He began a revision of the *Lay of Leithian* (the poem in rhyming verse telling the story of Beren and Lúthien that was abandoned in 1931) that soon became almost a new poem, of much greater accomplishment; but this petered out and was ultimately abandoned. He embarked on what was to be a long saga of Beren and Lúthien in prose, closely based on the rewritten form of the Lay; but that too was abandoned. Thus his desire, shown in successive attempts, to render the first of the 'great tales' on the scale that he sought was never fulfilled.

At that time also he turned again at last to the 'great tale' of the Fall of Gondolin, still extant only in the *Lost Tale* from some thirty-five years before and in the few pages devoted to it in the *Quenta Noldorinwa* of 1930. This was to be the presentation, when he was at the height of his powers, in close narrative and in all its bearings, of the extraordinary tale that he had read to the Essay Society of his college at Oxford in 1920, and which remained throughout his life a vital element in his imagination of the

Elder Days. The special link with the tale of Túrin lies in the brothers Húrin, father of Túrin, and Huor, father of Tuor. Húrin and Huor in their youth entered the Elvish city of Gondolin, hidden within a circle of high mountains, as is told in *The Children of Húrin* (p. 35); and afterwards, in the battle of Unnumbered Tears, they met again with Turgon, King of Gondolin, and he said to them (p. 58): 'Not long now can Gondolin remain hidden, and being discovered it must fall.' And Huor replied: 'Yet if it stands only a little while, then out of your house shall come the hope of Elves and Men. This I say to you, lord, with the eyes of death: though we part here for ever, and I shall not look on your white walls again, from you and from me a new star shall arise.'

This prophecy was fulfilled when Tuor, first cousin to Túrin, came to Gondolin and wedded Idril, daughter of Turgon; for their son was Eärendil: the 'new star', 'hope of Elves and Men', who escaped from Gondolin. In the prose saga of *The Fall of Gondolin* that was to be, begun probably in 1951, my father recounted the journey of Tuor and his Elvish companion, Voronwë, who guided him; and on the way, alone in the wilderness, they heard a cry in the woods:

> And as they waited one came through the trees, and they saw that he was a tall Man, armed, clad in black, with a long sword drawn; and they wondered, for the blade of the sword also was black, but the edges shone bright and cold.

That was Túrin, hastening from the sack of Nar-gothrond (pp. 180–1); but Tuor and Voronwë did not speak to him as he passed, and 'they knew not that Nargothrond had fallen, and this was Túrin son of Húrin, the Blacksword. Thus only for a moment, and never again, did the paths of those kinsmen, Túrin and Tuor, draw together.'

In the new tale of Gondolin my father brought Tuor to the high place in the Encircling Mountains from where the eye could travel across the plain to the Hidden City; and there, grievously, he stopped, and never went further. And so in *The Fall of Gondolin* likewise he failed of his purpose; and we see neither Nargothrond nor Gondolin with his later vision.

I have said elsewhere that 'with the completion of the great "intrusion" and departure of *The Lord of the Rings*, it seems that he returned to the Elder Days with a desire to take up again the far more ample scale with which he had begun long before, in *The Book of Lost Tales*. The completion of the *Quenta Silmarillion* remained an aim; but the "great tales", vastly developed from their original forms, *from which its later chapters should be derived*, were never achieved.' These remarks are true of the 'great tale' of *The Children of Húrin* as well; but in this case my father achieved much more, even though he was never able to bring a substantial part of the later and hugely extended version to final and finished form.

At the same time as he turned again to the *Lay of Leithian* and *The Fall of Gondolin* he began his new work on *The Children of Húrin*, not with Túrin's childhood, but with the latter part of the story, the culmination of his disastrous history after the destruction of Nargothrond. This is the text in this book from *The Return of Túrin to Dor-lómin* (p. 182) to his death. Why my father should have proceeded in this way, so unlike his usual practice of starting again at the beginning, I cannot explain. But in this case he left also among his papers a mass of later but undated writing concerned with the story from Túrin's birth to the sack of Nargothrond, with great elaboration of the old versions and expansion into narrative previously unknown.

By far the greater part of this work, if not all of it, belongs to the time following the actual publication of *The Lord of the Rings*. In those years *The Children of Húrin* became for him the dominant story of the end of the Elder Days, and for a long time he devoted all his thought to it. But he found it hard now to impose a firm narrative structure as the tale grew in complexity of character and event; and indeed in one long passage the story is contained in a patchwork of disconnected drafts and plot-outlines.

Yet *The Children of Húrin* in its latest form is the chief narrative fiction of Middle-earth after the conclusion of *The Lord of the Rings*; and the life and death of Túrin is portrayed with a convincing power and an immediacy scarcely to be found elsewhere among the peoples of Middle-earth. For this reason I have attempted in this

book, after long study of the manuscripts, to form a text
that provides a continuous narrative from start to finish,
without the introduction of any elements that are not
authentic in conception.

(2)

THE COMPOSITION OF THE TEXT

In *Unfinished Tales*, published more than a quarter of a century ago, I presented a partial text of the long version of this tale, known as the *Narn*, from the Elvish title *Narn i Chîn Húrin*, the Tale of the Children of Húrin. But that was one element in a large book of various content, and the text was very incomplete, in keeping with the general purpose and nature of the book: for I omitted a number of substantial passages (and one of them very long) where the *Narn* text and that in the much briefer version in *The Silmarillion* are very similar, or where I decided that no distinctive 'long' text could be provided.

The form of the *Narn* in this book therefore differs in a number of ways from that in *Unfinished Tales*, some of them deriving from the far more thorough study of the formidable complex of manuscripts that I made after that book was published. This led me to different conclusions about the relations and sequence of some of the texts, chiefly in the extremely confusing evolution of the legend in the period of 'Túrin among the Outlaws'. A description and explanation of the composition of this new text of *The Children of Húrin* follows here.

An important element in all this is the peculiar status of the published *Silmarillion*; for as I have mentioned in the first part of this Appendix my father abandoned the *Quenta Silmarillion* at the point that he had reached (Túrin's becoming an outlaw after his flight from Doriath) when he began *The Lord of the Rings* in 1937. In the formation of a narrative for the published work I made much use of *The Annals of Beleriand*, originally a 'Tale of Years', but which in successive versions grew and expanded into annalistic narrative in parallel with the successive 'Silmarillion' manuscripts, and which extended to the freeing of Húrin by Morgoth after the deaths of Túrin and Niënor.

Thus the first passage that I omitted from the version of the *Narn i Chîn Húrin* in *Unfinished Tales* (p. 58 and note 1) is the account of the sojourn of Húrin and Huor in Gondolin in their youth; and I did so simply because the tale is told in *The Silmarillion* (pp. 158–9). But my father did in fact write two versions: one of them was expressly intended for the opening of the *Narn*, but was very closely based on a passage in *The Annals of Beleriand*, and indeed for most of its length differs little. In *The Silmarillion* I used both texts, but here I have followed the *Narn* version.

The second passage that I omitted from the *Narn* in *Unfinished Tales* (pp. 65–6 and note 2) is the account of the Battle of Unnumbered Tears, an omission made for the same reason; and here again my father wrote two

versions, one in the *Annals*, and a second, much later but
with the *Annals* text in front of him, and for the most part
closely followed. This second narrative of the great battle
was, again, expressly intended as a constituent element in
the *Narn* (the text is headed *Narn II*, i.e. the second
section of the *Narn*), and states at the outset (p. 52 in the
text in this book): 'Here there shall be recounted only
those deeds which bear upon the fate of the House of
Hador and the children of Húrin the Steadfast.' In
pursuit of this my father retained from the *Annals*
account only the description of the 'westward battle' and
the destruction of the host of Fingon; and by this simpli-
fication and reduction of the narrative he altered the
course of the battle as told in the *Annals*. In *The Silmarillion* I of course followed the *Annals*, though with some
features taken from the *Narn* version; but in this book I
have kept to the text that my father thought appropriate
to the *Narn* as a whole.

From *Túrin in Doriath* the new text is a good deal
changed in relation to that in *Unfinished Tales*. There is
here a range of writing, much of it very rough, concerned
with the same narrative elements at different stages of
development, and in such a case it is obviously possible
to take different views on how the original material
should be treated. I have come to think that when I composed the text in *Unfinished Tales* I allowed myself more
editorial freedom than was necessary. In this book I have
reconsidered the original manuscripts and reconstituted

the text, in many (usually very minor) places restoring the original words, introducing sentences or brief passages that should not have been omitted, correcting a few errors, and making different choices among the original readings.

As regards the structure of the narrative in this period of Túrin's life, from his flight out of Doriath to the lair of the outlaws on Amon Rûdh, my father had certain narrative 'elements' in mind: the trial of Túrin before Thingol; the gifts of Thingol and Melian to Beleg; the maltreatment of Beleg by the outlaws in Túrin's absence; the meetings of Túrin and Beleg. He moved these 'elements' in relation to each other, and placed passages of dialogue in different contexts; but found it difficult to compose them into a settled 'plot' – 'to find out what really happened'. But it seems now clear to me, after much further study, that my father did achieve a satisfying structure and sequence for this part of the story before he abandoned it; and also that the narrative in much reduced form that I composed for the published *Silmarillion* conforms to this – but with one difference.

In *Unfinished Tales* there is a third gap in the narrative on p. 96: the story breaks off at the point where Beleg, having at last found Túrin among the outlaws, cannot persuade him to return to Doriath (pp. 115–19 in the new text), and does not take up again until the outlaws encounter the Petty-dwarves. Here I referred again to *The Silmarillion* for the filling of the gap, noting that there follows in the story Beleg's farewell to Túrin and his return to Menegroth 'where he received the sword Anglachel from Thingol and *lembas* from Melian'. But it is in fact demonstrable that my father rejected this; for 'what really happened' was that Thingol gave Anglachel to Beleg after the trial of Túrin, when Beleg first set off to find him. In the present text therefore the gift of the sword is placed at that point (p. 96), and there is no mention there of the gift of *lembas*. In the later passage, when Beleg returned to Menegroth after the finding of Túrin, there is of course no reference to Anglachel in the new text, but only to Melian's gift.

This is a convenient point to notice that I have omitted from the text two passages that I included in *Unfinished Tales* but which are parenthetical to the narrative: these are the history of how the Dragon-helm came into the possession of Hador of Dor-lómin (*Unfinished Tales*, p. 75), and the origin of Saeros (*Unfinished Tales*, p. 77). It seems, incidentally, certain from a closer understanding of the relations of the manuscripts that my father rejected the name *Saeros* and replaced it by *Orgol*, which by 'linguistic accident' coincides with Old English *orgol*, *orgel* 'pride'. But it seems to me too late now to remove *Saeros*.

The major lacuna in the narrative as given in *Unfinished Tales* (p. 104) is filled in the new text on pages 141 to 181, from the end of the section *Of Mîm the Dwarf* and through *The Land of Bow and Helm*, *The Death of Beleg*, *Túrin in Nargothrond*, and *The Fall of Nargothrond*.

There is a complex relationship in this part of the 'Túrin saga' between the original manuscripts, the story as it is told in *The Silmarillion*, the disconnected passages collected in the appendix to the *Narn* in *Unfinished Tales*, and the new text in this book. I have always supposed that it was my father's general intention, in the fullness of time, when he had achieved to his satisfaction the 'great tale' of Túrin, to derive from it a much briefer form of the story in what one may call 'the *Silmarillion* mode'. But of course this did not happen; and so I undertook, now more than thirty years ago, the strange task of trying to simulate what he did not do: the writing of a 'Silmarillion' version of the latest form of the story, but deriving this from the heterogeneous materials of the 'long version', the *Narn*. That is Chapter 21 in the published *Silmarillion*.

Thus the text in this book that fills the long gap in the story in *Unfinished Tales* is derived from the same original materials as is the corresponding passage in *The Silmarillion* (pp. 204–15), but they are used for a different purpose in each case, and in the new text with a better understanding of the labyrinth of drafts and notes and their sequence. Much in the original manuscripts that was omitted or compressed in *The Silmarillion* remains available; but where there was nothing to be added to the *Silmarillion* version (as in the tale of the

death of Beleg, derived from the *Annals of Beleriand*)
that version is simply repeated.

In the result, while I have had to introduce bridging
passages here and there in the piecing together of different
drafts, there is no element of extraneous 'invention' of any
kind, however slight, in the longer text here presented.
The text is nonetheless artificial, as it could not be otherwise: the more especially since this great body of manuscript represents a continual evolution in the actual story.
Drafts that are essential to the formation of an uninter-
rupted narrative may in fact belong to an earlier stage.
Thus, to give an example from an earlier point, a primary
text for the story of the coming of Túrin's band to the hill
of Amon Rûdh, the dwelling place that they found upon
it and their life there, and the ephemeral success of the
land of Dor-Cúarthol, was written before there was any
suggestion of the Petty-dwarves; and indeed a fully-
developed description of Mîm's house beneath the summit
appears before Mîm himself.

In the remainder of the story, from Túrin's return to
Dor-lómin, to which my father gave a finished form, there
are naturally very few differences from the text in *Unfinished Tales*. But there are two matters of detail in the account
of the attack on Glaurung at Cabed-en-Aras where I have
emended the original words and which should be explained.

The first concerns the geography. It is said (p. 230) that
when Túrin and his companions set out from Nen Girith

on the fateful evening they did not go straight towards the
Dragon, lying on the further side of the ravine, but took
first the path towards the Crossings of Teiglin; and 'then,
before they came so far, they turned southward by a
narrow track' and went through the woods above the
river towards Cabed-en-Aras. As they approached, in the
original text of the passage, 'the first stars glimmered in
the east behind them'.

When I prepared the text for *Unfinished Tales* I did not
observe that this could not be right, since they were certainly not moving in a westerly direction, but east, or south-
east, away from the Crossings, and the first stars in the east
must have been before them, not behind them. When dis-
cussing this in *The War of the Jewels* (1994, p. 157) I
accepted the suggestion that the 'narrow track' going southward turned again westward to reach the Teiglin. But this
seems to me now to be improbable, as being without point
in the narrative, and that a much simpler solution is to
emend 'behind them' to 'before them', as I have done in the
new text.

The sketch map that I drew in *Unfinished Tales*
(p. 149) to illustrate the lie of the land is not in fact well
oriented. It is seen from my father's map of Beleriand,
and is so reproduced in my map for *The Silmarillion*,
that Amon Obel was almost due east from the Crossings
of Teiglin ('the moon rose beyond Amon Obel', p. 241),
and the Teiglin was flowing south-east or south-south-
east in the ravines. I have now redrawn the sketch map,

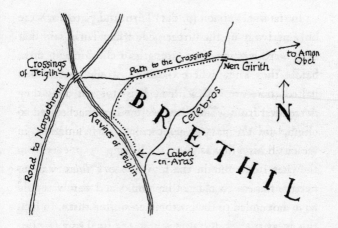

and have entered also the approximate place of Cabed-en-Aras (it is said in the text, p. 225, that 'right in the path of Glaurung there lay now one of these gorges, by no means the deepest, but the narrowest, just north of the inflow of Celebros').

The second matter concerns the story of the slaying of Glaurung at the crossing of the ravine. There are here a draft and a final version. In the draft, Túrin and his companions climbed up the further side of the chasm until they came beneath the brink; they hung there as the night passed, and Túrin 'strove with dark dreams of dread in which all his will was given to clinging and holding'. When day came Glaurung prepared to cross at a point 'many paces to the northward', and so Túrin had to climb down to the river-bed and then up the cliff again to get beneath the Dragon's belly.

In the final version (p. 235) Túrin and Hunthor were only part way up the further side when Túrin said that they were wasting their strength in climbing up now, before they knew where Glaurung would cross; 'they halted therefore and waited'. It is not said that they descended from where they were when they ceased to climb, and the passage concerning Túrin's dream 'in which all his will was given to clinging' reappears from the draft text. But in the revised story there was no need for them to cling: they could and surely would have descended to the bottom and waited there. In fact, this is what they did: it is said in the final text (*Unfinished Tales*, p. 134) that they were not standing in Glaurung's path and that Túrin 'clambered along the water-edge to come beneath him'. It seems then that the final story carries an unneeded trait from the previous draft. To give it coherence I have emended (p. 236) 'since they were not standing right in Glaurung's path' to 'since they were not right in Glaurung's path', and 'clambered along the water-edge' to 'clambered along the cliff'.

These are small matters in themselves, but they clarify what are perhaps the most sharply visualised scenes in the legends of the Elder Days, and one of the greatest events.

LIST OF NAMES IN
THE TALE OF THE CHILDREN
OF HÚRIN

Names that appear in the map of Beleriand are followed by an asterisk.

Adanedhel	'Elf-man', name given to Túrin in Nargothrond.
Aerin	A kinswoman of Húrin in Dor-lómin, taken as wife by Brodda the Easterling.
Agarwaen	'Bloodstained', name taken by Túrin when he came to Nargothrond.
Ainur	'The Holy Ones', the first beings created by Ilúvatar, who were before the World: the Valar and the Maiar ('spirits of the same order as the Valar but of less degree').
Algund	Man of Dor-lómin, member of the outlaw band that Túrin joined.
Amon Darthir *	A peak in the range of Ered Wethrin south of Dor-lómin.
Amon Ethir	'Hill of Spies', a great earthwork raised by Finrod Felagund a league to the east of Nargothrond.
Amon Obel *	A hill in the midst of the Forest of Brethil, on which was built Ephel Brandir.
Amon Rûdh *	'The Bald Hill', a lonely height in the lands south of Brethil, abode of Mîm.
Anach *	Pass leading down from Taur-nu-Fuin at the western end of Ered Gorgoroth.
Andróg	Man of Dor-lómin, a leader of the outlaw band that Túrin joined.

Anfauglith *	'Gasping Dust', the great plain north of Taur-nu-Fuin, once grassy and named *Ard-galen*, but transformed into a desert by Morgoth in the Battle of Sudden Flame.
Angband	The great fortress of Morgoth in the North-west of Middle-earth.
Anglachel	Beleg's sword, the gift of Thingol; after its reforging for Túrin named *Gurthang*.
Angrod	Third son of Finarfin, slain in the Dagor Bragollach.
Anguirel	Eöl's sword.
Aranrúth	'King's Ire', Thingol's sword.
Arda	The Earth.
Aredhel	Sister of Turgon, wife of Eöl.
Arminas	Noldorin Elf who came with Gelmir to Nargothrond to warn Orodreth of its peril.
Arroch	Húrin's horse.
Arvernien *	The coastlands of Beleriand west of Sirion's mouths; named in Bilbo's song in Rivendell.
Asgon	Man of Dor-lómin who aided Túrin's escape after the slaying of Brodda.
Azaghâl	Lord of the Dwarves of Belegost.
Barad Eithel	'Tower of the Well', the fortress of the Noldor at Eithel Sirion.
Baragund	Father of Morwen; cousin of Beren.

Barahir   Father of Beren; brother of Bregolas.

Bar-en-Danwedh   'House of Ransom', name given by
                            Mîm to his house.

Bar-en-Nibin-noeg   'House of the Petty-dwarves' on
                            Amon Rûdh.

Bar Erib   A stronghold of Dor-Cúarthol south of
                            Amon Rûdh.

Battle of Unnumbered Tears   See *Nirnaeth Arnoediad*.

Bauglir   'The Constrainer', name given to
                            Morgoth.

Beleg   Elf of Doriath, a great archer; friend and
                            companion of Túrin. Called *Cúthalion*
                            'Strongbow'.

Belegost   'Great Fortress', one of the two cities of
                            the Dwarves in the Blue Mountains.

Belegund   Father of Rían; brother of Baragund.

Beleriand *   Lands west of the Blue Mountains in the
                            Elder Days.

Belthronding   Beleg's bow.

Bëor   Leader of the first Men to enter
                            Beleriand; progenitor of the House of
                            Bëor, one of the three Houses of the
                            Edain.

Beren   Man of the House of Bëor, lover of
                            Lúthien, who cut a Silmaril from
                            Morgoth's crown; called 'One-hand' and
                            Camlost 'Empty-handed'.

Black King, The   Morgoth.

Black Sword, The   Túrin's name in Nargothrond; also the
                            sword itself. See *Mormegil*.

Blue Mountains   The great mountain chain (called
                    Ered Luin and *Ered Lindon*) between
                    Beleriand and Eriador in the Elder Days.

Bragollach   See *Dagor Bragollach*.

Brandir   Ruler of the People of Haleth in Brethil
                    when Túrin came; son of Handir.

Bregolas   Father of Baragund; Morwen's
                    grandfather.

Bregor   Father of Barahir and Bregolas.

Brethil *   Forest between the rivers Teiglin and
                    Sirion; *Men of Brethil*, the People of
                    Haleth.

Brithiach *   Ford over Sirion north of the Forest of
                    Brethil.

Brodda   An Easterling in Hithlum after the
                    Nirnaeth Arnoediad.

Cabed-en-Aras   'The Deer's Leap', a deep gorge of the
                    river Teiglin where Túrin slew Glaurung.

Cabed Naeramarth 'The Leap of Dreadful Doom', name
                    given to Cabed-en-Aras after Niënor
                    leapt from its cliffs.

Celebros   Stream in Brethil falling down to Teiglin
                    near the Crossings.

Children of Ilúvatar   Elves and Men.

Círdan   Called 'the Shipwright'; lord of the Falas;
                    at the destruction of the Havens after the
                    Nirnaeth Arnoediad he escaped to the
                    Isle of Balar in the south.

Crissaegrim *   The mountain peaks south of Gondolin, where were the eyries of Thorondor.

Crossings of Teiglin *   Fords where the old South Road to Nargothrond crossed the Teiglin.

Cúthalion   'Strongbow', name of Beleg.

Daeron   Minstrel of Doriath.

Dagor Bragollach (also *the Bragollach*)   The Battle of Sudden Flame, in which Morgoth ended the Siege of Angband.

Dark Lord, The   Morgoth.

Deer's Leap, The   See *Cabed-en-Aras*.

Dimbar *   The land between the rivers Sirion and Mindeb.

Dimrost   'The Rainy Stair', the falls of Celebros in the Forest of Brethil, afterwards called *Nen Girith*.

Dor-Cúarthol   'Land of Bow and Helm', name given to the country defended by Túrin and Beleg from their lair on Amon Rûdh.

Doriath *   The kingdom of Thingol and Melian in the forests of Neldoreth and Region, ruled from Menegroth on the river Esgalduin.

Dorlas   A man of consequence among the People of Haleth in the Forest of Brethil.

Dor-lómin *   Region in the south of Hithlum given by King Fingolfin as a fief to the House of Hador; the home of Húrin and Morwen.

Dorthonion *	'Land of Pines', great forested highlands on the northern borders of Beleriand, afterwards named *Taur-nu-Fuin*.
Drengist *	Long firth of the sea piercing Ered Lómin, the Echoing Mountains.
Easterlings	Tribes of Men who followed the Edain into Beleriand.
Echad i Sedryn	(also *the Echad*) 'Camp of the Faithful', name given to Mîm's house on Amon Rûdh.
Ecthelion	Elf-lord of Gondolin.
Edain	(singular *Adan*) The Men of the Three Houses of the Elf-friends.
Eithel Ivrin *	'Ivrin's Well', the source of the river Narog beneath Ered Wethrin.
Eithel Sirion *	'Sirion's Well', in the eastern face of Ered Wethrin; the fortress of the Noldor in that place, also called *Barad Eithel*.
Eldalië	The Elven-folk, equivalent to *Eldar*.
Eldar	The Elves of the Great Journey out of the East to Beleriand.
Elder Children	The Elves. See *Children of Ilúvatar*.
Eledhwen	Name of Morwen, 'Elfsheen'.
Encircling Mountains	The mountains encircling Tumladen, the plain of Gondolin.
Enemy, The	Morgoth.

Eöl	Called 'the Dark Elf', a great smith who dwelt in Nan Elmoth; maker of the sword Anglachel; father of Maeglin.
Ephel Brandir	'The Fence of Brandir', the enclosed dwellings of the Men of Brethil upon Amon Obel; also *the Ephel*.
*Ered Gorgoroth**	'Mountains of Terror', the vast precipices in which Taur-nu-Fuin fell southward; also *the Gorgoroth*.
Ered Wethrin	'Shadowy Mountains', 'Mountains of Shadow', the great range forming the boundary of Hithlum on the east and south.
*Esgalduin**	The river of Doriath, dividing the forests of Neldoreth and Region and flowing into Sirion.
Exiles, The	The Noldor who rebelled against the Valar and returned to Middle-earth.
Faelivrin	Name given to Finduilas by Gwindor.
Fair Folk	The Eldar.
*Falas**	The coastlands of Beleriand in the West.
Fëanor	Eldest son of Finwë, the first leader of the Noldor; half-brother of Fingolfin; maker of the Silmarils; leader of the Noldor in their rebellion against the Valar, but slain in battle soon after his return to Middle-earth. See *Sons of Fëanor*.

Felagund   'Hewer of caves', name given to King
                    Finrod after the establishment of
                    Nargothrond and often used alone.

Finarfin   Third son of Finwë, brother of Fingolfin
                    and half-brother of Fëanor; father of
                    Finrod Felagund and Galadriel. Finarfin
                    did not return to Middle-earth.

Finduilas   Daughter of Orodreth, second King of
                    Nargothrond.

Fingolfin   Second son of Finwë, the first leader of
                    the Noldor; High King of the Noldor,
                    dwelling in Hithlum; father of Fingon
                    and Turgon.

Fingon   Eldest son of King Fingolfin, and High
                    King of the Noldor after his death.

Finrod   Son of Finarfin; founder and king of
                    Nargothrond, brother of Orodreth and
                    Galadriel; often called *Felagund*.

Forweg   Man of Dor-lómin, captain of the outlaw
                    band that Túrin joined.

Galdor the Tall   Son of Hador Goldenhead; father of
                    Húrin and Huor; slain at Eithel Sirion.

Gamil Zirak   Dwarf smith, teacher of Telchar of Nogrod.

Gaurwaith   'Wolf-men', the outlaw band that Túrin
                    joined in the woodlands beyond the
                    western borders of Doriath.

Gelmir (1)   Elf of Nargothrond, brother of Gwindor.

Gelmir (2)   Noldorin Elf who came with Arminas to
                    Nargothrond to warn Orodreth of its
                    peril.

Gethron   One of Túrin's companions on the
                journey to Doriath.

Ginglith *   River flowing into the Narog above
                Nargothrond.

Girdle of Melian See *Melian.*

Glaurung   'Father of Dragons', the first of the
                Dragons of Morgoth.

Glithui *   River flowing down from Ered Wethrin
                and joining Teiglin north of the inflow of
                Malduin.

Glóredhel   Daughter of Hador, sister of Galdor
                Húrin's father; wife of Haldir of
                Brethil.

Glorfindel   Elf-lord of Gondolin.

Gondolin *   The hidden city of King Turgon.

Gorgoroth   See *Ered Gorgoroth.*

Gorthol   'Dread Helm', name taken by Túrin in
                the land of Dor-Cúarthol.

Gothmog   Lord of Balrogs; slayer of King
                Fingon.

Great Mound, The   See *Haudh-en-Nirnaeth.*

Great Song, The The Music of the Ainur, in which the
                World was begun.

Grey-elves   The Sindar, name given to the Eldar who
                remained in Beleriand and did not cross
                the Great Sea into the West.

Grithnir   One of Túrin's companions on the
                journey to Doriath, where he died.

Guarded Plain, The *   See *Talath Dirnen.*

Guarded Realm, The   Doriath.

Guilin   Elf of Nargothrond, father of Gwindor and Gelmir.

Gurthang   'Iron of Death', Túrin's name for the sword Anglachel after it was reforged in Nargothrond.

Gwaeron   The 'windy month', March.

Gwindor   Elf of Nargothrond, lover of Finduilas, companion of Túrin.

Hador Goldenhead   Elf-friend, lord of Dor-lómin, vassal of King Fingolfin; father of Galdor father of Húrin and Huor; slain at Eithel Sirion in the Dagor Bragollach. *House of Hador*, one of the Houses of the Edain.

Haldir   Son of Halmir of Brethil; wedded Glóredhel daughter of Hador of Dor-lómin.

Haleth   The Lady Haleth, who early became the leader of the Second House of the Edain, the *Halethrim* or *People of Haleth*, who dwelt in the Forest of Brethil.

Halmir   Lord of the Men of Brethil.

Handir of Brethil   Son of Haldir and Glóredhel; father of Brandir.

Hareth   Daughter of Halmir of Brethil, wife of Galdor of Dor-lómin; mother of Húrin.

Haudh-en-Elleth   'The Mound of the Elf-maid' near the Crossings of Teiglin, in which Finduilas was buried.

Haudh-en-Nirnaeth   'The Mound of Tears' in the desert of Anfauglith.

Hidden Kingdom, The   Doriath.

Hidden Realm, The   Gondolin.

High Faroth, The *   Highlands to the west of the river Narog above Nargothrond; also *the Faroth*.

Hírilorn   A great beech-tree in the Forest of Neldoreth with three trunks.

Hithlum *   'Land of Mist', northern region bounded by the Mountains of Shadow.

Hunthor   Man of Brethil, companion of Túrin in the attack on Glaurung.

Huor   Húrin's brother; father of Tuor father of Eärendil; slain in the Battle of Unnumbered Tears.

Húrin   Lord of Dor-lómin, husband of Morwen and father of Túrin and Niënor; called *Thalion* 'the Steadfast'.

Ibun   One of the sons of Mîm the Petty-dwarf.

Ilúvatar   'The Father of All'.

Indor   Man of Dor-lómin, father of Aerin.

Ivrin *   Lake and falls beneath Ered Wethrin where the river Narog rose.

Khîm   One of the sons of Mîm the Petty-dwarf, slain by Andróg's arrow.

Labadal   Túrin's name for Sador.

Ladros *   Lands to the north-east of Dorthonion
                    that were granted by the Noldorin kings
                    to the Men of the House of Bëor.

Lady of Dor-lómin Morwen.

Lalaith   'Laughter', name given to Urwen.

Larnach   One of the Woodmen in the lands south
                    of Teiglin.

Lord of Waters   The Vala Ulmo.

Lords of the West The Valar.

Lothlann   A great plain to the east of Dorthonion
                    (*Taur-nu-Fuin*).

Lothron   The fifth month.

Lúthien   Daughter of Thingol and Melian, who
                    after the death of Beren chose to become
                    mortal and to share his fate. Called
                    Tinúviel 'daughter of twilight',
                    nightingale.

Mablung   Elf of Doriath, chief captain of Thingol,
                    friend of Túrin; called 'the Hunter'.

Maedhros   Eldest son of Fëanor, with lands in the
                    east beyond Dorthonion.

Maeglin   Son of Eöl 'the Dark Elf' and Aredhel
                    Turgon's sister; betrayer of Gondolin.

Malduin *   A tributary of the Teiglin.

Mandos   A Vala: the Judge, and Keeper of the
                    Houses of the Dead in Valinor.

Manwë   The chief of the Valar; called *the Elder
                    King*.

Melian	A Maia (see entry *Ainur*); the queen of King Thingol in Doriath, about which she set an invisible barrier of protection, the Girdle of Melian; mother of Lúthien.
Melkor	The Quenya name of Morgoth.
Menegroth *	'The Thousand Caves', the halls of Thingol and Melian on the river Esgalduin in Doriath.
Menel	The heavens, region of the stars.
Methed-en-glad	'End of the wood', a stronghold of Dor-Cúarthol at the edge of the forest south of Teiglin.
Mîm	The Petty-dwarf, dwelling on Amon Rûdh.
Minas Tirith	'Tower of Watch', built by Finrod Felagund on Tol Sirion.
*Mindeb**	A tributary of Sirion, between Dimbar and the Forest of Neldoreth.
*Mithrim**	The south-eastern region of Hithlum, separated from Dor-lómin by the Mountains of Mithrim.
Morgoth	The great rebellious Vala, in his origin the mightiest of the Powers; called *the Enemy*, *the Dark Lord*, *the Black King*, *Bauglir*.
Mormegil	'Black Sword', name given to Túrin in Nargothrond.
Morwen	Daughter of Baragund of the House of Bëor; wife of Húrin and mother of Túrin and Niënor; called *Eledhwen* 'Elfsheen' and *Lady of Dor-lómin*.
Mountains of Shadow *	See *Ered Wethrin*.

Nan Elmoth *   A forest in East Beleriand; dwelling-place
            of Eöl.

Nargothrond *   'The great underground fortress on
            the river Narog', founded by Finrod
            Felagund, destroyed by Glaurung; also
            the realm of Nargothrond extending east
            and west of the river.

Narog *   The chief river of West Beleriand, rising
            at Ivrin and flowing into Sirion near its
            mouths. *People of Narog*, the Elves of
            Nargothrond.

Neithan   'The Wronged', name given to himself by
            Túrin among the outlaws.

Nellas   Elf of Doriath, friend of Túrin in his
            boyhood.

Nen Girith   'Shuddering Water', name given to
            Dimrost, the falls of Celebros in Brethil.

Nen Lalaith   Stream rising under Amon Darthir, a
            peak in Ered Wethrin, and flowing past
            Húrin's house in Dor-lómin.

Nenning *   River in West Beleriand, reaching the Sea
            at the Haven of Eglarest.

Nevrast *   Region west of Dor-lómin, beyond the
            Echoing Mountains* (*Ered Lómin*).

Nibin-noeg, Nibin-nogrim   Petty-dwarves.

Niënor   'Mourning', daughter of Húrin and
            Morwen, and sister of Túrin; see *Níniel*.

Nimbrethil *   Birchwoods in Arvernien; named in
            Bilbo's song in Rivendell.

Níniel   'Maid of Tears', name that Túrin gave to
            Niënor in Brethil.

Nirnaeth Arnoediad   The Battle of 'Unnumbered Tears',
also *the Nirnaeth*.

Nogrod   One of the two cities of the Dwarves in
the Blue Mountains.

Noldor   The second host of the Eldar on the Great
Journey out of the East to Beleriand; the
'Deep Elves', 'the Loremasters'.

*Núath, Woods of**   Woods extending westward from the
upper waters of the Narog.

Orleg   A man of Túrin's outlaw band.

Orodreth   King of Nargothrond after the death of
his brother Finrod Felagund; father of
Finduilas.

Ossë   A Maia (see entry *Ainur*); vassal of Ulmo
Lord of Waters.

Petty-dwarves   A race of Dwarves in Middle-earth of
whom Mîm and his two sons were the
last survivors.

Powers, The   The Valar.

Ragnir   A blind servant in Húrin's house in
Dor-lómin.

*Region **   The southern forest of Doriath.

Rían   Cousin of Morwen; wife of Huor Húrin's
brother; mother of Tuor.

*Rivil **   Stream falling from Dorthonion to join
Sirion in the Fen of Serech.

Sador	Woodwright, serving-man of Húrin's in Dor-lómin and friend of Túrin in his childhood, by whom he was called *Labadal*.
Saeros	Elf of Doriath, a counsellor of Thingol, hostile to Túrin.
Sauron's Isle	Tol Sirion.
Serech *	The great fen north of the Pass of Sirion, where the river Rivil flowed in from Dorthonion.
Shadowy Mountains	See *Ered Wethrin*.
Sharbhund	Dwarvish name of Amon Rûdh.
Sindarin	Grey-elven, the Elvish tongue of Beleriand. See *Grey-elves*.
Sirion *	The great river of Beleriand, rising at Eithel Sirion.
Sons of Fëanor	See *Fëanor*. The seven sons held lands in East Beleriand.
South Road *	The ancient road from Tol Sirion to Nargothrond by the Crossings of Teiglin.
Spyhill, The	See *Amon Ethir*.
Strawheads	Name given to the People of Hador by the Easterlings in Hithlum.
Strongbow	Name of Beleg; see *Cúthalion*.
Talath Dirnen *	'The Guarded Plain', north of Nargothrond.
Taur-nu-Fuin *	'Forest under Night', later name of Dorthonion.

Teiglin *	A tributary of Sirion rising in the Shadowy Mountains and flowing through the Forest of Brethil. See *Crossings of Teiglin*.
Telchar	Renowned smith of Nogrod.
Telperion	The White Tree, elder of the Two Trees that gave light to Valinor.
Thangorodrim	'Mountains of Tyranny', reared by Morgoth over Angband.
Thingol	'Greycloak', King of Doriath, overlord of the Grey-elves (Sindar); wedded to Melian the Maia; father of Lúthien.
Thorondor	'King of Eagles' (cf. *The Return of the King* VI.4: 'old Thorondor, who built his eyries in the inaccessible peaks of the Encircling Mountains when Middle-earth was young').
Three Houses (of the Edain)	The Houses of Bëor, Haleth, and Hador.
Thurin	'The Secret', name given to Túrin by Finduilas.
Tol Sirion *	Island in the river in the Pass of Sirion on which Finrod built the tower of Minas Tirith; afterwards taken by Sauron.
Tumhalad *	Valley in West Beleriand between the rivers Ginglith and Narog where the host of Nargothrond was defeated.
Tumladen	The hidden vale in the Encircling Mountains where the city of Gondolin stood.
Tuor	Son of Huor and Rían; cousin of Túrin and father of Eärendil.

Turambar	'Master of Doom', name taken by Túrin among the Men of Brethil.
Turgon	Second son of King Fingolfin and brother of Fingon; founder and king of Gondolin.
Túrin	Son of Húrin and Morwen, chief subject of the lay named *Narn i Chîn Húrin*. For his other names see *Neithan, Gorthol, Agarwaen, Thurin, Adanedhel, Mormegil (Black Sword), Wild Man of the Woods, Turambar.*
Twilit Meres *	Region of marshes and pools where the Aros flowed into Sirion.
Uldor the Accursed	A leader of the Easterlings who was slain in the Battle of Unnumbered Tears.
Ulmo	One of the great Valar, 'Lord of Waters'.
Ulrad	A member of the outlaw band that Túrin joined.
Úmarth	'Ill-fate', a fictitious name for his father given out by Túrin in Nargothrond.
Unnumbered Tears	The battle of *Nirnaeth Arnoediad.*
Urwen	Daughter of Húrin and Morwen who died in childhood; called *Lalaith* 'Laughter'.
Valar	'The Powers', those great spirits that entered the World at the beginning of time.
Valinor	The land of the Valar in the West, beyond the Great Sea.

Varda   The greatest of the Queens of the Valar,
                 the spouse of Manwë.

Wildman of the Woods   Name taken by Túrin when he
                 first came among the Men of Brethil.

Wolf-men   See *Gaurwaith*.

Woodmen   Dwellers in the woods south of Teiglin,
                 plundered by the Gaurwaith.

Year of Lamentation   The year of the *Nirnaeth Arnoediad*.

Younger Children   Men. See *Children of Ilúvatar*.

NOTE ON THE MAP

This map is closely based on that in the published *Silmarillion*, which was itself derived from the map that my father made in the 1930s, and which he never replaced, but used for all his subsequent work. The formalised, and obviously very selective, representations of mountains, hills and forests are imitated from his style.

In this redrawing I have introduced certain differences, intended to simplify it and to make it more expressly applicable to the tale of *The Children of Húrin*. Thus it does not extend eastward to include Ossiriand and the Blue Mountains, and certain geographical features are omitted; while (with a few exceptions) only names that actually occur in the text of the tale are marked.